Readers love
MARY CALMES

Chevalier

"This story was long awaited, and it didn't disappoint."

—Joyfully Jay

"…I couldn't keep the grin off my face as I read."

—Oh My Shelves

Lay It Down

"I absolutely fell in love with this book the minute I started reading it. Hudson is absolutely adorable and so perfect!"

—Alpha Book Club

"If you love a quick read with a bit of fun and some ooey-gooey love-at-first-sight, you just might eat this up!"

—The Novel Approach

Sleeping 'til Sunrise

"I loved every minute I spent reading this book and know both fans and new readers of Ms. Calmes will love it as well."

—Top 2 Bottom Reviews

"This short novella is a classic kind of Calmes with great dialogue, delicious heat and sexy times, and a breakneck romantic pace."

—Gay Book Reviews

By Mary Calmes

Published by DREAMSPINNER PRESS
www.dreamspinnerpress.com

TIMING

Mary Calmes

Published by
DREAMSPINNER PRESS

5032 Capital Circle SW, Suite 2, PMB# 279, Tallahassee, FL 32305-7886 USA
www.dreamspinnerpress.com

Timing
© 2016 Mary Calmes.

Cover Art
© 2016 Reese Dante.
http://www.reesedante.com
Cover content is for illustrative purposes only and any person depicted on the cover is a model.

ISBN: 978-1-63477-711-7
Digital ISBN: 978-1-63477-712-4
Library of Congress Control Number: 2016913865
Published October 2016
v. 2.0
First Edition published by Dreamspinner Press, 2010.

Printed in the United States of America

This paper meets the requirements of
ANSI/NISO Z39.48-1992 (Permanence of Paper).

For my mother, who believed in grace,
and for Elizabeth and Lynn for theirs.

CHAPTER 1

IT WAS unfair of my boss to order me to go.

"I don't understand why this is a big deal. We're only talking about the morning of one of the days. We're not talking about your entire—will you look at me, please?"

But I didn't have time. I was sorting paperwork on my desk in preparation for being away. I had different people doing different things, and so I was making piles. "My best friend is getting married, Knox. I don't want to think about—"

"I need you to meet this woman, Stef. You're the only one who can close the deal, so you're the one who's going."

"I'll go when I get back," I responded absently, checking the inbox of my internal e-mail, hoping he'd get the hint and just leave.

"Look at me."

But I was so busy. There were things I had to finish before I could leave and not worry. My assistant was amazing, but I couldn't leave her everything. She'd kill me.

"Stefan."

I lifted my gaze from my computer screen to meet his.

"That makes sense to you, does it? You're going to fly to Amarillo—"

"What?"

"*Stefan.*" His voice dropped irritably as he realized I had stopped listening to him.

"Are we still talking about this?"

"You're going to Amarillo for your—"

"Lubbock," I corrected him. "I'm flying into Lubbock."

"Whatever. You're telling me that you're going to fly to Lubbock and drive to the small town where your friend is getting married—which, it turns out, is one town over from where Mrs. Freeman is—and then you're going to come back here to Chicago only to turn around and make the same trip back out again? That seems logical to you?"

It didn't, no. And even though I had no intention of telling him so, my best friend, Charlotte Holloway, soon to be Charlotte Cantwell, had told me the exact same thing when I explained what my boss was planning.

"Just take the meeting." She had laughed at me over the phone. "I mean, for crissakes, Stef, it'll only take the morning of that Wednesday, and the wedding stuff doesn't even start until that night. I *so* don't care, I swear to God."

"You'll resent me for making your wedding into a business trip."

"I will only resent you if you're not there when I need you. Other than that… I'm good."

"But—"

"Stef, I'm in Winston. Where you're going is in Hillman. Seriously, it's like an hour drive away, tops."

"I just want you to know that my trip is all about you."

"Yes, dear, I know."

"Stefan!" Knox barking at me brought me sharply back to the present.

"Are you listening to me?"

I had been daydreaming, so the answer was no, I was not listening to my boss, Knox Bishop, Director of Strategic Operations and Marketing.

"Just go see Mrs. Freeman. I already said I would pay for your ticket, what more do you want?"

"I don't do sales," I repeated for what felt like the millionth time. "You know I don't. I'm in acquisitions, not sales."

"It's a title, Stef. You're in sales, believe me."

"No." I squinted at him. "I assess what property we should or should not purchase and how much money should or should not be offered to purchase said property. After a pitch is made and the deal is closed, I—"

"This is important."

"Then send one of the sales—"

"I need it to be you."

"Why?"

"Because a great deal of money is riding on us closing this deal," he explained, taking a seat across the desk from me.

Knox Bishop was one of those high-powered corporate men who always looked like he had just walked off the cover of a fashion magazine. He was model perfect. All the designer labels he wore, the way his steel-blue eyes never missed anything, the wisps of silver that had started to show in his thick, gray hair—he was flawless. The only thing more amazing than the way his suits fit or how broad his shoulders were or how his eyes twinkled when he was happy was his ever-calculating mind. The man was a first-class schemer, and he never missed a thing. The fact that he wanted me to go to Texas instead of someone else had already been carefully calculated. I just needed to figure out his angle. After four years of working for the man, it should have been easier for me to figure out what that was.

"Are you listening to me?"

"I just don't understand. Make me understand."

"It has to be you."

"Why?"

"Do it as a favor to me."

Favor to him? "Something must be really wrong."

"Don't concern yourself with that, simply get Mrs. Freeman in Winston, Texas to sell."

"Why is it so important?"

"We need the land."

"There's other land."

"Not anymore."

"I read the file, you know."

"So you get it, then."

I squinted at him. "What I get is that your seller, Grace Freeman, is the lone holdout in this whole mess. Everyone else on all four sides of her has sold their ranches. She's hedging and you don't know why. You don't know if she wants more money or if it's the idea of selling the ranch that's freaking her out."

"Which is why I need you to—"

"You know, my friend Charlotte's brother has a ranch, and he would never sell for anything, so how in the hell do you expect me to get this woman to say yes?"

"Stef—"

"You need a salesman to go talk her into it, not me."

"But do you get the—"

"I get that someone promised Armor South that land six months ago based on how fast the other ranchers were selling. So we took an advance, which we've probably already allocated to different projects, and now Armor South wants their land so they can build another one of those megastores. I get it. I get that we're in the hot seat because if we can't secure the deal for the land then we need to reimburse Armor South for, I'm guessing, millions of dollars?"

"Something like that." He smiled at me.

"Then I suggest you send the top sales guy out there to—"

"We did that already." Knox sighed deeply. "Mrs. Freeman threw him off her land."

I arched an eyebrow.

"Yeah, I know."

"That seems pretty clear to me." I chuckled. "The deal is off. Give Armor South their money back or start looking for a new—"

"There is no other place."

"Then just—"

"Stef—"

"Here's the thing, Knox. I may go there and she may throw me off her land too."

"And if she does, we'll pay back Armor South, but I'll bet she sells to you."

"This is a job for the money guys. Go throw cash at her and see what happens."

"We did that. It didn't work."

"Knox." I sighed, deflating. He wasn't going to stop. "What do you expect me to say that this woman has not already heard to get her to sell?"

"I think you should explain the benefits of a Green Light Megastore to the community."

I groaned. "We don't have any in Chicago, I've never even been in one, and, furthermore, I don't work for Armor South or Green Light; I work for Chaney and Putnam Acquisitions, just like you do."

"I know, Stef, but it has to be you."

I let out another deeply annoyed sigh.

"You're not always going to like all your assignments. There's bound to be some you hate."

"Like this one."

"Stef."

"I'm going to a wedding and you want me to work in a meeting while I'm there. That doesn't sound cheesy to you?"

"This is really a tremendous opportunity for you to prove yourself."

To whom did I need to prove myself? "I don't *prove* myself. I work off of sound—"

"I know, Stef. God, I know. Everybody knows." Knox rolled his eyes, obviously done with me. "They want you there, Stef—you're going, end of story."

"You want me to go. Don't blame anyone else."

"Fine, whatever, I want you to go."

"You don't need me. You need a salesman."

"You're who I need, and you're only missing the point because you don't want to do it and you're fighting me so hard. If you just think about it for a minute, you'll get the logic."

"No, I won't."

"Stef, no one can get things done like you can. Getting buy-ins from all parties is your strong suit. You close like nothing I've ever seen."

"I don't close; it's not closing. It's getting signatures."

I would have had to be stupid not to realize that I had a way with people, but still, I had no idea what that had to do with what we were talking about. I had not done any research, so I had no way of knowing what was best for the community, and I didn't want to lie and act like I did. I always operated from the premise that what I was doing was actually in the buyers' and sellers' best interest, but in this case, I couldn't honestly make that claim.

"Stef."

"I really don't think this is a good idea."

Knox's smile was wide as he sighed heavily. "I promise you that it's possibly the best idea I've ever had."

I stared at him.

He waggled his eyebrows at me.

"I really hate you."

"No," he said, leaning back in the chair to look at me. "You'd take a bullet for me if it came down to it. You're the most loyal person I've ever met in my life."

I groaned, letting my head fall back, raking my fingers through my hair. "You don't think sending a gay man to Texas is suicide?"

"You were going already, which is why I thought of you. It was like the answer to my prayers."

"I'm going for a wedding, not to talk to ranchers."

"You said your friend's brother was a rancher."

"Yeah, and we don't talk. In fact, he hates me, and I hate him right back."

"Well, un-hate him, because you might need his help," Knox suggested.

I groaned loudly. "That's not even possible."

Knox grinned at me. "Sounds like maybe you like him."

"That's it, I'm not going. Fire me, but I'm not going."

"You people are so dramatic."

"'You people'?" I repeated, aghast.

He sighed loudly.

I gave him a look, and he snorted out a laugh.

"Gay in Texas is an oxymoron."

"Just don't have a pride parade or anything."

"Oh God."

"And make sure you don't take your rainbow flag."

"I don't own a rainbow flag," I growled at him.

Knox started laughing.

"Shit, don't they have the Klan there or something?"

More laughter that was harder and louder.

"I don't have the wardrobe for the country."

Knox's head fell back, and he laughed so hard he could barely breathe. At least one of us thought it was funny. I was not amused at all.

CHAPTER 2

I ENJOYED the afternoon visiting before my best friend's four-day wedding extravaganza weekend for a full ten minutes before I saw her brother leaning against the bar, looking out of place and uncomfortable, talking with the groom-to-be.

"Oh my God, Char," Tina Jacobs said from the other side of me. "How did you get your brother off that ranch of his on a Tuesday?"

I turned slowly to look at my friend Charlotte Holloway.

"Oh look." She forced a smile. "Rand's here. Isn't that great, Stef?"

I just stared at her.

She smiled wider.

I scowled.

"Okay, fine," she said sharply, because she felt guilty, and we both knew it. "I lied. My brother will in fact be at my wedding." She grabbed my bicep tightly, making sure I couldn't go anywhere. "But this weekend isn't about you, it's about me and Ben. You're not here for fun; you're here to keep us both sane."

I shot her a look.

"Stefan Michael Joss," she snapped, using my whole name, which she never did. "You will stop being annoyed this instant! This is my wedding, for crissakes!"

But she had sworn up, down, and sideways that her brother and I would not cross paths. If she had never brought it up, I would have prepared myself, but as it was, I thought he had to stay home and brand something or round something up or shoot something.

"Like I was really going to get married without Rand. How is that even possible? He's the head of my family, Stef."

Since when did she care?

"Use your head, Stef. We both know you didn't actually think you were getting out of here without having to see Rand."

But I had, because she had promised.

"He lives, like, an hour away, Stef. Did you seriously think he wasn't going to come?"

"You promised me he was too busy to leave the ranch." I repeated what she'd said to me over a month ago when I had been hedging.

"I lied, obviously."

I arched an eyebrow for her.

"I'm sorry for lying, but you can't leave. Your name is on the damn wedding program."

She had a point. Two hundred had been printed, and they weren't cheap. I knew because she had told me a thousand times—lots of handmade banana leaf paper and ribbon.

"And besides, you have that work thing tomorrow."

I growled at her.

"Quit. I know you and Rand can be civil for the next four days. It won't kill you."

I wasn't so sure.

Ten years ago, Charlotte Holloway had walked into my dorm room at Arizona State University and announced that she was my roommate. Since I was a boy and she was a girl, I had seriously doubted it. Coed dorms were one thing, coed rooms a whole different story. But when we compared sheets of paper, our room assignment was correct. The error was a clerical one, her name listed as Charles instead of Charlotte, but after an hour together, we both agreed that it was actually fate. We were destined to be friends, best friends. We fit seamlessly, and it felt like we'd known each other forever. When I told her I was gay, she told me that I couldn't be any more perfect. By the time the admissions office discovered the mistake, we had already pooled our money and moved off campus together. Everything was sailing along great until Charlotte's older brother came for a visit.

Rand Holloway had made the trip from a small town close to Lubbock, Texas to Tempe, Arizona to check on his little sister a month after she moved. Charlotte's father was too busy running the ranch, so the task fell to Rand, the man who would someday be head of the family, to either give his approval or drag her home. I was cautioned to be on my best behavior, and I was prepared to be a saint. I was not, however, prepared for Rand Holloway. He walked into our apartment without even a knock of warning, and when I looked up, I had not been able to contain my gasp. I was young, only eighteen at the time, and there, standing in front of me, was easily the most beautiful man I had ever seen in my life.

He was tall, probably six-four, built like a swimmer with broad shoulders and a wide chest that narrowed to lean hips, and from the way his clothes clung to him, he was covered from head to toe in thick, corded muscle. His hair was so black it had blue highlights in it, and his eyes were a piercing turquoise blue, like the sky on a cloudless day. From the chiseled features to the bulging biceps to the way his jeans hugged his long, muscular legs and tight ass, he was utterly breathtaking, and I completely lost my power of speech. Unfortunately, he did not.

"So I guess you're the fag, right?"

First words out of the man's mouth and they set the tone for every interaction we've ever had from that moment on.

Charlotte had told her family that I was gay because she didn't want them to worry about her roommate being a guy. Rand had come to check out Charlotte's school, her living conditions, and, most of all, me. When I had looked over at my new roommate, I could tell she wanted to crawl under a rock and hide. But I wasn't mad at her. She had merely been passing along information as if I had been black or red or green or blue, but her brother... her homophobic, cowboy, shitkicker, redneck, small-minded, small-town, prejudiced piece of crap brother, thought I was the Antichrist. It was written all over his face, from the scowl to his crossed arms to the disdain that I could feel radiating off him. He hated me simply because of who slept in my bed. It was stupid, and so was he. I gathered up my things and left until I knew he was gone. The worst part of all was that the man was hot. If he'd been ugly, if I hadn't thought he was gorgeous before I knew he was an asshole, it would have been easier for me. As it was, there was guilt for initially thinking the enemy was glorious, mouthwatering perfection.

A year later, when Charlotte's father died unexpectedly from a heart attack, I made the trip to Texas with her to hold her hand, tell her jokes, and just keep her sane. Rand wanted her home, but both she and her mother thought that the best place for her was in school. I was the one who finally told him off, telling him that what he wanted didn't mean shit to anyone. His father, Charlotte's father, James Holloway, had sent his daughter to school because he wanted what was best for her. Just because it would be easier for Rand if his sister went home didn't mean she was going to go.

When he roared back at me that the tuition could no longer be paid, I told him that he didn't have to worry. I would help my friend stay in school. I would get as many jobs as it took to make sure that she didn't have to be stuck living anywhere near him and his narrow-minded view of the world. While Charlotte and her mother hugged and kissed me, Rand had stalked from the room like a wounded animal. It became clear that it wasn't just gay men her brother had a problem with, it was also women who wanted to be more than housewives and mothers. And while Charlotte wanted a husband and lots of cute kids, she also wanted the job that a college education could provide.

As soon as we got back home to Tempe, my best friend got two jobs and I got another in addition to the one I already worked five nights a week. It was hard: sleep became a treat and not a given, but we paid her tuition plus our bills. When we both got promotions, we could actually go out again and do some drinking and dancing, even see the occasional movie. A year later, when Rand offered to start paying her tuition, as he had the ranch back to where it was making money, I took great pride in the fact that she said thanks, but no thanks. He called me on my cell phone to tell me to stop being such a self-righteous prick and pressuring his little sister into decisions she didn't need to make. With Charlotte listening, I told him to go to hell. She had her own mind, and if she trusted me more than him, maybe that had more to do with him and less to do with me. It was a priceless moment when I got to hang up on him and not pick back up the other twelve times he called. Charlotte had dissolved into laughter watching me dance around the apartment.

Over the next two years, the animosity just escalated. When we graduated, I was sad because I would miss her, but the bright spot was that I would never be subjected to Rand Holloway again, nor the mandatory trips to Texas.

I didn't go near the Lone Star State, and with Rand never leaving the ranch, my vacations with my friend were evil-free. I was not surprised when Charlotte called to tell me that Rand's wife had left him after only a year of marriage. I had been more surprised over the news that he had gotten someone to marry him in the first place. She called me a jerk, but her new boyfriend Benjamin Cantwell had agreed with me. Rand wasn't his favorite either.

Six months ago, Charlotte had asked me to show up for her mother's sixtieth birthday party. The day afterward, the three of us—Char, Ben, and I—were flying out to Cancun to meet friends. When she told me we were going to the ranch, I was worried, but I figured it was only one day. What was the worst thing that could happen?

I was standing with Charlotte's uncle Tyler, having a good time, asking him questions while he barbequed, when Rand came by. He told his father's oldest brother not to waste his time talking to me because I wasn't really listening anyway.

"I am, actually," I had snapped at his retreating back.

"Bullshit," he barked back at me, having wheeled around. "Stefan Joss never listens to anything anybody says."

"No," I said coolly, staring directly into his eyes. "I just don't listen to you."

The muscles in his jaw clenched, the veins in his neck corded, and his eyes narrowed. "Well, that's certainly good to know."

I shrugged, and he walked away without another word.

"You know—" The older man had chuckled, which brought my attention back to him, "I have never seen anyone get a rise out of Rand like that."

"Sorry," I said, ready to walk away.

He stopped me with a gentle hand on my arm. "No." His smile was wide. "It was fun."

"Yeah, it was," I smirked at him, which sent him into choking laughter. I wasn't the only one who thought that Charlotte's big brother was an ass.

Later that night, Rand had stopped on his way into the house to say good night to his family and found me sitting between two of his uncles, drinking beer, talking, all three of us with our feet up on the railing of the porch. More of his cousins were crowded around us, everyone laughing. I was the only one without a cowboy hat on.

"You comfortable?" he asked snidely after he told everyone else he was heading up to bed, since some people had to get up early in the morning to work the ranch. "Think you'd still be if everybody knew?"

"Knew what? That I'm gay?" I asked him, grinning like crazy. "I dunno, maybe."

Watching his face fall was priceless.

"Stef told us about that," his uncle Lincoln told him. "I say what a man does in his own bed is his own business. Ain't that right?"

"It's just like a man that likes big women." His uncle Tyler shrugged. "If that's your taste, why not, I say."

"He likes big girls," Lincoln assured everyone, in case any of us had missed it.

Rand's sky-blue eyes were locked on me as he spoke under his breath. "You're lucky my family is full of open-minded, good-hearted—"

"Except you," I cut in, then took a quick breath and smiled wide even as I saw his jaw clench. "No one ever accused you of being a good guy, huh?"

He pointed at me. "You're a cocky piece of—"

"Aww, are you tired? Is that why we're name-calling?"

If looks could kill, I would have been dead right there.

"Better get on up to bed, Mr. Holloway. We wouldn't want you to be tired in the morning and be a dick or anything."

"You know, one of these days you're going to get yourself in a mess that—"

"Oh." I waggled my eyebrows at him. "I love a good mess."

Everyone laughed, and he stalked across the porch, fuming, fists clenched at his side.

"Stefan Joss, you cannot leave me!" The whispered threat brought me back from my wandering thoughts to Charlotte.

"Please."

Who was she kidding? I would never, ever leave her.

I rolled my eyes, and she leaped into my arms, wrapping herself around me as tightly as she could.

"Uh-oh, look out. Your man's coming," I said, putting her down.

We both turned to see Benjamin Cantwell crossing the room to us. He was dodging people trying to talk to him, making sure he didn't get caught in someone's clutches, and finally broke into a jog to get to me. It was easy to see, by the way his eyes lit up and his pleased smile, that the man really liked me. I opened my arms for him, and he lunged at me. The hug was hard and hurt a little, so that way I knew it was real.

"You're late," he said when he let me go, shoving me away from him. "I was worried you weren't coming until Thursday or something and by then my girl'd be a basket case."

"Oh shut up," she snapped, smacking him in the arm before moving to my side, leaning against me. "I'm perfectly fine."

I kissed the top of her head as I squeezed her tight. "Aww, Char, you know I had to show. I mean, who else is gonna watch out for your man at all the strip clubs?"

She laughed, and it was deep and throaty, one of many things I loved about her. I gave her a last hug before I let her go and she went into Ben's arms. She wrapped hers around his waist, and he anchored her there next to him.

"I was sorry to hear that your guy couldn't make it, Stef," Ben said softly, sympathizing.

I squinted at him. "What guy is this?"

"Oh." He sounded surprised. "Um, Cody, right? Wasn't that his name?"

"Oh, Ben, Cody is so six months ago." Charlotte chimed in.

"Less," I corrected her, "but yeah, he's done."

"Need a damn scorecard to keep up with these guys, Stef."

I shrugged.

"He's just picky," Charlotte defended me.

"So." I squinted at her. "You were kidding on the phone, right?"

She deflated, and Ben gave her a sympathetic shoulder squeeze.

"It's so awful," she said, her eyes locked on mine. "The dress, the bridesmaid dresses… the tuxedos… Stef, it's just… just…." She turned and looked up at Ben.

He squinted at me. "It's bad. Wait'll you see the tuxedo you're wearing."

When she had called, hyperventilating, to tell me that everything she had done in preparation for her wedding had been undone by her mother, her aunts, and her cousins, I had laughed on the phone. How bad could it really be?

But now, as I stood beside her in her room, staring at the atrocity hanging over the mirrored side of the armoire, I was speechless. I didn't know a dress could have that much beading and lace and….

"What are those… rhinestones?"

"Yeah, I think so."

"Huh."

"You see?" She waved at the dress.

"Huh," I grunted again.

"Oh God," she said, throwing herself down very dramatically across her bed.

"Maybe if we pull stuff off," I offered, fingering the lace and brocade.

"Thank God you're here," she muttered into the comforter on the bed. "I can't do this without you. Nobody gets me like you get me."

"I know," I said, because it was true, but also because it was an easy response and I was distracted. "I bet if the sun hit this just right you could, like, blind people."

She groaned loudly.

"Whose dress was this again?"

"Ben's mama's."

"Huh."

"There's a veil too."

"No, really?"

She lifted her head up off the bed so she could see me. "I'm sorry that you have to deal with the whole 'man of honor' thing, but if I had you stand with the groomsmen, it would have been a lie. You and Ben are friends, but Stef—you belong to me."

"Yes, I do, you poor, dumb bitch."

Her smile, with the dimples, was luminous.

Back downstairs in the living room of the enormous three-story bed and breakfast we were all staying at, Charlotte clutched my arm for dear life. I felt her fingers dig into my arm as a man and woman stepped in front of us, followed closely by a younger couple.

"Charlotte, is this your best friend that we've heard so much about?"

"Yes, Linda," she said softly, leaning against me. "This is Stefan."

I looked at Ben's mom and smiled wide.

She caught her breath.

"Wow," I said, offering her my hand. "Jesus, Char, you didn't tell me she was hot."

Charlotte squeaked her surprise as I yanked her soon-to-be mother-in-law into my arms and gave her a quick kiss before I hugged her tight.

She pressed against me, her fingers digging into my back.

"Hey." Ben's father laughed. "Give my wife back."

I let her go but put my arm around her shoulders, holding her beside me as I looked down into her face. "Whaddya say—can we revisit the dress, Mom?" I asked softly, using the full weight of my arsenal, my voice and my face. Having been told constantly from a very young age that I was gorgeous, I knew I was. The blond hair, dark green eyes, and the permanent tan that I had been born with, all of it blended together made people stop and watch me walk by on the street. I took no credit for any of it—it was just genetics, after all—but I used it to my advantage when I had to, and I *had* to get that dress altered.

Ben's mother giggled and wrapped her arms around my waist. "Yes, darling, whatever you want."

"Oh my God," Charlotte breathed out on the other side of me.

"Hello there," Mr. Cantwell said, smiling at me, extending his hand. "It's a pleasure, Stefan. My girl's face lights up every time she says your name."

"Yessir, I know," I said, smiling at him, taking his hand, gripping it firmly. Nice that he was calling his soon-to-be daughter-in-law "his girl."

"I know this was a long way to come, but Charlotte said you would do anything for her and Ben," he said, his eyes warm as he stared at me.

"Yes sir, absolutely."

He liked me. It was there in his twinkling eyes and the firmness of the handshake. He liked that I appreciated his wife's beauty and that his son was already important to me.

"Tell me all about yourself. What is it you do, Stefan?"

Before I could open my mouth to speak, Charlotte answered for me.

"Stef's an acquisitions manager at Chaney and Putnam. It's a real estate holding firm."

"Oh." Mr. Cantwell chuckled. "Well then… maybe I can talk to you about some land I'm thinking of purchasing, get your thoughts."

"Absolutely," I assured him.

He nodded, then let out a deep breath before turning to his right. "Let me introduce the rest of my family."

I met Ben's sister, Renee, and her husband, Stuart, and was then taken outside on the enormous patio and introduced to her grandparents and all her extended family. Aunts, uncles, cousins—I met everyone, Ben's mother Linda never relinquishing my hand, Charlotte never leaving me either, her body molded to my side. When the music started, I took the bride-to-be to the dance floor and into my arms. When she started to cry, I scooped her up and spun her around until she started laughing.

"Oh God," she groaned suddenly a few minutes later.

"What?"

"Look, it's the angel of death."

I followed her gaze and saw Ben standing with Nick and Clarissa Towne.

"You know, I seriously thought about not marrying the man because of his best friend."

"Why?"

"Are you kidding?" She shot me a look. "You know why. The guy's an idiot."

"Well, Ben's probably not thrilled that your best friend is gay."

"Ben couldn't care less. You know why?"

"I'm afraid to ask."

"You are not a total pig like Nick Towne."

"He's not that bad."

She gave me a look.

"I hesitate to even ask."

"He asked Ben if he had to marry me. *Had* to marry me, Stef, *had* to."

I just smiled at her.

"Like the only way I can get Ben Cantwell is if he knocks me up."

"Well, his family is very rich."

She smacked me really hard.

"Shit," I groaned, rubbing my arm.

"He's an ass."

"Stop," I teased.

"And his wife," she moaned. "My God, my desk at work is more animated than she is."

"God, you're a bitch," I said, grabbing her hand and dragging her after me off the dance floor.

I raised a hand, and Clarissa saw me. Instantly, her head tilted to the side as her smile made her eyes sparkle.

"Holy shit," Charlotte breathed out.

"See," I said over my shoulder. "She shines."

"Only when she sees you, Stef. Just like everybody else."

I let go of Charlotte's hand as I reached Clarissa, and she leaped at me. We hugged tightly, and she buried her face in my shoulder.

"It's so good to see you," she said, inhaling me.

"You, too, sweetheart." I smiled into her hair.

I let her hold me until she was ready to let go. When she did, I held out my hand to her husband and Ben's best man, Nick Towne, and he pulled me into the guy clench and patted my back hard. His face showed his ease in my presence.

"Hey."

I turned to Ben. "What?"

He just looked at me.

"What?"

"Nothin'." He smiled at me after a minute. "Look," he said as he raised his chin.

I heard my name before I even had time to turn. Charlotte's mother, May Holloway, was crossing the room, looking very uncomfortable until I waved. She stopped, and I went to her. There were arms held out waiting for me. A half an hour later, as I took a break from dancing, flopping down in the seat beside Ben at the end of the long table, I felt a hand trailing through my hair. When I lifted my head, I found Charlotte. She was looking at me oddly.

"What?"

"You're amazing, you know."

I arched an eyebrow for her, and she snorted out a laugh.

"Classy," Ben teased her.

"I just… you made Ben's mom say yes to altering my dress, you made me see a totally different side of Nick and our parents… I mean, look at them over there," she said, staring across the room. "You'd think they were old friends instead of meeting today for the very first time. It's all working out."

I was glad.

"And what started it all?"

"I have no idea," I yawned, folding my arms on top of the table and laying my head down. Six hours on a plane after pulling an all-nighter at work the previous day was taking its toll on me. Not to mention the copious amount of alcohol I had downed.

"You idiot." She bumped my side. "You took Ben's folks over to my mom, and since everyone is crazy about you, they were all so open and receptive. It was awesome."

"Okay," I placated.

She pinched my side, but I didn't even flinch.

"God, Stef," she said, running her hand down my torso. "Feel that stomach under that shirt; it's hard as a rock."

"Not fair," Kristin Barnes, one of her bridesmaids, said from the other side of the table. "If you're over there feeling Stefan up, then we should all get a turn."

"Well, then, come here."

"Kris, leave him alone," Ben ordered even as he made room for two other girls on either side of me.

"You're a big help," I told him.

There were hands in my hair, under the back of my shirt, on my chest, my biceps, and Kristin's fingers sliding over my eyebrows. I was drowning in women.

"Holy shit, Char." Someone laughed. "Your best friend is gorgeous."

"I know." She laughed. "I've been telling him since freshman year. With those eyes and that hot body, he could have whoever he wants."

"Oh, most definitely," Kristin chimed in. "The boy is smokin' hot."

I arched a brow for her, and she dissolved into giggles.

"Do you dye your hair, Stefan?"

Before I could answer, Charlotte did.

"No, honey, that's all natural. The gold tan, the dark green eyes, the dirty blond hair, that's all him. He looks like that every day when he first rolls out of bed in the morning. The only thing he works at is the body, and he doesn't work that hard, let me assure you."

"Hey," I protested. "My gym workouts are exhausting."

"Please." She put up her hand. "An hour a day out of your life is nothing, Joss."

"I think he's right, Char," Kristin agreed. "I mean, there are washboard abs here; I'm thinking he works hard."

"Oh yeah, lemme see."

"Enough." Ben laughed, getting up and shooing all the girls away, taking a seat beside me. "Y'all should be ashamed of yourselves, groping a gay man. The boy ain't even enjoyin' it. Go grope Rand, he's straight."

"Oh, I would love to get my hands—" Alison Ford, another bridesmaid, began.

"Gross," Charlotte groaned.

"Or my mouth," Kristin added, "on that man."

"Oh God, that's so disgusting."

"He's your brother, that's why," someone else said. "But Char, the man is absolutely edible."

"Yeah, but he's way too serious and dark to mess with."

"'Brooding' is a good word."

They were all talking at once, and I just smiled. I loved girls. They were so much fun.

"And he always looks mad," another voice suggested.

"But so hot."

"Any of us would do him, Char, but he seems… angry."

"Really angry," Kristin agreed. "Which is why even when he looks like that, I wouldn't go near that man on a bet."

"Me neither."

There was a chorus of agreement from the table.

"Which is why we love Stef," another of the bridesmaids put in. "He's beautiful and sexy and the sweetest guy I've ever met in my life."

"He's not broken, he's healthy."

"If you weren't gay," Alison said, "you'd belong to me, Stefan Joss."

"Bullshit," Kristin assured her. "He'd be mine."

"You're all high; I would have married him in college if he was straight."

"Pardon me?" Ben interrupted, and the table dissolved into laughter.

"Oh honey," Charlotte soothed him, getting up to take a seat in his lap.

"Get off me," he grumbled, much to everyone's delight.

When all the girls kissed me before getting up to go mingle, I turned my head to Ben.

He let out a snort of laughter. "I wouldn't be you on a bet."

I smiled at him as his hand rested between my shoulder blades.

"And thanks for being good to Nicky. I know he ain't your favorite guy, but he's not a dick like Rand either."

"I know."

"But if you give him a chance, then so will Char, and that's the truth."

"Sure," I yawned, rubbing my eyes hard. "I think I'm gonna go up and unpack and maybe lay down for a while until the bachelor party. I don't wanna pass out later."

"Bachelor party is tomorrow night, buddy. Tonight is just all of us goin' out honky-tonkin'."

Good God.

"Do you have boots?"

"Ben."

"And a hat?"

"I'll just sit and drink, how's that?"

He nodded, smiling wide. "Sounds like a good plan," he agreed, and I felt his hand slip off me. "I'll get you up in time to eat in case you really pass out."

I nodded and rose up out of my chair, looking down at my friend. "I really am happy to be here, you know."

"I know." He smiled up at me. "And I appreciate it too."

I squeezed his shoulder before I started for the grand staircase. Almost there, I was suddenly faced with Rand Holloway. I waited for the attack.

He scowled.

I crossed my arms.

Seconds ticked by.

His Technicolor blue eyes darkened.

"Jesus, what?" I finally asked, already exasperated.

"This is your greeting."

"You're the one standing there not saying a word."

He nodded, and I threw up my hands, slipping around him to the stairs. I took them in threes and made it to the landing and around the corner.

"Joss!"

Rand was one of those guys who called everyone by their last name. I hated it because it had always seemed like such macho bullshit. I turned at my door and watched him jog down the hallway to me.

"Listen," he said, stopping in front of me. "I just want to call a truce for the next few days, all right? I've got enough on my mind without having to fight with—"

"Great, perfect," I cut him off. "You stay clear of me, and I'll do the same."

His eyes searched mine, and as always I thought how beautiful they were. No matter my feelings for the man, he was, without a doubt, stunning. Just the Caribbean blue eyes were enough to melt me into a puddle on the floor. To say the man was hot was an understatement.

"Anything else?"

He turned and left without a backward glance.

I flipped him off because I felt like it. That he had missed it because his back was turned really wasn't the point.

Inside my room, I shed my jacket and fell down on the huge four-poster bed. It was nice that Charlotte's uncle Lincoln had volunteered his business to house the wedding party. I hated big hotels, since I traveled so much with my job. Being at a nice, quiet, charming B&B was a treat. As I closed my eyes, I wondered who had put Rand up to making nice with me. I would have to ask Charlotte if it was her when I woke up after my nap… later.

CHAPTER 3

LINDA CANTWELL asked the groom-to-be and all the groomsmen, plus me, to wear their tuxedos downstairs before dinner so she could see the problem that her son was talking about. She had felt that white tuxedos with tails would be elegant. Ben and Charlotte and the rest of the wedding party had insisted it was a very dated look. I was the last down because I overslept, and when I walked over to Ben, he groaned.

"What?"

"You look fuckin' great." He gestured at me.

"Oh, now see," Linda said to Charlotte, taking hold of my hand. "Stefan looks like he could have walked off the cover of a magazine."

"Linda, you can put Stefan in anything and he'll look good; he doesn't count," she ranted, gesturing at her fiancé. "Look at your son, for crissakes."

"Hey!"

Everyone's laughter followed me back up the stairs.

Later that night, I realized I was having fun just watching everyone dance, and Rand's absence made the evening much more enjoyable for me. Somehow or other, I had gotten roped into being a designated driver, along with Charlotte's cousin, Weston. We had a long talk about TV shows and soccer and his job as a tax attorney. I zoned out a couple of times but managed to look interested. When Charlotte decided that all she wanted to do was be draped over me with her head on my shoulder, I let her. When Ben found us, we were in the back, sitting as we always did, me stretched out with my feet up and her in my lap, her legs between mine.

"You know, you all look like you're the ones getting married."

I smiled up at him, but I could tell from the steady breath on the side of my neck that his bride was asleep. She shifted position, and her lips opened against my throat.

"If she bites you, I'm gonna smack her," Ben grumbled. "That ain't right."

"She's asleep," I told him.

"Asleep or awake, that woman is crazy about you."

"It goes both ways."

He grunted. "Well, pick her up, boy, we gotta head home. The rest of us can sleep in, but don't you hafta go meet that woman tomorrow?"

"Yeah, don't remind me."

"You want me to come?"

It was a really nice offer. "No, but thanks, really."

Back at the house, I carried Charlotte up to her room, and Ben followed after me. Once she was in bed, I ended up following him to his room and lying on the bed listening to him. We talked until two in the morning.

WITH ONLY five hours of sleep, I hid my eyes behind my oversized Prada sunglasses when I came downstairs looking for coffee the following morning.

"Little early for acting like a rock star, ain't it?"

Looking up, I saw Rand Holloway sitting at the kitchen table.

"What? No snappy retort?"

Even the intoxicating smell of coffee could not lure me any farther into that room with the beast. I turned around and walked out, heading for the front door.

"Joss!"

I kept walking and slammed the door on my way out. My car was parked at the end of the large, gravel-covered circular drive, and I had almost reached it when there was a hand on my bicep. I was spun around so fast I almost lost my balance.

"Jesus, can you wait?" he barked at me.

Realizing it was Rand, I yanked my arm free, again almost falling down.

He grabbed the same arm and jerked me forward so hard that I had to put a hand on his chest to keep from slamming into him.

"What the hell?" I snarled at him, twisting free, taking several steps backward.

"You never listen."

"Go away." I sighed, looking up at him, realizing how close he was now that he had bent toward me. We were almost nose to nose.

The muscles in his jaw clenched. "Where are you going?"

"Why is that your business?"

He breathed in through his nose.

"Seriously?"

He pushed the cowboy hat back on his forehead, telling me, without benefit of words, that he would wait all day if I didn't answer.

"I have an appointment to see a lady about a ranch."

"What the hell does that mean?"

"Just go inside," I told him, trying to get around him.

"I want to talk to you."

"About what?"

He didn't say, just stood there staring at me.

"I hafta go."

"Where do you have to go?" he pried. "You're on vacation."

"Fine, do you happen to know a lady named Grace Freeman?"

He scowled down at me. "Sure, she owns the Dancing Horse Ranch down toward Hillman. Why?"

I took a step back to put a little distance between us, because if I didn't, I was going to attack him. The man smelled amazing, clean and spicy at the same time. His eyes were darkening pools of heat, and looking at his plump, pink bottom lip was giving me chills.

"I—I hafta see if she wants to sell."

He squinted at me. "You work for Armor South?"

"No," I cleared my throat, taking another step back. "I work for Chaney Putnam, and we're the ones acquiring the land for Armor South."

"Whatever." He advanced on me, one hand on the roof of the Lexus, pinning me back against the side of the car. "She ain't gonna sell."

"I think that's awfully naïve of you to say when everyone else did, in fact, sell."

"She's different."

"How so?" Maybe he knew something I could use.

"She knows things ain't always easy."

"Okay, but does everything always hafta be hard?"

His scowl could have peeled paint.

"And why do you even care?" I asked, looking up at him.

He took a quick breath. "Because every ranch is important. We all support each other."

"The other ranchers already sold. How is that support?"

"You don't know anything about working a ranch or about the pride that comes from that," he growled at me. "You have no idea."

"I don't need to," I shot back. "I only need to know about Mrs. Freeman and what's best for her and her family."

"You don't know anything."

"Fine, can you move?"

He took a step back, and I walked around the car and got in. I felt instantly better. Out on the highway, I breathed a huge sigh of relief. Being around Rand Holloway took so much energy, and I hadn't even had coffee yet. Maybe Mrs. Freeman would have some.

It turned out that not only did she have coffee, but she made me breakfast as well.

As I sat out on the porch sipping sweet tea with Mrs. Freeman after breakfast, I realized that she was in a real quandary about what to do. Her own sons had not wanted the ranch, and only one of her grandsons seemed interested in the life. On the other hand, some of the men that worked for her wanted to pool their money and buy the ranch, but none of those plans were a certainty. The money Chaney Putnam was offering was for sure, and her neighbors wanted her to take it. If she said no, they all had to go back to their struggling ranches. Who was she to sentence them to that when they all wanted to leave? But the land had been in her family for generations and she didn't want to be the person who sold it.

"Yeah, you're kinda screwed either way," I said, smiling over at her, holding my sweating glass of tea.

Her smile was wide. "That company of yours is mighty smart, Mr. Joss, to be sendin' me such a sweet boy to talk to."

I waggled my eyebrows for her, eliciting a deep laugh. "Please, call me Stefan, and I heard you didn't like the other guy at all."

"What other guy?"

"The first rep from Chaney Putnam. I heard you threw him off your land."

"Darlin', you're the first one who's come."

But that made no sense. Either she was mistaken, or Knox had lied. But why would my boss lie to me? What would be the point of that?

"Sweetheart?"

But suddenly, I knew what the point was. Knox had tried to make the whole situation that much more hopeless and dire so I would have no choice but to go. Between the two of us, he was infinitely more dramatic.

"Stefan?"

I cleared my throat. "So how 'bout I come back on Monday before I leave and we'll talk some more? How would that be?"

Her face showed her astonishment. "You... you're not going to try and get an answer now?"

"No, ma'am," I assured her. "You need to think hard. You know better than I do what the community needs. I mean, there are jobs associated with the opening of the kind of store that Armor South wants to put up, but you have to weigh that against the lives of your family and the men who work on your ranch."

"Yes," she agreed solemnly.

I leaned over toward her. "You have my number; call me if you just need to talk. I'm a really good listener. Maybe there are alternatives that neither of us has thought of yet."

When I reached out my hand, she took it.

"Whatever I can do," I said gently.

"Thank you, Stefan." She sighed deeply. "Thank you so much."

I GOT back after lunch, and Charlotte wanted me to go with her to shop for lingerie for the wedding night. Her girlfriends were thrilled to have me along and surprised that I had good suggestions for my friend. We met Ben and the rest of the wedding party out for dinner. I was pleased that we were missing Rand. I wasn't up to a second altercation with him.

After dinner, we went into Lubbock for the bachelor party, and after four strip clubs, the drink minimum plus more at each place, moving from bar to bar and club to club, everyone was drunk. Around one, once everything closed, we returned home. I was the last out of the car because I was carrying Ben. He had been awake in the car for twenty minutes of the hour ride back but had passed out in my lap shortly thereafter. At least he had not succumbed to barfing, like two of the other guys. Charlotte started giggling as soon as she saw me, and I asked her if maybe she wanted to take charge of him. She was marrying him, after all.

"Oh hell no," she said like I was high.

"God, Stefan, isn't he heavy?" Clarissa asked me.

"Yeah, he weighs a fuckin' ton," I grumbled, starting up the stairs. It was awkward, since he was taller than my own five-eleven, closer to six-three, but I managed.

"Is he all right?" She laughed at me.

"Yeah, he's just done," I assured her, waving without looking at her.

"Well, throw him in bed and come back down. I want to talk to you," Charlotte told me.

I loved her, but I was beat. "How 'bout I'll see you in the morning?"

"Okay," she called after me. "I'll see you then. Love you!"

"Right backatcha."

Upstairs, I eased him down on the bed as gently as I could. After I took off his shoes and socks, I decided to leave the rest. I covered him with a blanket and was almost to the door.

"You know, I've never been in a fist fight in my life."

Weird thing for him to say out of the blue, but he was drunk, so I went with it and turned around to face the bed in the darkness. "No?"

"No," he burped. "How many have you been in?"

"Too many to count. Now go to sleep."

"Wait."

I groaned but turned again from the door.

He sat up and flicked on the small light on the nightstand. "How come you've been in a lot of fights, Stef?"

"I dunno, just have."

"Because of being gay?"

"No," I yawned, "not once because I was gay. Mostly from drunks, some because of trying to break something up, and one because my roommate has a big fuckin' mouth."

He grinned, and in the faint light, his warm brown eyes glowed as he looked at me. "Oh yeah? Charlotte got you in a bar fight?"

"Yep." I nodded before I explained about the drunken brawl in the middle of the pool hall when we were in college. Charlotte had been running her mouth, not backing down from the table of drunken frat boys shooting pool alongside us. When they finally had enough, I was the one they came after, since they couldn't hit a girl.

"How many guys?"

"Just three," I lied. It had been more like five.

"Jesus, Stefan, you're a badass, huh?"

"I just wasn't as drunk as they were."

His mouth was curled up in the corner, his eyes slits, and his hair was sticking up on one side. He was a disheveled mess, and I had never seen him look better. "Go to sleep."

"Wait."

I looked back around the door, since I was already in the hall. "What?"

"What if I hafta barf?"

"The trash can's there next to the bed."

"You think of everything," he said softly, his eyes on mine.

"Always."

"Thanks for bein' such a good friend, Stef. You didn't hafta like me"—he burped—"'cause you're Char's friend and all, but you do, and I appreciate it."

"I'm your friend too."

"No, I know, I didn't mean it like that."

"You mean if you guys get a divorce you know she'll get me."

"Well that's a nice fuckin' thing to say right before I get married."

"I'm just sayin'."

"Shit."

I laughed at him. "Go to sleep already."

"Wait."

"What?"

"I used to be worried, you know, when I first met you. I thought maybe you'd wanna fuck me or something, and it sorta weirded me out."

"Uh-huh."

"But now I know it ain't like that."

"'Cause you're not my type," I teased him.

"Shut up." He burped. "I'm tryin' to have a moment here."

"Sorry."

"I just... you're the only gay person I know."

"I seriously doubt that," I told him honestly, "but I appreciate the sentiment. Can you go to bed now?"

"Yeah." He belched loudly, lying down on the bed. "I think maybe I should, but Stef?"

"What?"

"Come kiss me good night."

I flipped him off before I closed the door behind me.

CHAPTER 4

CHARLOTTE KEPT me busy the following morning. She came to my room way too early, but she brought coffee, so I didn't kill her. Once I showered and changed and we were off to see a friend of the family who was a seamstress. Hopefully she could do something with the scary wedding dress. The woman was hesitant when we got there, but once I assured her that no harm would come to her for messing with an heirloom, she went to work, gutting it starting with the antique, over-the-top beading. Charlotte had sketched out what she wanted, and after I made some suggestions, it sounded like it was going to be good. She was all over me as we left. We met up with everyone else for a late breakfast at a local place that Charlotte's family loved.

After we got home, everyone started playing croquet on the back lawn. I thought it was a little tame until I realized that everyone had to take a shot of tequila before each round and you had to have a beer in your hand at all times. If the beer was put down, you took another shot of Patrón. If the beer went empty, same deal. There were going to be balls and mallets flying all over the place in a very short time. I decided to send out e-mails I had been putting off so I wouldn't have to do it later. The sooner I finished up the last of my work, the sooner I could get down to some serious drinking.

By the time I got finished, there were cars cluttering the street, lots of people at the house, and a basketball game going on in the driveway that was more about trash talking and pushing and shoving than anything else. The girls were goading the men on, everyone was laughing and drinking, and inevitably, the longer the game went on, the more obnoxious everyone became. I went inside to get a bottle of water, and by the time I returned, Ben was preparing to take a shot from what I assumed was the foul line. One of the guys from the opposite team was harassing him, and I realized suddenly how serious he was.

"Take the shot, you drunkass piece of shit."

"I'm not the drunk asshole," Ben snapped at him, dribbling the ball where he was. "And if you would shut the fuck up, maybe I could shoot."

"Fuckin' asshole," he complained to Charlotte. "Make your punk-ass man shoot the ball!"

"Shoot the ball, Ben!" She laughed. "Before my cousin Brandon beats the crap out of you!"

"I was just fouled, Char. It's my free throw."

"Oh, will you shoot already!" the guy said, walking forward and shoving Ben hard.

"Get off me!"

"Gimme the ball, asshole," he snarled, shoving Ben again, trying to take the ball.

"Get off!" Ben yelled, pushing back.

Because the guy was drunk, when he got as good as he'd given, he nearly fell over, only his windmilling arms keeping him on his feet. Everyone thought it was hysterical, and the laughter at the guy's expense was loud. Ben was chuckling, walking away, and never noticing that the guy was suddenly charging after him. Since he wasn't paying attention at that point, involved instead in yelling over to see who else wanted to play, he never saw the fist swung at him. I had started moving the second Ben had turned around, so I was close enough to interfere.

I stepped in front of my friend, absorbing the impact in my shoulder that he would have taken in the back of the head. The guy lifted up and threw a roundhouse punch that connected with my jaw. There was instant pain before my adrenaline kicked in. When I fight, I get that strobe-light effect. I see pieces until it's over. So I saw the guy pull back and swing at me again before I had my hand on his throat, my other arm blocking the blow. He was more muscular than I was, but I was just as tall, and my leverage was better. I wasn't drunk, and as a result, my reflexes were faster. I spread my legs for balance, tightened my grip, pivoted, and hurled him up against the wall of the garage. The force took all the air from his body as I put my forearm on his throat.

"Are you insane?" I asked him, staring into his eyes as I applied slow pressure to his esophagus, making him raise his head. "You could have really hurt him."

His eyes were huge.

Everyone was talking at once.

"Let him go, Stefan, he's just drunk," someone said.

"Stefan," Ben said from beside me, his hand on my left shoulder. "You're bleeding. Let him go so I can look at you. I wanna look at you."

"Watch out," I warned him before I released my hold, spun the guy around, and threw him up against the side of the house as hard as I could. He grunted with the impact, and I twisted his arm up behind him, smashing his face into the hard brick. I leaned in close to whisper in his ear. "Get outta here, man, and if I see you anywhere near him again, I will break your fuckin' jaw."

When I let go, he slid down the wall and made a puddle at my feet. Somebody grabbed my arm, and I whirled around, ready to throw down.

"Wait-wait-wait," Rand half yelled, half laughed, his hands up. "It's me, it's just me."

I stared into the vivid blue eyes and realized that for the first time in all the years that I'd known the man that I had never, ever seen him smile. It was mind-numbing, even more so because it was directed at me. In the middle of chaos, his lip curled up at the corner, his eyes sparkling, the way he sighed, had me at an absolute loss.

His smile widened. "Not sure if you wanna hit me, too, huh?"

I stepped back as Charlotte brushed by Rand and flung herself into my arms.

"Are you all right?"

"Fine," I said, taking a quick breath.

"I had no idea he would—oh God, baby, you're bleeding." She caught her breath, clutching me tight before grabbing the front of my shirt and yanking me forward, away from the crowd.

"I'm okay, Char."

"Holy shit, Stef," Kristin breathed, suddenly there as well, having brushed by Charlotte, her hands on my face, her fingers in my hair. "That was amazing. I had no idea you could—"

"What? Fight?" I scowled at her, pulling back, wiping at my mouth. There was blood on my hand, and I could feel the sting from where I'd been caught in the lip and jaw. I pulled off my blue dress shirt first and then the white T-shirt underneath. It was already stained with blood, so I used it to clean myself off. I felt a hand on my back, and when I turned, another bridesmaid, Alison Ford, was there.

"Are you all right?"

I nodded as her hand ran down my spine.

"Look at you," she said before our eyes met.

"What?"

"Stefan." She cleared her throat. "You totally manhandled that guy."

"Oh yeah?" I smiled at her, throwing my T-shirt into the trashcan closest to me before I turned to face her. "That do it for you?"

She nodded, giving me a wicked grin. "A little bit, yeah."

I gave her a smile before Charlotte turned my face back to her.

"Now you know I know that you can handle yourself," she growled, her head swiveling around to look for her cousin. "But I am gonna kill Brandon Holloway."

"Don't kill anybody," I soothed her, "handcuffs on your big day would be really tacky." I headed toward the house. Halfway there, I saw Ben's father. He motioned me to him.

"I'm sorry about that, sir," I said as I closed in on him.

"No," he shook his head, looking into my face. "He was out of line, and he won't be at the wedding. Trying to cripple my son is not designed to make me happy."

I nodded. "I'm just gonna go clean up."

"I like Charlotte," he went on, and I waited, "but the rest of her people are trash. This is only the latest example of that."

I stood there frozen, mute. Charlotte's family was the salt of the earth type. Her cousin was drunk, and that was all. And besides, no family was without its loose cannons. One bad apple did not poison the whole bunch, no matter how the saying went.

He motioned to the house. "Go inside, son."

In the hall bathroom, I washed my face, checked my nose and my bottom lip, and was about to leave when Ben opened the door and came in.

"Hey," he said softly. "Are you all right?"

"I'm fine."

"He could have really hurt me."

"I know." I smiled indulgently. "That's why I stopped him."

"It was so fast."

"C'mon, let's go back out."

"Stefan." He caught his breath, blocking me from leaving, his eyes locked on mine.

"What's wrong?"

"Do you know what a hit in the back of the head could've done to me? I mean, what was I thinking looking away from that guy—that was so stupid."

"You didn't know he was going to try and attack you," I assured him. "What are you, psychic now?"

"But… nobody else could've… if you hadn't been here…." He trailed off, standing there, trembling and needing me to do something.

I grabbed the back of his neck and pulled him close. His gasp made me smile as he leaned into me, clutching me tight, his face buried in my shoulder.

"It's okay," I soothed him, rubbing circles on his back. "You're just scared. It'll pass."

His hand slid across the small of my back as he pressed against me. I could feel his heart hammering in his chest. The knock on the door was unexpected, and I was even more surprised to find Rand there.

"Ben," Rand said coolly, squinting at him.

"I just came in to check on Stefan."

"Good, now go comfort Charlotte, because she's freaking out."

He nodded but seemed hesitant to leave.

"Now," Rand ordered.

Ben was out of there without another word. I tried to leave, too, but Rand grabbed my arm, holding me there.

"What do you want?" I snapped, trying to yank my bicep free of his grasp.

"Can I just look at you, please?" he said calmly, letting me go.

"Why?"

"You're such an idiot," he said, moving forward, his hands on my face as he lifted my chin and checked me over.

I froze under his touch, not sure what to do.

"I had no idea you could fight, Stefan."

Since when did he call me Stefan? "Why? 'Cause I'm—"

"Stop." He sighed, brushing my hair back from my face, scrutinizing me. "You're a helluva lot tougher than I gave you credit for."

I wanted to laugh, wanted to make some smartass, snide remark about him underestimating homos, but I just couldn't bring myself to trade quips with him like usual. I didn't feel like sparring with him. I just wanted him to keep being nice to me.

Standing there, I realized again how massive Rand Holloway really was, especially in comparison to me. Not that he was one of those bodybuilder types—the man was more swimmer than linebacker—but the shoulders were broad and his chest wide, and I knew from seeing him without a shirt many a time that his stomach, with his six-pack abs, was a work of art. He had the whole vee-line to him, and he was big; the top of my head would have notched right under his chin if he were to ever pull me into his arms. I was aware of his size and the heat radiating off his body, the scent of his skin, and the tender way that he was touching me. I could barely breathe.

"Your right eye is gonna be beautiful tomorrow," he assured me, his voice hoarse.

I grinned, lifting my hands to his forearms, thinking to move them off me. It was hard to think with him touching me. "I'll look great in pictures."

"You always look good."

I always looked good? My fingers were closed around his wrists, but he didn't let me go, still holding my face in his hands.

I stared up into his eyes. "Ask you a question?"

"G'head."

"Are you drunk?"

His grin fired his eyes, made them glow a gorgeous shade of deep sea blue. "No. Are you?"

I shook my head just a little.

"What?"

I could only stare at him.

He chuckled, and the sound came from deep in his chest. "You're wondering why we're speaking, right?"

Among other things.

There was a quick exhale of breath from him. "I always try and talk to you, but you usually go right for my throat, and so by the time I get a chance to get a word in edgewise, I just want it to be the worst thing I can think of."

I was stunned. I had no idea I had any effect on him at all.

His fingers slid into my hair. "I'm not sayin' I don't deserve it. I reckon the first thing I ever said to you pretty much took care of us."

I was in *The Twilight Zone*, I just knew it.

"But since we're both in Char's life, I figure our paths are gonna keep crossin'."

I nodded.

"So how 'bout I'll try and not be such a bastard, and in return if you could maybe talk first and shoot second, then that'd be good."

My eyes were locked on his.

"How'd that be? We both give some."

I smiled at him. "I could do that." It would be a relief, actually. Hating Rand Holloway took a lot of energy every time I saw him.

He nodded and smiled slowly, his hands dropping off me to be shoved into the pockets of his jeans. "I have appreciated everything you've ever done for Char, Stefan, even when you were a self-righteous prick about it."

"Me?" I was incredulous.

He laughed then, and I couldn't help the smile that I gave him back. It was overwhelming, the sudden ease, and I was thankful.

"Let's go put some ice on that eye, all right?"

I nodded.

We walked in silence to the living room, and I took a seat where he pointed. I was no different from anyone else; we all wanted to do whatever Rand said.

"Stefan, honey, are you all right?"

Instantly, Charlotte was all over me, as were the rest of the bridesmaids. Ben came to check on me again, and so did Charlotte's mother. I was told to sit and eat and not move. Eating, of course, could fix anything that ailed you.

Everyone was sitting down around me by the time Rand got back with the icepack for my eye. Charlotte snatched it from him and covered the right side of my face. I was surprised when he didn't just leave but instead took a seat on the floor next to me. Ben's mother delivered me a plate piled high with food. After I ate, I settled back, slouching down, getting comfortable, listening to everyone talking, not wanting to move too much as Rand's shoulder was pressed along the length of my left leg. It was stupid, and I felt like an idiot, but I couldn't help my reaction. Not disturbing him was key.

I must have drifted off, but what woke me was Rand moving. He was no longer on the floor but beside me, shoulder-to-shoulder with me on the couch.

"You okay?" he asked, turning to look into my face.

"What?" I was groggy with sleep, aware only of his closeness, his knee against mine, and how hot my body was. Waking up to a beautiful man, there was only one place my mind could go: to the man in question buried inside me.

"You made a noise," Rand said, his cobalt eyes locked on my face. "Are you in pain?"

Was that a trick question?

"Stefan?"

I tried to think about anything other than being flat on my back under Rand Holloway. It proved very difficult. "I'm fine," I said, clearing my throat. "Excuse me."

I stood up fast. I needed air, lots of air, and wide-open spaces. My body was hot, my cock was hard; I had to put distance between Rand and me immediately. I had no idea that just a little of his attention would be mind-numbing.

"You all right? You need to lie down?"

He was trying to kill me. "I'm good." I barely got the words out, certain from the way he was looking at me that he had no earthly idea what was going on in my head.

Rand was just being nice to me, and all my thoughts had him sweaty and naked in my bed. I needed to work off some energy so my thoughts would turn from carnal back to normal. Going for a run seemed like a really good idea. I bolted upstairs as fast as I could. After changing into running shorts, shoes, and a long-sleeved T-shirt, I made my escape before anyone came looking for me.

It was soothing to be alone, and I enjoyed the solitude, thinking about everything I had to do when I got back home, wondering what Mrs. Freeman would decide and how whatever the outcome was would affect me.

The scenery was beautiful—the trees, the wildflowers, and the greenest grass I'd ever seen in my life—but still I was thinking about work until Rand suddenly filled my mind. What the hell was going on with Charlotte's brother, and how in the world had I gone that fast from hating the man to lust? How shallow was I? Had my initial feelings never changed and so as soon as he called a cease-fire I was free to want him all over again? And what about all the things I knew to be true about him? How could I even like anyone as homophobic as Rand Holloway? It was all running around in my head, and because of that, I never even saw the truck.

The horn jarred me, and when I turned, the roar of the engine came seconds before the grill would have been on top of me. I dove right and there was no ground, only air. I tucked my head and rolled. I didn't stop. The hill was much steeper than it looked like from the top, and I tumbled off a ledge before I was suddenly hurled down into thick mud. The last drop had to be at least five feet. I couldn't breathe, as all the air had been slammed from my body.

I lay there staring up at the solid blue sky and watched the way the branches above me whipped around in the breeze. It was actually kind of pretty.

"Hey!"

I couldn't have made a sound even if I wanted to. Now that I was no longer falling, I was a little nauseous, so I didn't want to move too quickly. I was trying to determine if I was hurt or not.

"Hey!"

He must have stopped right above me, because leaves rained down on top of me.

"Oh Christ," he groaned, jumping down beside me, splattering more mud on my face and neck.

"Could you not," I said sharply, finding my voice, looking up at his face. "Oh shit," I braced, positive that he was there to hurt me.

"Ohmygod, you're all right." It was the guy who had tried to hit Ben, Charlotte's cousin Brandon. He was there, kneeling down beside me with one hand on my chest and the other on my shoulder. "Can you move?"

"Get off me! You just tried to kill me!"

"No!" He sounded panicky. "I wanted to talk to you and apologize, but then I saw you go for a run, and I thought I'd follow and try and talk to you, but when I saw that other truck gettin' close to you, lookin' like it might hit you, I blew my—"

"Shut up." I cut off his rambling, incredulous, watching him sway just standing over me. "You're drunk and you're driving? How stupid are you?"

"I just—I never act like… I'm so sorry, you gotta believe—"

"You tried to run me off the road," I said, starting to sit up.

"No." He knelt down beside me. "It wasn't me. I saved you. Now lemme help."

"No, just—don't," I snapped, brushing his hands off me. "Just move back, all right?"

He tried to smile, reaching for me again. "Please lemme help."

I could feel my eyebrows furrowing. "Fuck you, no," I growled, pulling my knees up, taking a breath, and trying to get my bearings.

"Wow." He chuckled, stepping back, hands in his pockets. "You got a temper on you, huh?"

"Not usually," I growled again, getting slowly to my feet, bending over, hands on my knees. "God, I'm gonna be crippled tomorrow."

"Oh shit," he breathed out, pointing. "You're bleeding."

I looked down at my long-sleeved, once white, now mud-stained T-shirt and saw the blood stain. But I wasn't hurt. I knew my body. "It's not mine."

We both saw his arm at the same time. The cut was wide, but it didn't look deep. A flap of skin was hanging open. It looked like mine had when I had wiped out on a surfboard on the coral in Hawaii two summers before.

"You probably need stitches."

"Oh geez," he said softly.

When I looked up at him, I saw him start to sway before his eyes rolled back in his head. I shifted quickly and caught him before he passed out cold.

"Aw, for crissakes," I yelled hoarsely, holding him in my arms. Who actually fainted at the sight of blood? I dragged him a few feet to the right so I could see up the long hill. It was steep, but it was covered in grass and dirt. The climb was doable, just not something I was looking forward to, especially with the added weight. And he was not a small guy. He was taller than me, close to six-two and more muscular. But what was I going to do? Leave him in a ravine in a swoon? How safe was that?

"Fuck me," I said aloud, because even bitching to no one, I felt a little better.

I checked him for a cell phone and, finding none, resigned myself to carrying him, because I didn't have mine either. Who took a cell phone for a run? I was used to being close to everything. There wasn't a place at home where there wouldn't be people around to help me. This was what I got for running alone.

It's probably called "deadweight" because you feel like you're going to die when you carry someone who's passed out. What had taken seconds to fall down took hours going back up. And even though logically, I knew that I was exaggerating, it seemed like I could feel every muscle in my body when I finally made it to his huge Ford pickup. The driver's side door was hanging open, the truck still running as I reached it. I rested a second, leaning him against the hood of the truck, before I opened the door and dumped him in the passenger seat. When I went around to the driver's side, he was slumped over with his face on the dashboard. Once I had his head back against the headrest and he was buckled in, I slammed the door shut, put my forehead on the steering wheel, and closed my eyes. "Exhausted" didn't do it justice. I wouldn't need to run for a week.

Fortunately, he had a GPS system in his truck, and once I entered what I needed, I had driving directions for the University Medical Center.

Halfway there, the guy came around, only to swoon again when he saw my shirt. He was beyond useless. Half an hour later, I parked outside the ER where I wasn't supposed to, left the car there, and got out. Nobody yelled at me as I carried Brandon into the hospital.

Since I knew nothing about him and wasn't family, I got to wait outside. And wait, and wait some more. An hour later, a nurse called me in to explain as much as I could about his injuries, and when they looked at me, they insisted that I be checked out as well. I was covered in cuts and bruises and I was sore, but I was sure that was all. They wanted to be certain. I got to have pictures of my brain taken, and three hours later, when I was finally allowed back to my room, I was told that I didn't even have a concussion. I could have saved everyone a lot of time and effort if they had just listened to me to begin with. I actually did know my own body.

As I was changing back into my dirty clothes from the lovely hospital robe, Brandon slipped into the room.

"Gonna shoot me now or something?" I asked the guy who had nearly killed me.

"No." He shook his head before crossing the room to me. "Why?"

"Oh, I dunno—the whole running me off the road thing... that ringing any bells?"

"Stef, you gotta get it through your head; I ain't the one that run you off the road. If I hadn't honked at you, I reckon you'd be dead right about now."

"You were drunk," I said, my tone sharp. "You just thought there was another truck, but it's not like you meant to kill me. You were just trying to make amends."

"I was—do wanna make amends, but there were two trucks. The other guy drove away the second he saw you go over. I swear to God I—"

"Whatever." I cut him off, too annoyed to listen to it anymore.

"Jesus, you're pissed at me, huh?"

"Pissed was hours ago," I assured him.

He offered me his hand. "I'm Brandon Holloway, but you can call me Bran."

I squinted at him until he dropped his hand.

"I'm so sorry about the fight, Stef. I was so mad at myself—furious. I mean, I never act like that, but I'm at this wedding, and my girl, she won't even talk to me no more, and—"

"You're frustrated about your girl and you took it out on Ben?" Unrequited love, the one thing I had sympathy for. "Is that what you're telling me?"

He raked his hands through his hair. "Aww, man, I'm so sorry. I was sorry the second you grabbed me. I was like, 'oh fuck me, I should just let this guy kick the shit outta me for being such a stupid prick.'"

I grunted.

"And then you go and make it worse by carrying my ass up the side of that hill. What're you, a fuckin' saint?"

"Hardly."

"Stefan, I am really so very sorry about the fight."

"But not about trying to kill me?"

"That wasn't me," he insisted. "I swear to God, there was another truck."

I let out a deep breath. "Whatever. It's over, don't worry about it."

"Well I ain't worried, but maybe you should be, huh? I mean, somebody just tried to kill you."

I shot him a look, as I was fairly certain that he was the only one putting my life in peril. I noticed then that his eyes had darkened to a deep olive green as he stared at me. He was actually a very handsome man with a slight cleft in his chin, sharply cut features, and a warm smile. His hair was light chestnut brown and streaked blond from the sun.

"So you know I intend to take care of any charges that—"

"That's not necessary." I cut him off.

"Oh, I think it is," he assured me as he stared into my eyes. "You carried me up a hill just 'cause it was the right thing to do. You're a real nice guy, Stefan Joss. I hope you can give me another chance to get to know you."

I had an idea about how he could help me. "Can you drive me back?"

In his truck another hour later, Brandon let out a deep, settling breath. I had to drive because I didn't trust the level of alcohol still in his system. It was almost dinnertime when I turned into the enormous circular driveway of the sprawling ranch house. I thanked him for letting me drive his truck and, over his objections, climbed a little unsteadily out of the driver's side door. What he was upset about were his keys in my pocket when I went inside. He was walking home if he was going at all. He was still assuring me that he was sober as I closed the door behind me.

I needed food and lots of water, but I had to shower and change before anyone saw me. I went through the foyer, the living room, and up the stairs. In my room, it was cool, because the lights were off. I was glad I had left the air conditioner on. Before I even thought about it, I toed off my shoes and got on the bed, crawling up to my pillow before I collapsed and lay down, closing my eyes, feeling like I was sinking into the mattress.

"Are you hurt?"

I jerked awake, not even realizing that I'd fallen asleep.

"Stefan?"

Deep voice asking me questions. I lifted my head and looked over my shoulder. Rand was standing at the end of the bed, arms crossed, waiting for an answer.

"I'm fine." I sighed, putting my head back down. "Why wouldn't I be?"

"Oh, I dunno, a trip to the hospital tends to be tiring."

I groaned as the light went on and a flood of people came through the door. Charlotte and Ben and the rest of the wedding party filled my room fast. I rolled over on my back and covered my face with the pillow.

"I would smack you, but I don't know where you're hurt!" Charlotte ranted at me. "Twice in one day you scare me—must be a new goddamn record for you!"

I groaned into the pillow before it was snatched away.

"Stefan!"

She was really mad, and everyone stopped talking to look at her. Her voice was shrill. It sounded strange, unhinged, and her breathing was erratic, like she was going to hyperventilate.

"You are my best friend in the whole world, and I love you more than practically anyone! You were there through the worst moment of my entire life, and if anything ever happens to—"

I lifted up, grabbed her arm, and yanked her down beside me. She wrapped tight around me, coiling, and even though it hurt a little, I didn't make a sound.

"I didn't want to ruin the wedding," I told her, kissing her forehead, nuzzling my face in her hair.

"The only way it gets ruined is if you're not there beside me, you stupid ass."

I squeezed her, and the tears rolled out of her eyes.

The bed dipped as everyone sat down on it, Ben sitting up beside the headboard, the bridesmaids on the other side, soothing Charlotte. Rand was standing by the window, looking out at the darkening sky.

"You guys need to go," I told them. "There are more festivities planned for tonight, right?"

"Yeah, we'll all meet downstairs in, like, half an hour," Ben said softly. "I need to talk to Stefan and Char real quick, but the rest of you guys go on and get ready."

It was his wedding, so everyone did as he asked except for Rand. But I knew, just like we all did, that Ben had never actually thought Rand would listen to him. Rand didn't listen to anyone. When the room was finally clear, he asked his bride to look at him.

"Tell me about the worst thing that ever happened to you, Char. I'm gonna be your husband, I should know."

She clutched me tighter, buried her face in the side of my neck.

"Is it a deal breaker?" I asked him.

He squinted at me. "What're you talking about?"

"If she doesn't tell, is the wedding off?" I asked Ben, hoping it wasn't.

"What—no, of course not, I love—"

"Then not today," I said softly, giving Charlotte a final squeeze before I let her go and whispered for her to go to Ben.

She rose out of my arms and lunged at her fiancé. He grabbed her tight, and when she locked her legs around his hips, he carried her out of the room. I let out a deep breath, pulling my hair back from my face. What a day.

"My cousin Bran says that he didn't try to kill you," Rand said, moving from the window to stand beside the bed. "I think maybe if he hadn't been hyperventilating when he said that someone else ran you off the road then maybe Charlotte wouldn't have freaked so hard. I only heard a little of it before I came up here. Tell me what happened."

I looked up at him.

"Now."

Why I responded to him, I had no idea, but I heard more than the demand, I heard the underlying concern as well. So I told him everything that happened, including carrying his cousin up out of the ravine. I tossed him Bran's keys. Rand was nodding when I was done.

"I always thought you were sort of fragile, but you're not; you're strong," he breathed, and for some reason that revelation seemed to please him. "So now tell me about this Cody guy."

I was silent because I was both confused and unsure that I'd heard him correctly.

"Did you hear me?"

"I'm not sure, could you repeat the question?"

"Tell me about Cody."

"I'm sorry, what?"

"Charlotte said a while back that you were dating some guy named Cody but he didn't come along with you so I'm askin' you what's going on with him?"

I took a breath, squinting up at him. "Rand, why are you—"

"Did you break up?"

I nodded after a moment, completely confused by the entire conversation.

"Why'd you break up?"

What were we, girlfriends now? "Rand, are you aware of how weird this whole—"

"What was wrong with Cody?"

He seemed very intent about wanting to know.

I cleared my throat. "Well, it ended like a month ago."

"Why?"

I squinted at him.

"Just tell me."

"He was too serious."

"Whaddya mean?"

"Rand, do you really expect me to—"

"Tell me what went on."

He would wait all day for the answer, I could tell. It was such a weird conversation—at least I thought it was. But I was a little out of it, so maybe it was normal.

"Now."

"Why?"

"Why not?"

"That's not an answer."

He scowled at me.

I gave up. What did I have to lose? "Okay, so he was ready to settle down and buy a house and get a dog and all that shit. He was even talking about kids, and—"

"And you don't want any of that stuff."

"No, I do," I corrected him. "I just... he just—"

"Wasn't the one," he said softly.

"Yeah." I sighed. "He wasn't the one."

It was hard for me to explain to people, so I usually just skipped it, doing my patented disappearing act instead of having the big blowout that signified the end of a relationship. More than anything I wanted a home, wanted to belong to one man, but the men I always ended up with wanted to smother me and entrench me in their lives. I wanted to share my life with someone, not simply take on theirs. Most men didn't understand that, and so I ended up leaving. There was a man out there confident enough that he could keep me around without trying to change me. I just hadn't found him yet.

"Stef."

I looked up at Rand.

"You left because he wasn't strong enough to handle your bullshit, right?"

"What?"

He grunted.

"I'll have you know that I'm a catch, no matter what you think."

"Is that right?"

It was, but the way he was looking at me, daring me to say something else, I couldn't think of anything.

There was a long silence. "You should take a shower; you're a mess."

"Excellent idea," I said, getting up and walking by him toward the bathroom.

"I'll be back," he said, turning toward the door. "I'll bring you something to eat."

"Thanks," I said, closing the bathroom door behind me.

I stood under the water in the shower for a while, thinking about Rand. His questions, his demeanor... if he were bi, I would have known how to read him. If he were either bi or gay, I would have told him to put his hands on me. As it was, I was at a loss. But maybe he was like that with everyone. Charlotte had always said that I was lucky that Rand hated me because if he liked me, he would try to run my life. Maybe since he liked me now, he had some nice gay friend he wanted to set me up with and he was just trying to get a feel for me. He was asking questions to find out if I was looking for a serious relationship or if I just wanted to sleep around. And maybe that would have remotely made sense if it was anyone else but Rand. I just knew that Charlotte's cowboy brother didn't have any gay friends that he wanted to set me up with. I laughed as I stood under the hot, steaming water.

CHAPTER 5

.

I CHANGED into jeans and a T-shirt after taking a shower and sat down on the bed to wait for Rand to bring me some food. I must have dozed off again, because when I woke up, Rand was sitting up in bed beside me, on top of the quilt with me under it, flipping channels and eating a sandwich off a paper plate.

"I thought you were getting something for me?" I asked, sitting up beside him so that we were shoulder to shoulder.

He said something with his mouth full as he pointed with the remote control to the other side of me. On the nightstand was a plate with a sandwich and chips on it and a huge glass of iced tea. The glass was cold, so it had just arrived.

"Thank you," I said as I rolled toward it.

He just grunted.

"Remember you have to chew," I told him as I started on my sandwich.

He ignored me, flipped the channels some more, and then turned to look at me.

It was my turn to talk with my mouth full. "What?"

"Why didn't you just call me or Char to come get you from the hospital?"

"I didn't want Charlotte to worry, and honestly, I didn't even think of calling you."

"Why not?"

"Probably because we've only been on speaking terms for, like, a minute."

He shrugged. "Sure, but you gotta know that in an emergency, all bets are off."

I just looked at him.

Slowly, the wariness filled his eyes, and I watched his brows furrow. "Wait, you do know that if you needed me... whenever, that I would show up."

"What?"

"You do know that, right?"

"No."

He was genuinely surprised. "I've known you over ten years, Stefan. You're my little sister's best friend; how do you not get that you can count on me?"

"What does my relationship with Charlotte have to do with you?"

He stared at me, and I could tell he was trying to figure something out.

"Are you being serious?" His eyes were darkening.

"Sure. Me and Char have nothing to do with you and me."

"Is that right?"

The way he said it, like he was hurt, I sort of wanted to take it back.

"Screw you," he said as he climbed off the bed.

"Wait, why're you pissed at me?"

He turned and pointed at me. "It's nice how little you think of me."

"Rand—"

He turned for the door.

"Wait."

But he left, slamming the door behind him. I had no idea what was going on.

I tried to just watch TV, but the fact that I knew he was mad at me, for whatever reason, nagged at me. Normally, the man being annoyed was a good thing. Once, I would have basked in the knowledge that I had pushed his buttons, driven him to explosive anger. But it was different suddenly, so sleep was not a possibility. I headed downstairs to find him.

There was a small group sitting around, talking, telling stories, eating, drinking, and laughing. They were back from being out, and I realized that I must have slept a lot longer than I thought. I saw Rand sitting between two guys I had met the other night, but I couldn't recall their names. As I crossed to them, Charlotte called my name.

I went to her, and she slipped her hand into mine as she let her head fall back to look at my face.

"Sit here by me."

I let her pull me down, and after she was done grilling me about how I felt, she turned back to her bridesmaids and continued the conversation she'd been having before I showed up. She was sharing some wild and crazy moments from her past. I glanced over at Rand, but he was talking with others. I realized it had been a mistake to come downstairs. He wasn't going to let me talk to him and was in fact doing his best to ignore me.

Charlotte's mom brought me some tea, which I appreciated, as the girls had started talking about the sluttiest things they had ever done. Whoever thinks that men talk dirty has never listened to a bunch of women let loose. I have a theory that because women are better with details that they can do graphic a hundred times better. When someone shook my leg, I opened my eyes and found Charlotte smiling at me.

"Yes?"

Five sets of lovely eyes looked at me.

"Have you ever been tied up, Stef?"

"You know I have," I told the bride-to-be.

"Were you scared?" another bridesmaid asked me.

"No." I smiled at her.

"Ever been handcuffed?"

"Yes."

There were squeals of delight.

"Have you ever tied anyone up?"

"Yes."

Even more giggling as they all leaned in close to me.

"Was it fun?"

I arched an eyebrow for them. I didn't need to answer.

They erupted in laughter as someone brought over a board game. I started to get up, but Charlotte insisted, since I was feeling better, that I be on her team as a silent partner. I was going to beg off when Rand took a seat on the couch beside me. He was going to play, so I stayed where I was.

I paid attention, leaning forward, listening to categories being read and people try to come up with the answers. After the third time around, I looked up and noticed Ben staring at me. His eyes were flat, cold, and when I turned to Charlotte, she just gave me a quick shake of her head. What the hell?

"Maybe being the caretaker of secrets is overrated, huh, Stefan?" Rand asked, leaning in close to me. "Whaddya think?"

"Shit," I groaned softly, face down in my hands, closing my eyes.

His hand was on my neck, massaging, his fingers working up the back of my head into my hair. It felt so much better than good, and I let out a deep breath.

"You should go to bed."

"I need to talk to you."

"Why?"

I rolled my head sideways to look at him. "I had no idea that you could separate us being assholes to each other to us being friends. I've never had that, so I didn't know."

He was studying my eyes, and after several minutes, he nodded. "Okay."

"Okay? You sure?"

"I'm sure."

I released a breath I hadn't realized I'd been holding.

His hand slid back down to my shoulder and then off, as he had to roll the dice. Everyone talked, Ben's mother brought out photo albums, and there were funny, embarrassing stories to be shared. I listened, liking the banter, the family moments.

"Stefan, honey." Ben's mother looked at me. "Where's your family?"

I turned and looked at Charlotte. She waved.

"I don't understand?"

"I left home at fourteen. I never went back."

Her eyes were huge. "How do you leave home at fourteen?"

I shrugged. "My folks got divorced when I was three or so, and I never saw my dad again. When I was fourteen, my mom married this guy who really couldn't stand me, so… he threw me out, and she let him."

She looked horrified.

"It was a long time ago," I said.

"But I—"

"He got a job, he went to school, and he lived with a lot of different friends… he did it," Charlotte cut her off. "And then he went to college and met me. Voilà, instant family."

Ben's mom stared at me. "Have you spoken to her at all since you left?"

"No, ma'am, she passed," I told her. "Charlotte went with me to the funeral."

"Which you paid for," Charlotte added.

There was a long, suffocating silence. I felt like I was on display.

"Come here and hug me," Ben's mom said, motioning me over to her.

She wanted to comfort me. It was very sweet.

I declined more offers of food as a tray of pastries was brought out along with hot chocolate. The yawning was impossible to stifle, my eyes too heavy to keep open. All the inactivity was making me lethargic. Usually at ten on a Thursday night, I was done with dinner, moving on to clubbing and screwing. There was always someone new to take home and then ask to leave before morning.

"Scoot over."

They were making room for more people on the couch. Charlotte got up, and I moved to the end of the sectional, which was shadowed in the corner of the room. It was relaxing until Rand crowded up against me.

"So," he said, his mouth suddenly next to my ear, his breath hot down the side of my neck, "would you like me to tie you up?"

Taken off guard, I shivered from his words and his closeness.

"I figured," he said as his fingers slid up under the back of my T-shirt to touch my bare skin, which was now covered in goose bumps.

So slight a movement and so very erotic. I almost jumped up, and everyone looked at me oddly.

"Headache," I said, pressing a hand to my forehead before I walked out of the room.

He caught up to me at the bottom of the stairs.

"Stef."

I spun around to face him. "You're being an ass, for whatever reason."

His jaw clenched as he stared at me.

"Fuckin' fix it," I told him, turning around and heading upstairs without another word.

In my room, I yanked off my T-shirt and ran water and gel through my hair before crossing to the dresser to find a new shirt. I had to get out of there, go somewhere and drink, find somebody, and get laid. If I stayed, I would just climb the walls.

"Stefan!"

I didn't answer.

Another call came through the door after more knocking, which I ignored.

"Stefan!" he yelled for the third time.

"Yeah?"

"Don't say 'yeah'!" he yelled. "Open the goddamn door!"

"Fuck you, Rand!"

Momentary silence before his voice softened. He was right up against the door. "Lemme in, please."

"Screw you!"

"Please, Stef."

"What the fuck is going on with you? Are you fucking with me on a bet?"

"No." His voice cracked, lowered. "Please just open the door."

"I'm goin' out. I'll see you in the morning."

"You are not going out… no fuckin' way."

Obviously the man had lost his mind. "Are you high?" I asked as I opened the door.

He nearly fell in on me.

"What are you doing?" I snapped at him, shifting to take a step back to give him room.

He grabbed hold of my bicep to still my movement. "I was an idiot. Forgive me."

"Which time?" I barked back, peeling his hand off me, shoving him away.

"You're really mad, huh?" he asked, closing and locking the door behind him.

"Now what the fuck are you doing? I'm going out," I announced, moving around him to reach the door.

He stepped in front of me.

"Move."

He blocked my exit, arms spread. "I need you here, Stef. Right here."

I knew the look. Charlotte had the same one. He wasn't going to move without a fight.

Throwing up my hands, I pivoted around and went back to the dresser. "You're such an asshole."

"Oh, I'm sure that's true."

I took deep breaths, calming as I looked for the shirt that would get me laid. "Can you please just tell me what the fuck is wrong with you?"

There was no sound.

"You're never hot and cold, you're usually just cold."

"I know," he breathed out. "I work at it."

Whatever the hell that meant. "Is there something going on at home? Is the ranch in trouble?"

"No."

I looked back over my shoulder at him. "Then what is it?"

He crossed the room to stand close to me. "What are you looking for?"

"A new shirt."

"Why? I already told you you're not going anywhere."

I exhaled sharply and turned to look at him as he leaned on the dresser. "Is the wedding bumming you out? Are you thinking about when you were married?"

"No, but Jesus, your mind goes a lotta places, huh?"

I squinted at him.

"I like you worrying about me."

"Why?"

"Just do."

"Please, Rand." I sighed, at a loss as to what was going on. "What are you worried about?"

"I'm not worried," he said flatly. "I just have a problem." His eyes were so dark, studying me.

"You're drivin' me nuts. Either tell me or get the fuck out."

"You are a heartless creature, Stefan Joss."

I grunted, pulling out a tight, black short-sleeved shirt, ready to put it on. "It's true."

"No, it's not," he said, snatching the shirt away, balling it up and throwing it on the bed.

I tilted my head as I looked at him. "Just tell me what's wrong and I'll fix it."

His smile was instant, and it warmed his eyes, made them look like melting jewels. "You can do that, can you? Fix whatever ails me?"

"I just want to help if I can."

"All right."

Pleased that he had finally agreed, I crossed back to the bed to retrieve my shirt. I didn't expect to be shoved from behind so I went facedown onto the quilt.

"Better."

I rolled over on my back to look up at him. "What the fuck?"

"Oh." He swallowed hard, the muscles in his jaw working. "Look at your eyes."

My eyes... my brain stumbled. He was not playing by our rulebook, and I was at a loss as to what was going on in his head.

"Come here," he said, one knee on the bed as he reached for me.

"Oh shit." I jerked to my feet, his chin colliding with my chest as I scrambled off the bed, moving faster than I had thought I could. "What the fuck are you doing?"

He was smiling, and I saw how big and wide it was as he moved his jaw and rubbed where I'd clipped it.

I backed away, not taking my eyes off him. "Rand?"

His turquoise eyes were so dark they looked wet, the smile had become very sexy, and the way his gaze raked over me from head to toe... what the hell? Had I missed that he was drunk?

"Rand, are you drunk?"

He motioned me to him. "I'm so tired of fighting... just c'mere."

"Are you stoned?" Maybe he was stoned.

He shook his head. "Please come here."

"Rand," I said, feeling somehow naked standing there in just my jeans. "Do you have any idea what you're do—"

"I know exactly what I'm doing."

But I didn't think he did. "Rand, I think you need to sit down."

"That ain't what I need," he husked.

"Are you serious?" I blurted as he rose off the bed and started toward me.

"I don't know. I don't know about anything right now. All I do know is that I need you so I won't feel like this no more. I'm so sick of feeling like this."

Wait. What? "I'm sorry, what?"

He laughed softly. "You heard me."

"No, I don't think I did," I assured him. "See, because for starters, you're straight."

He nodded. "I am straight, with one seemingly very large exception."

I shook my head. "Listen, if you need to experiment, you—"

"It's not an experiment."

"That's bullshit. How could it be anything else but—"

"'Cause of how I feel."

He looked absolutely miserable and happy all at the same time. What in the world was going on? How could I have missed all this?

"Ask me how I feel."

"I... okay. How do you feel?"

"Sick," he confessed, reaching for me, lifting his hand to place his palm over my heart. "Every time I met some new guy you were fuckin', every time I saw you leave with somebody as I came in, every time... it killed me. I remember at Charlotte's graduation party, you were dancing with your boyfriend, some guy you dumped like a month later, but that night…. I was so fuckin' jealous of him 'cause you were all over him and it made me sick. It's been killing me since that first day when I walked in and you looked up at me and it was like I got hit by lightning."

I was stunned. What could I say? I thought he hated me. I had always thought he hated me.

"The way you smiled that day was… but I was scared, so scared, and you were young, Stef, but so was I," he flared, irritated at me. "You forget that I was young too."

"Rand, what are you—"

"I was only twenty-one, and I… I mean, how could I want you and still be me? There was no way."

My mind worked fast. "So you insulted me."

He nodded. "It was easy."

It had been easy, and I could own that piece years later. "I used to be hotheaded."

"You still are."

It was true.

"But then I wanted to fix it, but you wouldn't even talk to me, and then after a few years, you stopped even seeing me. Now it's like I'm a ghost."

"I ignore you."

"You try to."

"You make it hard," I conceded. He was always such an ass to me, almost like he went out of his way to get in his digs.

"I try my damndest."

"What are you talking about?"

He was silent, his eyes locked on mine.

At once, I understood. "All those times we… you… you did that on purpose? You picked those fights deliberately?"

He gave me a quick shrug. "If you were pissed at me, I knew you still cared enough to be mad. At least it was somethin'."

The confession left me reeling. Ten years of guerilla warfare with Rand Holloway and I had been the only one really fighting? "I don't know what to—"

"You know Charlotte used to come home and talk about you and all the men in and out of your bed, and I'd think how lucky I was that I didn't ever get near you."

My track record was bad, there was no denying it. I changed men like I changed clothes; the second they became clinging, I needed air.

"But how you are with Char, how loyal you are, what she tells me you're like with your friends…. I know how you really are, Stef. I've seen your heart in the way you are with her and with my mom. I see you."

Shit.

"And the way you look at me with those eyes of yours just about burns me up."

I had no idea what I was supposed to say.

"When you're really mad," he said, smiling sheepishly, raking his fingers through his thick hair, "your eyes get this color green that"— quick breath—"it's really somethin', is all."

What was something was that he was nervous, really nervous, and I was the cause.

"Fighting with you was all I had, you know?"

He had deliberately fought with me, antagonized me, and picked apart me and everything I did. The battles we had waged over the years, the words that had flown between us and the insults hurled… I had to wonder about the man. How had he always been able to push my buttons? I never got mad at anyone the way I did Rand Holloway. Maybe there was a reason?

"I know I should have told you all this before now." He sighed, fiddling with my hair, curling a long piece around my ear. "But you're not the easiest person in the world to talk to." The back of his fingers ran up my throat under my chin. "And besides… you hate me."

I took a step back and bumped into the wall behind me. I had thought to move beyond his reach, to get his hand to slide off me, but he wasn't having it.

"Look at you all flustered." He smiled down into my eyes.

Again I tried to lean out of his touch, but he fisted his hand in my hair. It was way too long, hitting my shoulders, but at that moment I was so glad.

"I always wanted to do this, put my hands in your hair."

My heart hurt.

He ran his hands down my chest. "And touch your skin."

I had to try to breathe. "Rand—"

"You sound like you're dying."

"I just—"

"You know how sick I am of watching other people touch you?"

I was silent.

"Charlotte and Ben and all the girls downstairs, everybody wants to touch you all the time. I'm the only one who can't when I want to be the only one that can."

The shudder tore through me, and I couldn't stop it.

"Kiss me," he said, his eyes locked on mine, absorbing me. "Just once. If it's bad, if I freak out or if you do… fine, we'll forget all this."

It wasn't a good idea.

"Come on, you have nothing to lose."

"I have you to lose, and I just got you," I confessed, terrified.

"You'll never lose me, I swear."

His hand slid around the nape of my neck, and I felt the strong fingers massaging gently as he eased me forward. His mouth hovered over mine, and he took a sharp intake of breath before he pressed the length of his body against me.

"Kiss me." His breath ghosted over my face.

I leaned in and plastered my mouth to his, harder and faster than I ever had before, trying to show him how fierce and grinding it was to kiss a man in comparison to the softness of kissing a woman. But he knew, somehow he knew what I was up to; his smile told me so, as well as the long, contented sigh. When his lips parted over mine, his tongue gliding into my mouth, his hands clutching at my skin, my legs nearly went out on me. I had never been kissed with so much yearning and so much heat. His kiss sent shivers rippling through me, making me tremble in his arms.

"I knew you would taste good," his voice rumbled in his chest. "And I knew kissing you would feel right."

"Then kiss me again," I urged him without thinking.

The second kiss was devouring, and I gave as good as I got, licking, biting, sucking, not letting him go, not letting him breathe. I felt his hand slide down the front of my jeans, under the waistband of my briefs, and fist around my hard, throbbing cock. I broke the kiss then as electricity tore through me, needing air, needing to get my bearings. He tried to follow me as I pulled back, but I reached up and put a hand on his collarbone.

"Stop," I breathed out, taking in gulps of air.

His eyes were heavy-lidded, his mouth curling in the corner as he looked at me. "I can feel your heart beating in your cock," he said, leaning in to bite the curve of my shoulder where it met my neck. "I need to taste you."

"Stop," I panted, feeling his words in the pit of my stomach.

"I don't wanna stop," he said, his voice hoarse, deep. "I just wanna touch you."

"Rand—"

"Stop fighting," he said, his fingers moving fast to unsnap the top button of my jeans, the zipper succumbing next. Opening the flaps, he pushed my jeans and briefs down fast with his one hand, the other still wrapped around my shaft. "Just let me have you."

He went to his knees and took me into his mouth. I smiled when he gagged, watched him look up at me with a mischievous grin, and then gasped when he instantly tried again. In seconds, he learned not to take all of me in at once, to use his hand and his lips together to make me catch my breath. He licked and sucked, and it was the worst and best blowjob I ever had. His utter joy, the way he surrendered himself so completely to his desire, and how wet and hot his mouth was, all of it nearly pushed me over the edge.

When I shoved him back, he looked like I'd hit him. The look was replaced instantly with wonder when I pulled him to his feet and pushed him down on the bed. I made quick work of his belt, his briefs and jeans yanked to his knees before I went to mine in front of the cock I had uncovered. It was beautiful, long, thick, and cut, the color a deep golden brown, and it was completely stiff and waiting for me. The musky smell of him and the bead of precome at the end of the flared head were intoxicating. When I took him into my mouth, the groan he let out was hoarse and deep.

"Jesus." He writhed under me, clutching at my hair as I swallowed him down, deep-throating him with practiced ease. I give a killer blowjob, and the way he called my name let me know that I was driving him out of his mind. "God… Stef, you gotta stop, I don't wanna… I'm gonna come if you don't stop."

I had no intention of stopping. The end to wanting Rand Holloway was in sight. The man I had lusted after since I was eighteen years old was lying under me, the hard silky length of him gliding in and out of my mouth. I wasn't about to let him get away. I sucked harder, the suction too strong for him to keep control. His hands were in my hair as he rocked into me, fucking my mouth. I swallowed hard as my throat was suddenly coated with his thick, salty come, taking it all, leaving nothing but his quivering release. When I lifted my head, smiling wickedly, he reached for me, pulling me up to him and then down into a kiss. His mouth opened for me, and his tongue tangled with mine, sucking, tasting himself. He couldn't get enough, arching up into me, his hands clutching at my skin.

I had to break the kiss so I could breathe. My head and my lungs were ready to explode. "We should stop... we can still stop and you can still say you're straight."

His smile was huge. "I don't think so."

"Rand, you—"

"Stef," he growled, rolling over on top of me, kicking off his boots, shucking out of his pants, pulling and yanking and pinning me under him so I couldn't move. Like I wanted to. I was having too much fun watching his frustration with his clothes, how disheveled and sweaty he looked, and how he had to bend his head every few seconds and lick my leaking cock. "I just want to be inside you, and I really doubt that wanting that makes me straight."

His confession was designed to give me heart failure.

He froze suddenly, every bit of his attention locked on me. "Is that something you would let me do... be inside you?"

"Oh God, yes," I nearly moaned.

His smile was slow as his eyes swallowed me. "I've seen you, you know."

I watched his long fingers as they worked over my shaft, sliding from the base to the head as it hardened and dripped precome. Did he know how good it felt?

"I was in town once when you were going out with that guy Brett. You didn't hear me come in. Charlotte had given me her key. You guys were in bed, and when I looked in your bedroom, I saw you."

He was gorgeous there above me, the hard, corded muscles, washboard stomach, and beautifully sculpted chest. I had always admired the beauty of the man, his permanently tousled black hair and sexy blue eyes. I was finally free to look at him for as long as I wanted.

"You had your legs over his shoulders and his cock was buried in your ass and he was jerking you off while he fucked you." He smiled seductively, his eyes barely open. "Let's do that."

I shook my head.

"Why not? Would it hurt you?"

"You hurting me is not the issue."

"Then what?"

"Rand, if you do this and then hate me afterward, I—"

"I could never hate you," he assured me. "What do we need?"

"Rand, you might hate—"

"Isn't there lube or something?" he demanded.

I pointed at the nightstand, and he stretched for it, lengthening out his beautiful body but not letting me move. He wanted me right where I was.

"Listen," he said as he settled himself back, straddling my thighs. "I haven't been with anyone since my ex-wife Jenny, okay? I have the paper at home that says I'm clean, but you gotta take my word for it and let me skip the condom."

I was overwhelmed. "Rand, you can't want to—"

"Oh fuck yeah, I want to."

I had to concentrate on breathing. "Listen, I'm clean, too, but you shouldn't just take my word for it. I've been with more guys than—"

"Not anymore," he said, leaning down to deliver a kiss that curled my toes. The man was so hot, and he really knew how to kiss me. "You're done with anybody else."

His words drove through me like a freight train. I didn't like people trying to control me. But Rand....

"And I know you think I'm fulla shit right now, but you wait and see," he said, leaning over and kissing me again, this time tenderly, his lips lingering over mine. When he pulled back, he was smiling. "Now tell me what to do."

"Here." I held out my hand for the tube. "Let me make you ready."

He handed it to me, and he shivered when I popped open the lid. The man had it really bad for me, and I never had a clue.

I coated his long, beautiful cock with the lube until it glistened in the faint light from the bathroom. My fingers sliding over his hot skin were making his breath falter.

"God, that feels amazing."

I knew it did.

"God, Stefan… please… please…."

He didn't need to beg me. I shifted under him, staring up into his now heavy-lidded eyes. "Put your arms under my knees."

As big and strong as he was, he lifted me effortlessly. "I want… can it be gentle next time?"

Permission needed to be given. "Yes."

I felt the head of his cock slide slowly between my cheeks before he pressed against me. "Are you sure?"

"Yes, Rand."

The thrust into me was hard and fast, and I moaned loudly as all my muscles tightened at once.

"Shit." He sounded pained. "Oh Stef, I'm so—"

"Stop," I ordered, wrapping my legs around him so he couldn't pull back out. "This is part of it, Rand, just stay."

His balls were against my ass, and his hands were on my thighs, his fingers digging into my skin. "You feel so good… and looking at you…. Jesus, Stefan."

"Fuck me," I begged him. "Do it now."

He reacted instantly, filling me, driving inside so hard and so deep that I was sure that I felt him in my abdomen.

"Oh God," he moaned, his body reacting like an electrical current had coursed through him. I was very pleased with myself for eliciting such a gut-wrenching convulsion. "Stefan." My name came out as a raspy groan. "You're so tight an' hot."

I felt the muscles in my ass clenching and tightening as he pushed in and out of me, burying himself to the hilt with each new thrust, over and over, setting a hammering pace.

"Stefan," he repeated.

"You're so hard, you feel so good. Move… don't stop."

He thrust deep inside, and I gasped, but when he checked my face, I smiled at him before asking to be fucked harder and faster still.

"I don't wanna hurt—"

"You could never hurt me. It's not in you."

I saw the muscles in his jaw clench.

"What?" I teased him, lifting my knees as he leaned forward, arching my back so my legs could slide over his shoulders, bring him deeper. "I should trust you. It's what you wanted, isn't it?"

"Yes." He swallowed hard, and his voice was husky and low.

"Tell me."

"I just…. This is how I always wanted to be… inside you," he said, bending toward me. "Kissing you… filling you up."

The angle slid his cock over my prostate. I nearly came up off the bed. "Oh God, Rand, please."

"Feel good?" he asked before he pushed down into me.

There were no words. Between the feel of him deep inside and knowing that it was Rand Holloway I held in my arms, I was lost. My body jerked under his, shuddering before I cried out, my head rolling back, my eyes closed as I rode out my throbbing, heart-stopping climax.

"Stefan!" He roared my name, and when I opened my eyes, I realized that he had never looked more beautiful. His body went rigid seconds later, and I felt the flood of liquid warmth in my ass.

We were silent, riding out the aftershocks, both of us trembling. When I could breathe, I looked up at him.

"Jesus Christ, I think I'm blind."

He sounded so serious that I had to laugh at him; then he collapsed on top of me, boneless and exhausted. I ran my hands down the sweat-dampened planes of his back, letting my fingers touch his hot skin, trace his spine, feel the rippling muscles. I felt more than heard his chuckle and rolled my head to look at his face. His eyes were dark and wet, his pupils huge.

"What's wrong?"

"Nothing's wrong," he promised, bending his head to nuzzle the side of my neck before placing gentle kisses down the column of my throat. "How could anything be wrong?"

"I just wanted it to be perfect."

"If it was any more perfect, I'd be dead." He exhaled deeply, pulling slowly out of my body.

I just stared at him as he lifted up off of me before leaning back down to kiss me, his mouth warm on mine.

And in that second, I was filled with a certainty that scared me to death. I broke the kiss and rolled over on my stomach. What the hell was I going to do?

He followed, rolled me over, then draped a leg between mine, and propped his head up on his elbow to look down into my face. "Freaking out?"

How was he so calm? "Yeah. Why, aren't you?"

He nodded, the evil grin back, making his wet eyes glow.

"You're amazing."

"No," he said, using his fingers to trace my eyebrow, then down my nose to my mouth. "You, my friend… you are amazing. I had no idea it would be like that."

I squinted at him as he traced my lips.

"I have never just…. It felt good… right."

"That's great," I muttered, shoving him off me, rolling to my side. "And now that your curiosity is satisfied… you need to get the hell outta my bed."

"Is that so?"

"Yep," I said flatly. "Just go or—"

His laughter washed over me, loud and deep and full of absolute relief.

"Fine, I'll go," I snapped at him, lifting up to move.

He grabbed my shoulder and pinned me down on the bed, hovering above me, his eyes locked on my face. "Don't be an idiot. I already told you I wasn't curious."

"Then what the hell is going on?" I never worried after sex. I never even cared, but I had never been in bed with the man who had starred in every fantasy I'd had since I was a freshman in college.

"What's going on is that I want to take you home with me."

My eyes lifted to his.

"Do you have any idea how long I've waited?"

I yanked him down to me, kissing him hard and deep, the kiss rough and claiming. I wanted to be gentle, but between the aching need in my chest and the overwhelming desire to make him mine, there was no way. I rolled him over and had him flat on his back seconds later. He smiled before parting his lips, sucking on my tongue, tasting me, kissing me back with as much heat as I was giving him.

"Stefan," he gasped, shoving me off him, breaking the kiss to capture my face in his hands, holding me still so he could look at me. "After the wedding, come home with me to the ranch for a few days, okay?"

I was lost in the depth of his eyes. There was lust and heat and absolute, undeniable need.

"Please, Stef," he said, leaning me down into him, his lips closing on my throat. "Just come see the ranch."

"I'll think… maybe," I said quickly. Having him under me was making me dizzy. I just wanted to breathe him in, hold him forever.

"I want you to see how beautiful it is there."

"Why?"

"So maybe it'll get you thinkin'."

"About what?"

He didn't answer. Instead, he sealed his lips over mine as he kissed me softly, tenderly, one of his hands sliding around the back of my neck, the other slipping down over my hip.

I caught my breath, and he smiled against my mouth as he rolled me over on my back, settling his big, warm, naked body over mine, pressing me down into the bed.

"You're gonna be mine."

"Rand." I sighed into his shoulder, my hands sliding all over him, touching the hard muscles under the silky skin. "This is only for—"

"Stop," he ordered me gently. "'Cause you have no idea what this is."

I stared up into his eyes, putting a hand on the back of his neck, my fingers massaging.

"I wanna stay here with you." He smiled before he bent and kissed me again. It was slow; he took his time, hands on my face, sliding over my brows, my cheekbones, and down my neck. "But what will Charlotte say when she walks in tomorrow morning?"

I jerked under him, and his smile was huge.

"I guess you should go," I said without any conviction whatsoever.

He arched a brow for me, and his eyes glinted with heat. "You know, you look really good under me. I knew you would."

"Rand—"

"I never thought guys could be… but you…." He trailed off, his eyes dropping from mine.

"Hey."

His eyes flicked back to my face.

"Tell me." I wanted to know everything he thought about me.

He took a breath. "I just…. I bet folks tell you all the time how beautiful you are."

I arched an eyebrow for him.

"I knew it," he breathed out, and I saw how heavy-lidded his eyes were before he rose over me, parting my thighs with his knee. "You know you're gorgeous."

"Rand, you gotta—"

"I never knew that men could be beautiful, Stefan. Not like this, not like you." He trailed off before he suddenly bent and took my hardening cock into his mouth. It was fast; I didn't even have time to think.

"Rand," I almost yelled, trembling under his hands, nearly coming up off the bed.

His mouth on me was ravaging, and as I stared at him, watching his lips move over my skin, feeling the hot, liquid heat swallow me, it was almost too much, too raw, too overwhelming. To go from nothing from the man to everything was making my heart hurt, my body throb.

"You need me."

And it was pointless to argue, as the truth was there in my panting breath, the way I was writhing beneath him, and my soft begging. I had forgotten about anyone but the man who had me pinned to the bed, wanting only my desire sated.

He laved my cock, sliding his tongue into the slit, tasting, sucking, and the simultaneous pumping of his hand was moving me quickly from fluttering heat to throbbing need.

"Ohmygod." I fisted my hand in his hair, yanking hard. "Come here."

His mouth came off me, and my wet cock tapped his cheek before he moved up my body.

"Rand." I licked my lips, squirming as he watched me. "I wish you could see your eyes."

"Why?" he asked as he hovered over me, grabbing the lube from under the pillow.

"They're so dark."

"'Cause I'm lookin' at you."

"Jesus." My voice was hoarse, low. "Since when are you—"

He sealed his mouth to mine, and I felt the fierce, hot kiss roll through my whole body.

I had to shove him off me so I could breathe.

"Rand." I panted out his name, arching up off the bed when I felt his slick fingers on my skin. He was fast with the lube, his fingers already slippery with it.

"Scream my name, Stef... scream loud."

"Jesus God," I moaned as he buried himself in me fast and hard and deep, grabbing my legs, wrapping them around his hips. I loved that he was rough with me because I craved the power and the dominance, wanting to submit but having never found a partner strong enough to make me or whom I trusted not to hurt me. I had to be careful, or I could fall really hard for my best friend's brother.

"Look at me," he ordered, and when my eyes drifted open, he fisted his hand again on my cock at the same time as he pressed deeper inside my body.

The first pulse of my orgasm beat at the base of my spine as I pushed up into him, watching the muscles in his abdomen contract, his chest heave, and his jaw clench.

"I have to be closer," he said before he suddenly sank down into me, wrapping me in his arms, molding his hot, sweaty body to mine.

Never had anyone held me crushed to their heart as they were buried inside of me. I felt exposed and vulnerable, hot tears blurring my vision.

"You fit me just right," he growled before he turned his head and kissed me, his voice low and sexy.

The sizzling heat tore through my body as I clung to him, arms wrapped around his neck, legs around his narrow hips. He lifted his head to breathe and thrust forward at the same time, filling me, finding his release as he clutched me tight, my name spoken over and over like a chant. We were frozen for long moments, both of us spent, heaving, just lying there, unable to do anything more.

"Are you okay?" I asked when I could.

"Yes," he breathed out, his face buried in the side of my neck. He had not pulled out of me, content to lie there between my thighs. "Are you?"

I nodded, sighing deeply, content not to move for the rest of my life.

"Stefan," he said before his mouth closed on my skin.

I understood the need to bite and lick, suck and bite again. He needed marks on me, *his* marks, compelled by some primitive desire to brand what was his. The slow, languid kissing that followed was almost too much to bear.

"You're shaking," he said finally, his breath warm on my face.

"'Cause of you."

He pressed his bicep against the side of my face, leaned my head close to his, and held me tight. "Is that bad? I didn't hurt you or—"

"No," I breathed out.

His sigh was long and loud. "I can't seem to let go."

"Fine, don't."

His smile was gentle, tender, one I had never seen before, just for me. I watched him, taking in the long lashes, the slight dimple in his chin, and the laugh lines in the corner of his eyes. He had always been gorgeous but was suddenly now breathtaking.

"You're looking at me funny." He chuckled, biting the side of my neck, licking it to take the sting away before biting again, harder. I made a noise of pure pleasure, and he sucked the spot, making it tender, sensitive as he bathed it with his tongue.

"I can't help it." I was in a daze from his attention.

He slid slowly out of my body before collapsing beside me.

"Tired?" I teased him.

Instantly, I was reached for and tucked against his side, one hand buried in my hair, the other on the small of my back, holding me gently. "You get that I'm not leaving your bed, right?"

I smiled at him as he reached behind his head and turned off the light on the nightstand. With the way the moonlight filled the room, it wasn't dark, but it was soothing and cool.

"Unless you want me outta here," he said, and I heard the catch in his voice. He didn't want to go, but he would if I asked him to.

I rolled to my side, drawing his arm around me as I did it. Instantly, he was spooned me and I was engulfed in hard muscle and warm skin. I never before wanted anyone to hold me after, sleep with me against their heart, nuzzle their face into the crook of my neck. I always leaped out of bed after sex and took a shower. Being covered in sweat and semen had never been something I cared for. But the man I had always thought hated me wanted to sleep with me wrapped in his arms, so I didn't care that sticky fluid was drying between us, cementing us together. The smell of our lovemaking, of his skin, was a tangible reminder of what we had just done, the consummation of years of yearning. The revelations of the day were phenomenal.

"Stop thinking and go to sleep already."

I was going to ask a question, but the soft kisses on my shoulder stilled me, and my mind went blank. While I was trying to think of it, with his hand stroking over my hip, I fell asleep. It had been a really long day.

CHAPTER 6

RAND WAS gone when I woke up in the morning, but there was a note under my cell phone telling me why. The ranch needed him, but he would see me that evening for the rehearsal dinner. Until then, I was to miss him and not be too mad about my neck. The last part of the note made no sense until I passed the mirror in the bathroom.

"Oh… shit," I groaned, leaning forward, looking at all the deep purple marks on my collarbone and the sides of my neck. There was one right at the base of my throat, but it was small, barely noticeable. Between my bruised eye and the hickeys, I looked like somebody beat me up.

After I showered and changed, I put on a dress shirt and left only the top button undone. I looked like I was ready to go to a business meeting instead of downstairs for breakfast.

"What's with the shirt?" Charlotte asked as I took a seat beside her.

"I'm running out of clothes," I lied, smiling at her.

"You didn't pack enough clothes?" she asked skeptically. "You didn't… you?"

"Yeah," I snapped at her. "I miscalculated."

Her eyes, a darker version of the ones her brother had, narrowed.

If for any reason I flinched, she had me. She knew me too well for me to be able to hide things from her.

"What?"

"I dunno, something's weird… different."

"Just hurry up and eat," I ordered her. "We've gotta go pick up the dress, and I've gotta check the wedding programs, and—"

"The programs are here. Nick and Clarissa picked them up."

"Where are they?"

She got up and brought me back the huge box, and the second I removed the lid, I saw a problem. It turned out to be only one of many, the least of which was that my name was not Stephanie.

"Who proofed these?" I asked her softly, slowly, my eyes lifting from the program to her face. "It wasn't you, was it?"

"No," she answered warily. "Why?"

I turned it around so she could see that her wedding was still more than a month away. I was surprised that all the glasses in the room held up to the scream instead of shattering right there on the spot.

"What's wrong?" Ben yelled as he came flying in from the kitchen with Nick behind him. He looked like he was ready to kill someone.

But it was impossible to understand Charlotte between the sobbing and intermittent shrieking. The wedding was making her crazy.

"Jesus," he yelled at her a few minutes later, finally understanding what she was crying about. "Could you save that particular bloodcurdling scream for when you're being murdered? Christ, Charlotte, you scared the shit outta me!"

The wailing continued as she collapsed into my lap, wrapping her arms around my neck, sobbing into my shoulder.

"Tell me where there's a printing place around here," I said to Ben, standing up with his fiancée clinging to me like a vine.

"Sure," he said, his eyes wild, concerned about the bride-to-be's state of mind.

"Now," I said flatly.

At which point he finally understood the magnitude of her breakdown.

Calming Charlotte took time, but once I got my laptop, she and I sat down and redesigned the program, and I e-mailed it over to the local copy shop, she was once again able to breathe. The glasses of white wine helped a lot, as did the amazing job the seamstress had done updating the dress. It was not Vera Wang, but neither was it the horror it had first been. The lace had been shortened to the bodice, and without the scary beaded sleeves, it fit like a mermaid gown, and her silhouette was stunning. My friend would be radiant, the train long enough to be elegant but still short enough to dance in, and the veil was enchanting. I was certain that there would never be a more beautiful bride.

In my room later, I tossed her a small, black velvet box.

"What's this?"

"It isn't a ring," I teased her.

"Well no." She giggled. "I didn't think it was."

"Open it."

"Stefan Joss, what did you… oh my God." She caught her breath when she lifted the lid.

Between the bridesmaids and her mother and mother-in-law to be, Charlotte had the old, borrowed, and blue all taken care of. They were missing the new, but I had supplied that.

"Oh Stef." Her bottom lip quivered as she stared down at the diamond earrings. At a carat each, it was not a small gift. But she was the only woman in my life, the only family I had, my touchstone, and my dearest friend. She deserved a medal for putting up with me.

"It's you who deserves the hazard pay," she said as she put the earrings on, finally releasing me after long minutes to screw on the backs.

"Happy?" I asked her.

"I'm never going to take them off."

"Good." I smiled at her, turning back to face the armoire, trying to figure out what else I could wear to hide the purple blotches on my neck. Rand Holloway was a dead man when I saw him.

THE AFTERNOON rehearsal was crazy. One of the groomsmen was AWOL, Reverend Ellis could not wrap his brain around Charlotte having a Man-of-Honor, and everyone was stunned at the very revealing dress that Ben's mother showed up in. It plunged in the front, and it plunged in the back, and I was simply speechless. The groom was mortified.

"Aw, c'mon, that's probably why they're still married," Nick consoled his best friend. "'Cause your mom still fires up your dad's engine, if you know what I mean."

Ben's stunned expression as he looked over at Charlotte and me made me snort out the water I was drinking. The bride just sounded like she was gagging.

"This is what I've been telling you." She smacked her fiancé in the back of the head. "The man's a pig."

"Stef," he whimpered.

"Char," I said, trying not to laugh.

She made the disgusted noise again.

"So, how are we all getting out to the ranch?" Tina asked as she arrived at my side.

I wasn't sure who she was talking to.

"Stef?"

I turned my head slowly to look at Charlotte.

"Hi." She smiled widely, looking guilty as hell.

"What's going on?"

"Well." Her voice went way up high, squeaking like it did when she was really nervous.

"Aren't we going out to Rand's for the rehearsal dinner?" Nick asked, confused.

Ben waggled his eyebrows at me. "Oh yeah, buddy—we're both in hell."

I scowled at Charlotte.

"Your face is gonna freeze like that."

"I'm not staying out there," I said so she wouldn't know it was all I wanted.

"You have to," she moaned. "I think it's in the best friend contract."

Ben could not contain his cackling laughter.

We ended up in a ten-car caravan driving out to the Red Diamond Ranch, and even though my stomach was full of butterflies, I made sure that my tradition with my best friend was observed. The second we got into the Mustang convertible that Ben had given Charlotte when they got engaged, I plugged in my iPod, and we got "Cruisin'" cranked up as loud as it would go.

"Aww," Tina gushed from the backseat. "How cute are they?"

"Adorable," Ben groused from behind Charlotte.

"You're just jealous because her boyfriend is so hot," Kristin taunted the groom.

"Not one person in this car is sane," he assured us all.

But he ended up singing along with us under the hot Texas sun as we went through an hour's worth of oldies.

The closer I got to the ranch, the more nervous I got. What if Rand ignored me when I got there? What if he had invited a woman to be his date? What if he was kind and warm but wanted me to stay only because of Charlotte? He would be engaging and charming, and then, at the end of the night, retire alone to his bedroom, allowing Charlotte and me our time together, our last night as *Will & Grace*.

"Oh, lighten up." Charlotte cuffed my arm as I took the first turn off the highway, and the down the driveway that would eventually lead to an enormous Folk Victorian house.

"Oh, look at this." Tina was in awe as she got out of the car. "There's a huge porch and a swing…. Is this where you grew up, Char?"

"Yes, it is." Charlotte inhaled the scent of wildflowers, grass, and freshly cut wood, just like I did. For whatever reason, the ranch always smelled good, everything mixed together on the breeze. "Don't you just love it?"

"I do," Kristin chimed in. "I love it. The huge porch and the swing and… oh…."

It was the long, drawn-out *oh*, said with such absolute, breathless wonder, that caught my attention. As the other cars began to roll up around us, parking wherever they stopped, I watched, along with everyone else, as Rand rode toward us. He was doing it on purpose, and I didn't appreciate it.

"Wha… ha… oh," Kristen gurgled out beside me, one long string of vowels emanating from her mouth, which she seemed unable to close.

"Oh my." Tina caught her breath.

"Holy shit, I almost forgot," Alison whispered fast.

"What?" Charlotte asked her.

"That your brother is a cowboy, and a damn fine sexy one at that."

"Are those chaps?"

"Dear God in heaven, the man is beautiful."

There was no argument to be made; the man was absolute fantasy material come to life. Up on his horse, riding in from the range, he was as close to heaven as most of us were ever going to get. As he dismounted, my eyes mapped every line of his massive frame. He looked amazing in the boot-cut jeans that hugged his long, muscular legs and ass, the brown leather chaps, and the weathered cowboy boots. The belt buckle was huge and drew your eyes to his groin, and between the flannel shirt, the white T-shirt peeking out from the open collar, and the cowboy hat, he was mouthwatering. And it wasn't just me noticing.

The sly, sexy way he smiled, the dimple in his chin, the veins in his hands, the way the shirt stretched across his wide chest, and his bright, glittering eyes… I needed to be dumped into a pool of ice water. When he reached us, leading the beautiful Appaloosa mare, I felt my mouth go dry.

"Hey, you," Charlotte greeted her brother, stepping forward to touch the brim of the hat that shaded the upper part of his face. "Are you ready for all of us?"

"I've got dinner covered," he assured her, passing me the reins of the horse, "but I've only got room for you and Stef out here tonight."

"No, I know." She smiled at him. "I appreciate you hosting this for me. I know that traditionally the rehearsal dinner is for the groom's family to do, but since they're paying for the wedding... I wanted us—our family—to do this."

"'Course," he said, turning to me. "You okay to hold her?"

I nodded, looking at the horse, reaching out to stroke the side of her neck. "Yeah. She's so beautiful, Rand."

"Yes, she is."

"She's not one of your brood mares, though?"

"No," he said slowly, "she's not."

I felt myself scowl. "What?"

He shook his head. "Nothing. It's just funny that you know anything about brood mares."

My face got hot. "No, I—"

"So tell me—how many brood mares do I have, Stef?"

"I dunno... fifteen?" I asked, looking up into his glittering eyes.

"That's right," he said, delight plain on his face. "And how many other horses on the ranch?"

"Four stallions, and what'd you tell Char last time—thirty saddle horses?"

His smile was out of control. "Yep, and what kind of cattle are here on the Red Diamond?"

I was aware of everyone's attention. Charlotte was looking at me like I had grown another head, and Rand's wicked smile was making his eyes glitter. I was making an absolute fool of myself, and that would not do. I dropped the reins before turning to walk toward the house.

"Is your mom here?" I asked casually.

"Yeah, she's inside." He chuckled.

I nodded, moving fast, not liking the fact that he was making fun of me. I had cared enough to remember details I had overheard about his ranch, and he found that amusing. Screw him! Nobody got to laugh at me. The only comforting thought was that after years of practice, my emotions were not easy to read on my face. I might feel warm, but I never blushed. I might have trouble speaking, but it only made my voice, when it did come out, lower, huskier, sexier. A string of my mother's deadbeat boyfriends, culminating in a vicious stepfather, had taught me how to keep everything from showing on the surface.

"Stef!"

I kept walking.

"Stefan Joss!"

His voice had been a roar, so I stopped and looked back over my shoulder.

"I fired the butler," he said sarcastically, pushing his hat back before pointing to the trunk of the car. "So you should probably bring in your and Char's stuff."

My look must have scared Ben.

"I'll bring the bags," the groom offered quickly, putting up his hands. "Just go in already."

On the porch, the wood creaked under my wing tips, and I smelled the garlic and onions even before I reached the screen door.

"Hello," I called out as I opened it and went in.

"Stefan, honey, I'm in here," May replied from the kitchen.

You never realize how hungry you are until you're faced with sautéed onions. Even if you hate them, they still smell amazing.

"There's my boy," Charlotte's mother greeted me warmly as I came through the swinging door to join her.

After we finished the hugging and kissing portion of the evening, I listened as she explained about the twice-baked potatoes that were in the oven and the gravy she was making to go over the barbecue ribs.

I was leaning against the counter when Ben came in with my duffle and Charlotte's garment bag. I saw him out of the corner of my eye.

"Thanks. Sorry."

"No." He shook his head, waving at me, wanting my attention.

When I was really looking at him, giving him the full weight of my stare, he mouthed out that Rand was a dick. Since Rand's mother was in the room with us, I understood why I was reading his lips and not listening to his voice. No one wanted to hear a criticism of their child, even if it was true.

"I couldn't agree more," I assured him, leaning against the counter as Charlotte's mother walked up beside me, her hand on my back, patting gently.

"I made peach crumb cobbler for you and Charlotte for later."

She knew it was my favorite. "Thank you for thinking of me."

"I always think of you, sweetheart… you're my angel."

I had taken care of Charlotte when she couldn't, helped fulfill her late husband's wish that his girl get a college degree. For the rest of my life, I was golden in her book.

"Which room is mine?"

"The one next to Rand's at the top of the stairs." She smiled at me. "Charlotte's is across the hall."

Grabbing my duffel, I slung it over my shoulder and headed for the stairs. I loved the feel of the house and noticed on the many occasions I had been forced to be in it over the years that, for whatever reason, I always felt comfortable. There were lots of windows, wooden floors, rugs that resembled Navajo blankets, and leather furniture with the brass rivets in it. It was a man's home, and there were no delicate feminine touches, even though Rand's mother visited often. She had left the ranch after her husband died and now lived in a condo in Lubbock.

My room for the night was small but airy, the Casablanca fan spinning slowly on the ceiling, all the windows open, the breeze bringing in the smell of wildflowers and charcoal. The grill had been fired up.

"I wasn't laughing at you."

Turning, I found Rand leaning against the doorframe.

"I swear, Stef, I would never laugh at you."

"It felt like it."

He shook his head. "Nope, I was just surprised."

"About what?"

"That you knew anything at all about this ranch."

I looked at him and felt my stomach flip over.

"So I'm sorry, all right?"

All I could do was nod.

His smile came fast as he tipped his head at me. "Nice collared shirt you got on there."

I flipped him off, turning back to the bed, needing to take a breath since looking at Rand made moving air through my lungs difficult. He needed to go away so I could calm down.

Grabbed hard, I landed on my back in the middle of the bed under my best friend's brother. It took me a second to realize that I had been tackled and that the man with the dancing eyes looming over me seemed very pleased with himself.

"Rand...." I tried to shove him off me. "What're you—"

He bent and kissed me, sucking my bottom lip into his mouth, biting it gently. The result was instantaneous: I forgot about everything but him. My brain emptied; nothing mattered except Rand Holloway and the way I was being kissed, like if he didn't, he'd die. He made me feel like I was all he needed.

I arched up into him and felt the answering tension, his hard thigh pressing into my groin, his arms wrapping around me tightly.

"Did you miss me?" he asked against my lips.

I coiled around him so he'd know, turning my head to offer up my neck for more of his marks. His teeth closing on the base of my throat felt like heaven, as did the hand sliding down my thigh, lifting my leg up over his hip.

"I wanna be buried back inside you, Stef. It's all I could think about all day long."

My eyes lifted from the kissable mouth to eyes filled with need. "Close the door and I'm all yours."

He chuckled before he bent and ground his mouth down over mine, kissing me so hard, so deep, his tongue driving me out of mind, stroking over mine until I was sure I had melted into the bed. His hands were on me everywhere, under my shirt, on my burning skin. I didn't even realize he had tugged the button-down out of my pants.

"You're just saying yes 'cause you know I can't do shit about this right now."

I reached up and took his face in my hands. "I'm saying yes because I want you to fuck me 'til I pass out."

The groan was low; he sounded like he was in agony. "Jesus, Stef… why you gotta say shit like that when you know it'll be all I can think about now?"

"Because I can," I said with a smile up at him.

"Aww, man." He sighed before he suddenly clutched me tight to him, his face pressed into the crook of my neck. "This is good too."

I had no idea what was going on. Hot pillow talk promising hours of fucking I could do. Intimacy was a totally different thing. The man was not trying to rip off my clothes; he was hugging me tight to his heart as he rolled over on his back, keeping me in his arms.

"Stay here with me after the wedding. I wanna wake up with you in the morning and take you riding and eat dinner, just you and me. Please… just stay here."

I pushed against him, and he let me untangle myself. I sat up, straddling his thighs as I looked down into his eyes.

"Oh yeah." He shifted under me, drawing his knees up behind my back, running his hands up my thighs. "This works."

When I put my hands down on his chest and lifted up only to sink back down, pressing my ass over his groin, I felt him shudder under me.

"Stef." My name came out as a sultry whisper. "Forget what I said... fuck me now."

I licked my lips. "Can't... you've got a house full of people to entertain."

"Stef, I—"

"Stef!" Charlotte called as she clomped up the stairs.

I scrambled away from Rand and off the bed and was standing by the window when she strolled into the bedroom.

"What're you doing?" she snapped at me. "Get downstairs and deal with these people with me."

Rand muttered something as he stalked from the room.

"What?" she called after him. "What?"

I moved toward the door, but her eyes, suddenly back on me, froze me where I stood.

"What did he say?"

"What?"

She squinted at me.

"Seriously, what?"

"Did he just say that I shouldn't yell at you?"

"No," I assured her, tipping my head at the door. "C'mon, I'll follow you."

She was staring at me. "Why would my brother care what I do to you?"

"He doesn't."

But she did not look convinced as I walked out of the room.

THERE WERE over a hundred people just at the rehearsal dinner; I could only imagine what the wedding the following day was going to be like. As I sat at the table with the rest of the bridal party, I watched Rand as he stood talking to people I didn't know. Every time I tried to look away, I found my eyes wandering back.

His black hair fell into his eyes, long in the front and running down the back of his neck, but not hitting his shoulders like mine did. The inky waves looked soft, and I knew from brand new firsthand experience that they were. The blue eyes looking out between the strands of hair that caught on his lashes were very sexy. I found that just looking at him— his profile, the chiseled features, the sharp, clean lines—made my heart beat funny. I needed to take a walk and clear my head so I could process everything that had happened.

I walked down toward the stable, and halfway there, I heard footsteps behind me. Turning, I found Nick. He was weaving, tripping as he closed in on me, so very drunk.

"You better get your ass back up there and—"

"Stef," he cut me off, lunging at me, wrapping his arms around me, trying to pull me close.

But while Nicholas Towne was taller than me, six-three to my own five-eleven, he was not the wall of solid muscle that Rand Holloway was. I had him shoved back and flat on his back in the dirt seconds later. The maneuver I had performed had swept his legs out from under him before he even realized he was falling.

"Shit," he coughed after a minute. "I think you broke my legs."

"Hardly," I said, squatting down beside him. "What the fuck was that?"

He coughed again. "I don't…. I'm just drunk."

I nodded. He was most definitely drunk, but that did not mean his agenda was fuzzy in any way. Had I been receptive to it, he would have kissed me and maybe done more. The look, when he came at me, had been pure lust. But making him explain himself was a mistake. Better to just let it go and not have any awkwardness for Charlotte's big day.

"Take my hand."

He took the assistance I offered him, letting me pull him up to his feet.

"Sorry, Stef."

"It's fine," I assured him, turning away. "I'll see you back up at the house."

"You won't tell Ben," he said behind me.

"Shouldn't you be more worried about explaining it to your wife?"

"Stef, I—"

"Just forget it."

"Thanks, Stef," he called after me.

I waved to let him know I'd heard him but didn't turn around. I was having the weirdest few days.

The farther I walked, the calmer I got. It was twilight; the breeze was warm, and the smells of grass and flowers and the faint trace of smoke filled the air. It was nice, slow and easy, and as I climbed up on the fence to look out at the pasture, I had the strangest feeling of calm. Four men on horseback were riding toward the house, and when they saw me, they all lifted their hands to wave. It was nice, friendly, and I smiled as I waved back. Minutes later, hoofbeats in the dirt turned my head back toward the house. I doubted I would ever get tired of seeing Rand up on a horse. He belonged on the cover of a romance novel.

"Hey." I nodded to him as I stepped off the fence, looking up into Rand's bright blue eyes.

"What're you doin' out here?"

I shrugged. "Just needed to clear my head."

"Why?"

"You know why."

He nodded, patting the side of the horse's neck. "C'mon, lemme give you a ride back before anyone attacks you again."

My head snapped up. "You saw that?"

He smiled, leaning forward to give me his hand. "Yessir, I saw that," he told me. "Which is why I nearly rode him down on my way to you."

"Rand, he just—"

"C'mere," he ordered me. "Hurry up."

I grasped his warm, callused hand, and he hauled me up behind him.

"Put your arms around me."

"I shouldn't," I told him. "Everyone will see."

"See what?"

"How much I'll be enjoying it."

His rumbling laughter made me smile as he looked at me over his shoulder. "Hold on tight, Stef. I don't wanna lose you."

My thighs were plastered behind his, my arms wrapped around him, and I rested my cheek between his shoulder blades.

"Tighter." His voice came out as a rasp.

I clutched at him, and I felt his hand over mine, his fingers between my fingers, pressing my palm over his heart so that I could feel his pulse through the flannel shirt.

"Call whoever you have to, but promise me you'll come back here with me tomorrow after the wedding and stay here, just for a week or so."

But how could I promise that when my life was in Chicago?

"Stef?"

"I'll see."

He was silent as we rode, just holding my hand until he cautioned me to stop squirming if I didn't want to be pulled into the barn and thrown down in the hay.

"That sounds really hot," I assured him.

"It's not, actually," he growled at me. "It itches."

How matter-of-fact the man was in the face of passion made me smile.

"What's funny?"

"Nothing," I squeezed him tight, heard his grunt when I did it before his deep sigh.

I made him drop me off at the end of the drive and watched him ride away. I had no idea what he really expected me to do, while at the same time I wondered what I was capable of. I was normally so in control when it came to sex. I had been called cold, aloof, and distant, but I couldn't manage to be anything but shockingly eager whenever Rand got near me. What the hell was I supposed to do?

IT WAS the evening I was certain Charlotte had hoped for, wished for. There was music and dancing and food... so much food. It was all so warm—the picnic tables with the red gingham tablecloths, the wildflower bouquets on every table, the pitchers of sun tea—the rehearsal dinner was more like a big family gathering than a planned event. Everyone got caught smiling. Even Ben's father, whose comments about Charlotte's family had disturbed me, was touched by the charm of the ranch. There was no way to miss the beauty, the quality of life that had not changed in generations, and the strength and character of the man who owned it and the men who worked it. Ben's father, along with everyone else, was impressed with the Red Diamond Ranch.

As I watched Charlotte and her brother dancing on the end of the gravel drive, I took in the fluid way the man moved, the play of muscles under his shirt, and the way his jeans hugged his firm, round ass. When our eyes locked, I realized that I had been caught not only staring, but probably salivating. His arrogant smile told me he was pleased. I took quick refuge in the house, but it was a mistake. Had I not run, the torture would not have been instigated.

Later in the evening, back outside, I was having a slice of red velvet cake, listening to Charlotte's uncle talk about the day she was born and what her daddy had said to him, Rand moved in beside me. The bite I was ready to eat was taken from me, along with the fork.

He grinned lazily, brushing against me. "It's good, ain't it?"

I could feel the warmth radiating off him. "Sorry?"

"Don't you think?"

Any thought that had been in my head had been abandoned the second he gave me his full attention.

"Stef?"

"What?"

"The cake?"

"Cake?"

"Yeah." His smile made his eyes sizzle. "The cake you're eating. It's really good."

Watching him eat off my plate was what had been good. The muscles in his jaw, the line of his throat, the way he licked his lips—all of it combined had short-circuited my brain.

He leaned forward, his voice dropping low. "You like watching me."

"Yessir, I do," I said, licking my lips, my eyes narrowing. "And you like looking at me, too, don't you?"

He sucked in his breath. "Yes, I do."

"Good," I said before I levered myself off the wall and walked back toward the house.

"Where are you going? I thought you were gonna play with me?" He sighed when he caught me at the back door with a hand on my bicep.

I looked down at his hand on my arm. "Can't do this out here where someone might see us. What would they say?"

"Who?"

"Anyone."

"Jesus, Stef you don't have to get all serious alluva sudden. Do you even know how to play?"

"So this is a game?" I clarified with a chill in my voice.

"You're bein' an ass."

"Let go."

"No." He smiled at me, tightening his grip, stepping in close to me so his chest was against my shoulder and I had to tilt my head back to hold his gaze. "I ain't lettin' go."

"You have to," I assured him, and for some reason I was flooded with sadness.

His eyes locked on mine, and when I eased out of his grip, he did, after all, let me go.

MUCH TO Charlotte's annoyance, no one was leaving. I knew she wanted her quiet alone time with me, but by eleven, two hours after the dinner had officially ended, the entire wedding party and a few assorted cousins were still sitting around in Rand's living room. I was stretched out on the couch, listening to everyone talk and laugh, the alcohol making for interesting conversation.

"Here you go, guys," Ben said as he took a seat beside me, having used getting another round of beers as an opportunity to swap places. I knew that sitting next to strangers made him uncomfortable—he wasn't a big extrovert. He felt better flopping down between me and Charlotte.

"Thanks," I said, liking the way his thigh rested against mine. It spoke volumes about how comfortable he was with me. The fact that I was gay and he wasn't didn't matter in the least.

"I should have brought clothes with me too," he groused, turning his head to look at me.

I shrugged, feeling good. I had taken a shower and was now sitting there in a white cotton button-down, white T-shirt, and jeans, barefoot, with my arms back over the seat; I was ready to drink or talk or do whatever anyone wanted. I was at their disposal.

"Tell me again what's with the dress shirt," Charlotte pressed me.

"I told you, I'm short clothes."

"Which has like never ever happened to you before, care to explain?"

"I'm getting old and forgetful."

Her scowl was immediate, and she would have said something, but the doorbell chimed and Clarissa got up to get it. She returned leading four women into our midst. It turned out to be Charlotte's cousin Bethany, from Lubbock, and she had brought three friends with her.

"Those are the girls I told you about," Charlotte said under her breath, leaning forward to talk to her brother, who sat beside the couch in an overstuffed wingback chair. "At least two of them might actually want to live way out here in the boonies with you, cowboy, so don't mess up."

He laughed at her. "Is that right? You're setting me up the night before you get married?"

"A true matchmaker never sleeps," she assured him, inhaling. "Well, at least you smell good for once, not like horses."

The man's scent was a hundred times better than good. The aroma of musk and soap was rolling off him. He looked and smelled good enough to eat.

"Well, let's bring on the buffet." Rand waggled his eyebrows at her, his eyes flicking to mine before returning to his sister.

"Here," Ben yawned, shoving a Wii controller into my hand. "I wanna kick your ass at tennis again, alright?"

"I'm sorry?" I asked him, grinning as I stood up. "When did you kick my ass before?"

As I played, I could not stop glancing over at Rand. His warm smile lifted his eyes, crinkling their corners and turning them a startling aegean blue. One of the girls, Gillian, a pretty brunette with creamy olive skin and big dark eyes, put her hand on his forearm as she talked to him about hunting. Apparently, she wanted him to take her. She preferred to hunt wild boar, but whitetail deer or mule interested her as well. He seemed pleasantly surprised as he listened to her talk about growing up on a ranch.

"Christ, Stef, are you even paying attention?"

I wasn't, no. When my eyes flicked back to Rand and the woman who wanted to bear his children, I was startled to find him staring.

"Can I play the winner?" he asked me.

I swallowed to make sure I could speak. "Sure."

"Come on," he said as he invited all the girls to sit behind us on the couch. As he walked by me, he put a hand in my hair, rubbing the back of my head quickly, gently, and the touch, coupled with the warmth in his eyes, made my heart hurt.

Ben beat me because I could not focus to save my life. I took a seat on the floor, not wanting to wedge myself in between the girls, and when Rand lost as well, he sank down beside me. When the girls offered to make room for him, he shook his head, leaning his knee into mine.

"I'm good here," he assured them before he leaned sideways, his mouth hovering close to my ear. I could feel his moist breath down the side of my neck. "Don't worry, baby, you're the only thing here I'm interested in."

Baby? I sucked in my breath. On what planet was I worried? When my head swiveled to look at him, he waggled his eyebrows for me.

"You should see your eyes," he whispered, his smile making his eyes glitter. "How pissed off are you?"

I got up quickly to go to the kitchen.

"Hey, Stef," Rand called after me, "bring me back another beer, will you?"

"Me too," Ben chimed in. "Thanks, hon."

I shot Rand a look over my shoulder, and he snorted out a laugh. I hit the swinging kitchen door with both hands. He would be lucky if I came back without a firearm. I was standing out on the enclosed porch when I heard a sound from behind me. Rand was slouching in the doorway when I turned to look.

His eyes were hot, and I saw the muscles working in his jaw. "I had no idea you were so possessive, Mr. Joss."

"I already told you that I don't like to be teased and I don't like to be laughed at."

"Yeah, well, so what?" He shrugged. "You need to learn not to take yourself so goddamn serious and stop bein' such a pain in the ass."

My eyes felt huge as I looked at him.

"Stop tryin' to push me away 'cause I'm crazy about you."

What was the proper response for that?

"You could say you're nuts about me too."

"That's awfully presumptuous," I said without thinking.

He chuckled, moving closer. "Jesus, how did I ever fall for such a coldhearted man?"

I was often accused of having no heart at all, because even though my friends saw it, the men I went to bed with never did.

"Shit, you're too cool for me, Stefan Joss."

I just stood there, staring at him as he got closer and closer.

"Or maybe not, huh? Maybe you're not as unaffected as you pretend to be."

I cleared my throat. "Better get back to the girls, Rand," I said, shoving my hands in my jeans, taking a quick breath. "They'll be missing you."

"Shut up," he growled at me, hands on my shoulders so I couldn't bolt. "God, I've never met anyone who needed a kick in the ass more than you."

I stared up into his eyes as he slowly lifted his hand and placed his palm on my cheek.

"You think I'm like all those others guys that can't really see you, but I'm not. I know you better than that. I've seen you with Charlotte and my family, I watched you save Ben the other day, put yourself between him and my idiot cousin, and with me…. God, Stef, with me you're so gentle and sweet—"

"Now wait," I warned him, trying to tug away from him to no avail. He was not letting go. "I may be many—"

"Stop," he ordered. "Last night, when you were lookin' at me, kissin' me… I saw you clear as day, Stefan Joss, and even though you don't think you trust me or even wanna trust me… you do. You already do."

I shivered hard.

"You ain't gotta be strong all the time." He exhaled, lifting his other hand to rest on the side of my neck, touching the pulse beating wildly at the base of my throat. "'Cause you don't have to be on your guard with me. I ain't laughin' at you, I'm laughin' along with you, and you need to learn the difference."

"Rand—"

"Teasin' you is all kinds of fun," he rumbled, the backs of his fingers sliding up and down my throat.

I wanted him to put his hands all over me, so I bit the inside of my cheek to make sure I didn't give voice to the desire.

"I don't want you to worry no more about them girls."

I coughed before clearing my throat. "I was never worried."

"Like hell you weren't."

"Rand—"

"You done staked your claim, boy. Ain't nobody takin' that away from you."

He was insane. "I did no such thing."

"You wanted to sit in my lap."

He had no idea how much I had wanted that.

"I wouldn't've minded at all."

I pulled free of him and took several steps back. "Really? That would have been all right with you if I just outed you in front of everyone?"

"It would've been better'n the silent treatment I got since this afternoon."

"Rand, that's stupid. I'll be gone in two days. Why mess up your life for nothing?"

"So this is nothing to you."

"No—you just—"

"Wait," he ordered me, moving forward, the mountain of hard muscle that was Rand invading my personal space. "Just, let's try a truce again, for the rest of tonight and tomorrow. I just don't wanna fight with you no more."

As I stared up at him, the light from the enclosed porch gave off just enough of a glow for me to see the hope and need in the big man's eyes.

"Okay."

"Okay?" The smile came blazing back to life, wicked and hot.

"Yeah, fine, whatever."

He grabbed hold of the front of my shirt, fisting his hand on the collar. "You should see how you're lookin' at me."

"How am I looking at you?"

"Like you wanna be kissed."

"Are you drunk?"

He looked me up and down, missing nothing, eyes settling on my lips. "Your bottom lip is wider than your top one—just made to be bit."

"Rand—"

He lifted a hand, turned, and disappeared back into the house. I was surprised that he left me and just as surprised when he reappeared on the porch seconds later.

"What are you doing?"

He held up an olive oil cruet and flipped a dishtowel over his shoulder.

I pointed at him. "I get to go home, cowboy, but you're the one that gets to live with it if anybody sees us. You ready for that?"

"I'm ready; you're the one who's chicken."

"Is that right?" I asked, walking backward away from him, toward the shadows where the dryer was, and beyond. "Maybe for that, you get to wait to get laid until all those people clear out of your living room."

"I can't wait," he said, following me, stalking me. "You smell so good, Stef, and lookin' at you all stretched out on the couch, that beautiful body just needin' some attention, and those jeans... how are you even moving in them?"

"Come see if you can get them off."

He charged over to me. "Oh, I'll get 'em off," he promised.

I leaped at him, arms and legs wrapping around him tightly, kissing him savagely as his hands cupped my ass, grinding his groin into mine.

It felt so good—the friction, the way he rubbed against me, how rough he was as he kissed me.

"Fuck, Stef," he growled at me, shoving me up against the washing machine, both hands on the fly of my jeans. Then his voice went up sharply. "Shit!"

He had to lunge sideways to catch the glass cruet and keep it from falling off the dryer, and the ridiculousness of the situation made me laugh.

"What?"

I tried not to giggle. "We're outside sneakin' around like a couple of kids, ready to use olive oil as lube, no less."

"Yeah, it's hysterical." He smirked at me before he spun me around and pushed me forward, steering me past the dryer to a small folding table I hadn't noticed in the dark. Seconds later, the snap of my jeans surrendered to his dexterous fingers, and the zipper followed. All I heard was his indrawn breath before I was bent forward over the table, my jeans and underwear shucked roughly to my knees. I parted my legs as far as I could and let my head fall back.

"Rand." I trembled when I felt his slippery fingers coating my crease.

"Say I can. Tell me it's okay."

"You know it's okay."

"You're so beautiful, Stef. I mean it. I ain't never seen the likes of you."

He rubbed his face in my hair at the same moment his oily hand wrapped around my cock. A hoarse moan tore out of me.

"I love the noises you make," he said, his voice a throaty whisper as he prodded against my entrance. "Fuckin' love 'em."

I could feel the muscles in my ass clenching and unclenching, ready for him, wanting him, needing him. "Fuck me."

"Yessir." He exhaled as he thrust inside, sheathing himself in me, the burn white-hot for seconds before the pleasure twisted quickly into bliss.

He felt so good. I was so full, and his cock buried inside me felt somehow more intimate than it had ever felt with anyone else. "Rand." I barely got his name out.

"God, Stef, your body just swallows my cock and then holds it so fuckin' tight... how is that even... baby," he moaned, sliding in and out of me, stroking deep, the movement sensual and slow. The pace of his movement let me know that he wanted to feel all of me squeezing all of him.

I pushed back as he pushed in, the two of us rocking together hard, the sound of skin slapping on skin filling the open space. The fingers tracing my lips were salty when I tasted them, and Rand let out a harsh groan when I sucked his thumb inside my mouth.

"Christ, I have never wanted anyone this bad," he almost snarled, tangling his hand in my hair only to yank my head back hard, making my back arch as he shoved into me, stretching me tight. The angle was perfect, and he stroked over my gland, causing a hoarse moan to well up from deep inside me.

I felt my balls tighten, heat gathering at the base of my spine as the strokes became harder, pounding thrusts before I was lifted and twisted sideways, folded in half, his hand like a vise around the back of my neck. Rand slid his hand to the small of my back and held me there, anchored, the hammering thrusts pushing up as I was forced down. Every gliding stroke nailed my prostate. I couldn't scream—only panting came out.

His balls slapped against my ass, his thighs plastered to mine as he pushed in and out of my clenching hole, fucking me so hard, so deep. I writhed on his cock, and I heard the sharp intake of breath.

"Fuck yeah... come for me. You're fuckin' drippin', Stef... you're so hard in my hand... let go, just let go."

His name tore from my throat in a strangled whisper, and semen splashed the floor at my feet. The muscles in my ass clamped down on him, gripping his cock tight, and I instantly felt my insides filled with heat.

"Stef!" He got out my name before I was yanked up roughly by my hair, and arms like iron wrapped tight around me. His face was buried in my shoulder, and I registered the moisture seconds later.

"It's okay," I soothed him, trembling hard, so thankful to be held.

"I'm not...." he started, but couldn't continue.

I knew he wasn't crying; it was simply that the emotions were overwhelming, the pleasure so intense that there was no way to process it without breaking down just a little.

"I don't wanna let go," he said, his mouth opening on the side of my neck, sucking hard.

The man really enjoyed leaving marks on me. "You gonna stay inside of me 'til you go soft?" I smiled, letting my head bump against his, my body boneless in his embrace.

"Stef!" I heard Charlotte yell from inside.

"I guess not." He chuckled, and because he was still buried inside me, plastered to my back, I felt the rumble spread through me like a ripple on the surface of a lake until my entire body vibrated with his happiness.

When he slid out of me, I had to grip the edge of the table to keep myself standing. Everything in me wanted to beg him to stay buried to his balls in my ass.

"I wanna lie down with you," he said, kissing up the side of my neck to my ear, breathing out sharply, covering me in goose bumps from head to toe. "Don't you wanna get in my bed, Stef? Don't you wanna wrap yourself around me?"

I groaned, unable to stop shaking.

He took a quick breath. "Lookin' at your sweet little ass with my stuff dripping out of it is makin' it hard to breathe."

His words were having the same effect on me.

"Stefan Joss, where are you?"

The yell was shrill—she wanted me now. Without another word to him, I bent, yanked up my briefs and jeans, and bolted from the porch.

"You smell like come and olive oil." He laughed at me as I threw open the screen door.

I had just enough time to flip him off before Charlotte appeared in the kitchen doorway.

"Jesus Christ, Stef," she barked at me. "I've been looking for you for a half an hour!"

But even though she was mad, all I could hear was Rand's throaty laughter. He really needed to get it together. It wasn't that funny.

ONCE THE crowd thinned out, I went upstairs with Charlotte and lay down on her bed. I listened to her talk about Ben and the wedding flowers and the appetizers and how much she hated vegans and why my idea of having a photo booth had been so inspired. She had wanted to have cute pictures of everyone, and now she was sure to have them. The photo booth would make two prints of every picture, one for the guest and one for Charlotte's wedding album.

"How did you ever get so brilliant, Stef?"

It was a photo booth; I had not found the cure for the common cold. "Seriously, how tired are you?"

She groaned loudly and flung herself facedown on the bed.

"What's wrong?"

There was a long, muttering explanation spoken into the pillow.

"Look at me, because I didn't hear a word of that."

She rolled her head to the side, her eyes fastened to mine. "I said that Ben wants to know about the worst day of my life."

My stomach did a slow roll.

"What should I say?" she asked, her fingers featherlight across my jaw.

"What do you want to say?"

She took a shaky breath. "I want to tell him, but I'm just afraid that he'll look at me different after. I should have told him a long time ago."

Her face looked pained.

"Honey, do you—"

"Will you hold my hand?"

"What?"

"When I tell him"—she swallowed hard—"will you hold my hand?"

I took a quick breath. "Cut out my heart instead."

Her sigh touched my face. "I already did that."

Laying there, my face inches from hers, I watched her eyes fill, saw the tiny rosebud lips purse and the delicately arched brows tighten slightly.

"Ben's downstairs."

"He's drunk."

"Maybe that's better."

We sat up at the same time.

"It's a lot to take in the night before your wedding," I told her.

"And I should do what?" she asked me seriously. "Begin my life with him with this hanging over us?"

"What's hangin' over you?" I snapped at her. "If he never knows, who cares?"

"Easy for you to say." Her sigh moved my hair. "You know already."

I rolled my head back so I was looking at her.

"Sorry, that was a shitty thing to say."

Only at that moment, staring into her eyes, did I realize how terrified she was. I grabbed her hands tightly, startling her, as evidenced by her gasp.

"You know… whatever happens…."

She nodded quickly, the tears spilling over, trailing down her cheeks. The reassuring smile she gave me, trying to comfort me, was painful. "Go get him."

I didn't say anything; I just got up and went to the door.

"And Rand."

My head swiveled back to her.

"I want Rand to know."

"Why?"

"Because he should," she said, her tone telling me that she was resigned to the idea.

Halfway down the stairs, I remembered to breathe.

Maybe it was my face, or the way I couldn't bring myself to speak, but when Rand saw me, he got up from where he was sitting apart from the others. Instead of sharing space on the couch, he was alone in the wingback chair.

"Stef," he said softly, moving quickly to step in front of me. His hand slipped around my neck, his thumb sliding down my throat. I doubted that he even realized he was touching me, wearing his affection and possessiveness for anyone to see. It was fortunate for him that everyone was drunk. They didn't even spare us a glance.

"Can you and Ben come upstairs with me?"

"'Course," he said, turning only his head to look over his shoulder at Ben. "C'mon."

"Stef, what—"

"Now." Rand's voice dropped into his chest, and I heard Ben's quick intake of breath before he was up and standing beside me. "We'll follow you."

When I opened the door of the bedroom minutes later, I found Charlotte standing at the window. Her face, when she turned, was panicked.

"Shit," I muttered, crossing the room to her, taking the trembling hand she reached out to me. She was already a mess.

"Char?" Ben asked, and I heard the click of the door closing behind him.

She took a breath, forcing a smile. "Okay, so the other day I blurted out about the worst day of my life, and you said you really wanted to know."

He was stunned; it was all over his face. The man had been laughing and having a good time earlier, and now, suddenly, he was stone-cold sober. "Charlotte—"

"And I know it wasn't just that, because you've known from other things I've said, how weird I get sometimes in the dark or when we went to that swingers'—"

"Charlotte!" He raised his voice, glancing at me and Rand. "I don't think—"

"I was excited to go." She smiled, even though her eyes were starting to moisten, redden. "I told Stef all about the retreat."

His eyes snapped over to me. "She told you about that?"

But before I could answer, as she did in most situations, she answered for me. "Seriously, Ben there's nothing—and I mean really, nothing—I don't tell Stef."

He opened his mouth to speak.

"Like remember the time you shot your wad so hard you hit the cat?"

"Charlotte!" he coughed.

I smiled at him, giving him the big thumbs-up. "Nice distance, by the way."

His eyes were huge as he turned to look at Rand.

Charlotte's brother clapped him on the back. "Not bad, but I don't have a cat. If you can hit one of my hunting dogs, I'll be impressed."

I could tell from his expression that of all the revelations of the past few minutes, Rand joking around with him was the biggest. Ben was looking at him like he'd grown another head. When his eyes hit me, I just shrugged. I'd had no idea the man could laugh or tease or be funny either. I had been just as surprised.

"So anyway—" Charlotte cleared her throat. "The point is I really wanted to go. I mean, I'm as twisted and kinky as the next girl, but when we got there, it was just…. I wasn't expecting the bondage part of it, and even that would have been okay, but—"

"You freaked when those two guys grabbed your arms."

She nodded fast. "Yeah, I mean if the girls had strapped me in, I probably would have been all right, because the straps themselves, the harness… that wasn't like what happened, so it wouldn't have reminded me."

"Char," Ben began softly, taking a step toward her, "I don't think you really want Rand and Stef here when you—"

"Oh no," she cut him off, lifting a hand to stop his progress. "I have to have Stef here, and Rand…. I mean, I should feel weird telling him that his baby sister is willing to take part in a ménage or even an orgy, but even though I talk a lot of trash about my brother… he's still my brother, and c'mon, I tell my family everything. Even my Mom knows about the weekend with the swingers."

"She does?" Ben gasped.

"Oh sure." She nodded. "My family is not emotionally stunted like yours is, Benjamin. We all talk about things."

"Char—"

"But the only thing I've never told my mother or my brother or you is about the worst day of my life," she cut him off, squeezing my hand, shifting on her feet so she was pressing against me. "And you should know… I mean, I was telling Stef that I should've just told you before, but I just—I never—"

"You were raped, weren't you?" Ben swallowed hard, the muscles in his jaw working.

I saw Rand's brows furrow as he crossed his arms, waiting.

"Honey." Ben's voice was soft, caressing. "I don't—"

"No," she said, her voice small, nasally, as tears filled it, welling up in her eyes. "I wasn't raped. My friend Mandy was."

No one moved or made a sound, and Charlotte took a breath.

"See, I had this great idea in junior year that for me to really date and meet lots of guys that I would move in with another girl and have the cool bachelorette pad." She nodded, taking another breath, swallowing before she found her voice again. "And so I moved in with my friend, Mandy Woods."

"I don't remember you living with anyone but Stef," Rand said, letting her focus on the most mundane part of the story for a moment so she could get herself under control.

"I know." She smiled through her tears. "Because it was so short. I think it was like two months, and then I was back home… with Stef." She wiped quickly at her eyes, taking another quick breath.

"Love…." Ben moved closer, and when her hand didn't stop him, she retreated just a little behind me. It was enough to stop him.

"I can't confess if I can't get it out," she told him.

He stopped, and his eyes flicked to mine. "I hate that you know whatever this is and I don't. It's killin' me."

It had nearly killed me at the time.

"Okay," she growled, shaking it off. "Sorry, I'm stronger than this shit. Here's what happened. I woke up because I heard screaming, and there was a man in my bed choking me."

"Ohmygod, Char—"

"Shut up," Rand said, his eyes never leaving Charlotte.

She gave a quick smile. "He told me that he'd kill me if I made any noise, so of course the second he let me go, I screamed my head off."

No one made a sound.

"When he came at me again, I made it off the bed and out of the room, and I would have made it out of the apartment, but I tripped over Mandy," she managed to get out before the sob took her voice.

My arm went around her, and she turned into me, face in my shoulder, hands digging into my back as she clutched at me.

"I thought… maybe I'll write it down," she cried and then suddenly laughed, looking up at me. "Fuck, it's like a goddamn oral book report."

I grunted out my agreement.

"Did you have to do those?"

"'Course. Your teacher gives you a choice. You can either stand up in front of the class for three minutes or write a six-page report." I smiled down at her, wiping away her tears. Her eyes were already getting puffy. "I always stood up."

"Oh, I'm sure you did." She sighed. "I always wrote the six pages."

"Well." I shrugged. "I am fantastic at oral."

She coughed before snorting out a laugh. "God, leave it to you to tarnish my memories of elementary school."

"It's a gift," I assured her, wiping away more of her tears with my hands. "Don't cry anymore. You're gonna look like shit for pictures tomorrow."

She giggled. "I know, right? I mean, you with your black eye and me looking like ass, what're people gonna think?"

"Who knows," I grunted before blowing cold breath on her face. "There, now finish. It was your brilliant idea to do this tonight."

"Could… maybe you…." She shook her head, waving her hand at me. That was it; her voice was gone.

"Shit," I muttered under my breath. Somehow I had always known that the explanation would fall to me. Looking over at Rand and Ben, I realized how hurt Charlotte's fiancé looked, and saw plainly the fury stamped on her brother. Quick was better, the Band-Aid theory, and so I took my own breath to settle the butterflies in my stomach. "There were two men in the apartment. The police agreed that the screaming Char heard was Mandy. She made it out of her bed after being raped, but she didn't make it out of the apartment. They caught her and hit her, and she was just a little tiny thing, and…." How could I explain all the blood? How broken she had looked with her throat cut?

"So Charlotte fell down, but she got up fast." I smiled down at my friend for a moment. "And when she got up, she ran into the kitchen and grabbed a knife."

"You fought," Rand said flatly, and Charlotte turned to look at him and nodded.

"She did," I told him. "And when Kevin Kramer went after her and tried to grab her, he ended up dead." I looked back down at her. "Like he deserved to, in that apartment with the girl he raped and murdered."

Charlotte nodded.

"Mandy's parents think you're a fuckin' superhero."

Another quick nod.

"But what about—"

"Stef came," Charlotte gasped like she was surfacing from deep underwater. "I turned around after I stabbed"—gulp of air—"Kevin in the throat, and the other guy grabbed me and punched me, and he was kicking me when the door opened and there was Stef."

Two sets of eyes on me.

"I had a key," I told them. "I called earlier, and she told me to come and sleep over after I went out 'cause we were supposed to do something the next day. So I got to the apartment and opened the door and…." I shrugged.

It was hard, even after so long, even being so far removed from it, to put everything into words. The blood, the man beating the shit out of my friend, Charlotte's face, the weight of knowing that in that instant, I was all she had.

"Oh." She sighed, easing away from me, and I saw her smile. I opened my mouth to stop her. "No—no, you know I'm good during this part. I can tell it from here, it's just before, when I was scared and alone… but then you came," she said, turning to look at the two men she had trusted with this story. "Stef just ran in, and the guy, Jared Kenny, he tried to stab me, but Stef was there before he could."

Adrenaline was a scary thing. I had seen pieces. The guy, Jared, had lunged at me, and before I even registered my action, my fist had connected with his jaw. He fell hard and fast, and the second he hit the ground, I kicked him. My motorcycle boot made mush of his face, but I wanted to make sure he stayed down.

"When the police got there, it was all over."

"Did Jared go to jail?"

She nodded. "He did."

"And is he still there?"

"No, he died three weeks into his sentence."

"Do you know—"

"Yes," she cut Ben off. "The detective who took care of my case told me. Another prisoner killed him."

"Why?"

"The detective didn't say."

"How did the men get in the apartment?"

"Through Mandy's window. She was forever leaving it open. I told her all the time to…. Stef even put a lock on it so all she had to do was shut it, and it would…. But she forgot."

"Char—"

"When the police interviewed Jared, he told them that he and Kevin were out shooting pool when they saw Mandy and decided to follow her home."

"Jesus."

She shrugged. "They got in through her window and raped her, and when she got away and went to call the police, Jared stopped her. He beat her up pretty bad before he slit her throat."

There was a long silence.

"Is it okay," Ben finally whispered, looking at Charlotte. "Could I maybe hold you now?"

She lifted her arms for him, and he lunged forward, grabbing her tightly, crushing her against him.

"Oh baby," he breathed into her shoulder, shivering hard. "I'm so fuckin' proud of you. You were so strong, and you were so brave, and you never gave up."

"It was just survival instinct," she sobbed. "That's all. I'm not—"

"You're amazing," he assured her, "and I knew it all along, but it's even clearer now. Goddamn, woman, you're a lion!"

I was so pleased with him, so touched watching Ben hold my best friend, that I didn't realize that Rand was speaking to me for several minutes.

"What?" I asked softly.

"Thank you."

I smiled up at him, into the azure eyes, before he moved to go to Charlotte and Ben. As I watched the three of them, I understood the magnitude of what my best friend had done. She had exorcised all her demons, had come clean to the two most important men in her life, and now she was ready to be married the following night with no secrets, nothing hanging over her. It was a triumph for her, and I was so proud and so happy, even though I knew our relationship had just changed forever.

Because she had told Ben and Rand, I was no longer the caretaker of her secrets, no longer her champion. Her husband was taking my place as her safety net, and while that was the way it was supposed to be, I had no job if I wasn't the person in Charlotte Holloway's life who reassembled the pieces after she broke. If I didn't ride to the rescue, what use was I? When I slipped from the room, no one noticed.

CHAPTER 7

I WOKE up broken. Sleeping on a chair in Rand's den had been a bad idea, but it was where I had fallen asleep watching television. I felt all of my twenty-eight years, and even though I was in pain, when I told that to Rand's uncle Tyler, he laughed at me.

"We'll talk again when you're seventy-five," he told me, pouring coffee for both of us.

The look I shot him made him laugh, as did my comment that I was in real pain.

"Drink the coffee, and I'll make you some breakfast. You can come down to the barn with me and watch Chase and Pete help deliver a calf. You ever seen a cow get born?"

"No sir." I shook my head, not sure if it was something I wanted to see after all.

"Well, come on then, it ain't somethin' you'll wanna miss."

Walking in my jeans and T-shirt beside the older man, listening to him talk, shivering in the early morning air and wishing the whole time that I hadn't ditched my dress shirt, I felt better. Just moving was uncurling my spine, and I found the fact that I was not expected to speak comforting.

No one had come looking for me. Charlotte had forgone the traditional separation between bride and groom the night before the wedding, and she and Ben had stayed up late talking. I went up once to see if he had left but heard whispered voices through the door. I didn't want to intrude.

Rand was gone. He wasn't in his bedroom, the house, or anywhere I could find. Worst of all was that he obviously hadn't needed me. It was sobering. Hot sweaty sex on a major appliance had not translated to Rand wanting me spooned around him in the night. I was hoping for the caveman scene, the one where he came and found me, threw me over his shoulder, and carried me upstairs to his bed. That I had been seemingly forgotten was devastating. I wanted to run away instead of facing him, embarrassed about being so needy.

The iron grip on my bicep brought me from my thoughts.

"You all right there?"

"Yes, sir." I smiled at him.

As I followed the older man, I looked around at the ranch. The two-story house we had just come from really was beautiful, and even the stables and the bunkhouse where the ranch hands ate and slept had a homey appeal. Veering left toward the barn, I was stopped instantly with a hand clamped down on my shoulder.

"Where are you goin'?" the older man asked me.

I tipped my head toward the wooden structure. "To the barn."

"Nothin' in there that'll give birth. That's where we keep the tractor and such."

The man enjoyed teasing me, and so I fell back into step beside him, realizing as we walked that his hand was still on my shoulder. It was nice, and I felt the tension that had been hanging on from the night before start to drain away.

I WAS dozing when I heard my name. Lifting my head, I saw Rand standing at the edge of the porch scowling at me. I just waited.

"What the hell are you doing here?"

No greeting, just straight to the inquisition. "Nice," I muttered, closing my eyes.

"Stef!" he barked at me.

"Resting," I said, since it should have been very obvious that I was well on my way to drifting off into a coma.

"Charlotte's been lookin' for you for hours."

I grunted, letting my head fall back.

"Goddammit, Stef, what—"

"Why are you yellin'?" I heard Uncle Tyler yell himself from the house, followed by the harsh, protesting squeak of the screen door as it was opened. "That boy done real well this mornin'. You got no cause to be fussin' at him, Rand Holloway."

"Why is he wet?"

"I hadda hose him off 'fore I let him walk up here to the house. He was a mess."

"Why?" Rand asked, and I heard him cross the porch, the sharp strike of his boots on the wood.

"Well, I went down to the barn this mornin' 'cause Chase called and said that we was due for a calf and—"

"Yeah, I know, that's why I told Pete to—"

"Pete never showed."

The silence stretched so long my body started to get heavy.

"What?" Rand finally said, his voice low and ominous.

"That's right, bossman; Pete forgot to show up again. I already done called Mac, and even though it ain't my place no more—I ain't foreman—Mac did exactly what I woulda and fired that useless boy the second he got back from his whorin' around."

"Shit," Rand groaned.

"Shit is right; you're a terrible judge of men, Rand Holloway. Let Mac do the hirin' from now on."

"Maybe you're right."

"Well of course I'm right. I'm always right, but that don't make no never mind. Pete's gone, but Chase says he's got himself a cousin needs a job, so—"

"What does any of this have to do with Stef?"

I didn't mind him talking about me like I wasn't there since I didn't want to talk to him anyway. I was nothing to him, after all; he hadn't even bothered to look for me when he went to bed. I was of no consequence to him.

"Well, once I got to the barn and found out it was just me and Chase, I needed Stef to help. I ain't a young man no more, Rand, I can't pull no calf, I ain't got the back."

"Shit, why didn't someone call me?"

"Like I was sayin', there weren't no time, that calf was comin', and when we realized that it needed to be turned and... well, you know how it goes."

"And?"

"And Stef did real fine, and both mama and baby are doin' real good."

"You saved them both?"

"Yessir we did, just an old man and a green cowboy and... what is it again, Stef?"

"An acquisitions manager."

"What he said."

"So Stef did what, the pulling?"

"Yes, he did."

The hand on my shoulder made me open my eyes and look up. I was rewarded with a smile on the face of the man staring down at me.

Crap. Just looking up at Rand Holloway made my stomach twist into a knot. Whatever I told myself, the truth was that I wanted him to care because I wanted to matter to him. I needed to know that he had missed having me beside him, close to his heart.

"Got covered in blood and all kinds of shit, didn't you?"

I groaned. The miracle of life was beautiful and disgusting all at the same time. "He's really cute, Rand," I told him, smiling slightly. "You should go see him. I named him Phil."

He looked pained. "I'm sorry?"

"He looked like a Phil."

Rand looked over his shoulder at his uncle Tyler. "Is he kidding?"

I looked over at him, too, and saw him shrug. "What's the problem? The boy bein' there saved the cow and her calf. If he wants to name the damn thing, I say g'head."

Rand made a noise in the back of his throat before he turned back to look down at me. "You look like shit."

I had no doubt. I had been hosed off, but there was still some sticky stuff dried in my hair, and I smelled really bad. My T-shirt, which had started off-white, was brown and red and just needed to be tossed. The jeans needed to be washed several times, and as for my hiking boots, I had already thrown them out.

"So Mac fired Pete?" he asked the older man.

"Yessir he did, and it's about time, if you ask me. Everett and Jackson took him off the ranch an hour ago."

"Did Mac pay him out?" Rand asked, turning his head to look at him.

"I'm sure he did, but you should be askin' Mac about that, not me."

"And so you and your buddy Stef are going to do what now?"

"You ain't got no cause to be givin' us none of your—"

"Sorry." Rand sighed. "I didn't mean nothin'."

"And for your information, your mama's bringin' Stef and me some lunch and we're havin' us a beer."

Rand squatted down beside my chair as I lifted my hand for the Budweiser his uncle passed me.

"I'll be right back with the salsa, Stef. Little girl I know in Guthrie makes it for me. It's real good."

"It's real hot is what it is," Rand mumbled under his breath.

"What's that, boy?"

Rand shook his head, and I watched the screen door bang shut behind the old man, who was in a lot better shape than I was.

"Hey."

I turned my head to look at Rand.

"So you helped a cow give birth this morning. How do you feel?"

"Like I need to sleep." I yawned. "But sitting with your uncle and your mom is gonna be just as good."

"Why don't you come back up to the big house with me?"

"You mean your house."

"My house, big house, since when does—"

"Never mind."

"What's going on?"

"Nothing."

"Listen, Charlotte needs—"

"Charlotte has her bridesmaids and Ben. She doesn't need me."

"Little dramatic, ain't it?"

I took a long swallow of my beer and let my head fall back and my eyes close. I was ready to stretch out and go to sleep.

"She needs you, you jackass. She's gonna fall apart without ya."

She was a rock now. She had unburdened her soul. There would be no more crying over wedding programs or wedding dresses or wedding flowers. She was woman; hear her roar.

"I seriously doubt that."

"Where were you last night?"

"In the den."

"Why didn't you come to my room? I waited up, but I must've fallen asleep."

My eyes flicked open as I looked at him. "I checked your room, you weren't there."

"When?"

"I dunno, little after one."

"I was bringin' in the dogs and checkin' on things. You shoulda come on back, 'cause I was there."

"Why didn't you look for me?"

"Because you were supposed to come to me."

"Yeah, but—"

"You was the one wantin' to be in my bed. Why would I go lookin' for you?"

"Why would you think I wanted to be in your bed?"

His smile was wicked. "Oh, I dunno, maybe 'cause I fucked you on my back porch and I figured maybe you'd like it better in bed."

"Really? Is that what you thought?" Again he was taking me for granted, and I hated it.

He snorted out a laugh. "Damn, you are a touchy thing, ain't cha?"

"Go away," I grumbled, suddenly tired and much too edgy to banter with him. I looked out toward his house to where I hoped to see his mother coming from the back porch.

"And cold as ice and stubborn," he said, hand on my chin, bringing my eyes back to him. "You are the most stubborn man I have ever met."

I had no doubt that was true.

"Jesus, Stef, I promise not to think I own you if you confess to likin' me just a little."

I stared into the electric blue eyes.

His fingers slid over my jawline, stroked down my throat, and then made the return trip to my lips. "Tonight, after the wedding, when everybody's gone, I'm gonna bring you back out here to the ranch and put you in my bed."

I sighed deeply. "That sounds real nice."

His eyes sparkled. "Does it? Real nice?"

I grunted.

"Sounds like some Texas creepin' in there to me, Stefan Joss."

"Oh my word," Rand's mother said from behind him. "Stefan Joss, what did my brother-in-law let you get yourself into?"

"He's covered in blood an' shit, Mama." Rand laughed, rising to his feet. "And he looks damn fine."

"Well, yes, but... Tyler!" she yelled toward the house, carrying a tray by me. "Rand, open this door for me—Tyler!"

I was smiling as Rand moved fast to hold the screen door open for her.

"Tyler, what did I tell you about Stefan? He doesn't belong to you, he belongs to Charlotte! You have no right to...."

Her voice trailed off as she went deeper into the house.

Rand was smiling as he walked to the edge of the wraparound porch at his uncle's home. "I won't tell Char that you're down here at Tyler's, but you need to get on up to my house as soon as you're done with lunch, you understand? They'll be leavin' soon, and you need to go with them."

"Sure," I lied to him.

He pointed at me. "Knock it off and quit bein' such a prick. This here day ain't about you, Stefan Joss. It's about her, and you're here for her, just like the rest of us. Don't be a selfish bastard, or you'll never forgive yourself."

I sat up fast. "Listen—"

He cut me off. "No, you listen. You're right, Charlotte don't need you the same no more. You and her… there are things she's gonna share with Ben that you ain't never—"

"I know that," I snapped at him. "Don't you think I—"

"Lemme finish."

I knew that my relationship with Charlotte would never be the same; he didn't need to reiterate the point for me.

"But just because you don't belong to her no more don't mean you should worry that you got no home," he said, stepping off the porch. "'Cause my mama's wrong."

"What?" I asked, standing up to go to the edge of the porch so I could look down at him. "Rand?"

He stopped and looked up at me. "What she said to Tyler ain't right."

"Oh," I said, something about the look in his eyes making my legs go weak.

"You don't belong to Charlotte. You belong to me."

I swallowed hard, my mouth dry, my throat tight. "You shouldn't just—"

"Eat and then get your ass back up to the house right quick. Don't mess with a woman that's about to be married. Her sense of humor is all gone."

I would have said something else, but he was walking away too fast, whistling for his dogs, all of which came charging across the paddock to reach him. Watching him kneel and pet them, seeing their absolute joy at his attention, I realized that if I had a tail, I would have wagged it every time the man got near me too.

"Stef, honey, come eat."

I practically bolted into Uncle Tyler's house.

TO ME, it was nice that the whole Holloway family had lived on the ranch all together at one time. Charlotte's father had owned the ranch, and his brother Tyler had been ranch foreman and lived in the house that was still his. When Tyler had retired as foreman, Rand should have let

Mac Gentry move into Uncle Tyler's house, but instead, Rand had built another house for his new foreman and allowed Tyler to remain on the land. He had not wanted to pressure the older man into moving in with him, and it turned out that his uncle liked living alone. Currently, he was courting a widow from Dumont, and not sharing space with Rand was a good thing. The older man didn't want Rand cramping his style. Rand, he said, was much too much of a homebody to live with. The man never left the ranch and as such was always underfoot.

"He don't do nothin' or go nowhere," Tyler told Charlotte's mother and me over lunch. "I tell you what, May, that boy of yours needs a good woman."

"He needs someone, yes," she said, nodding, "but we thought Jenny was the woman for him, and look how that turned out."

Tyler scratched his head. "Y'know, I reckon I still don't know what happened there. She was the perfect gal for him. She taught school, she was a homemaker, her family was ranch folks... but something wasn't right, and I still don't know what."

"Don't you remember?" Charlotte's mother said gently. "It was the way he looked at her. From the beginning, he liked her just fine, he would smile whenever she looked at him, but the problem was that when she wasn't, he never smiled."

"What are you goin' on about?"

"She means like Ben," I clarified for Tyler. "Whenever you catch him looking at Charlotte, even when she doesn't notice him... he's smiling or just looking at her with that goofy, lovesick face of his. You know he's crazy about her."

"Exactly," she agreed. "That's what I mean."

Tyler rolled his eyes. "Well, I don't rightly know what you two see that I don't, but mostly it has to be sex."

"Ty!" May Holloway yelled, as I choked on my ice tea.

"The man didn't enjoy sleepin' with his own wife—I know, she told people, and it got around. She wanted him and he didn't want her, can't get no plainer'n that."

"Tyler Wade Holloway!"

He threw up his hands as I started laughing.

"I'm just sayin', might been she weren't his type. She was a bit small-chested for a woman, and maybe he needed a little more to hold."

I was laughing so hard, and watching May beat Tyler with her napkin wasn't helping me regain my composure.

After lunch, I offered to do the dishes but was turned down twice, so instead of being at the sink, I was sitting with Tyler on the porch when Ben came walking down to the house with Nick in tow.

Tyler and I both waved with our beer bottles. It was a nice day, now close to one, the morning having been spent birthing cows and the early afternoon eating, drinking, and talking with two of my favorite people in the world. Funny that Charlotte's mother, the mother of the bride, had opted to spend a little over an hour of her time with me instead of up at the house with her daughter. Maybe she was feeling a little useless as well.

"What the hell are you doing?" Ben yelled at me as he came up the three stairs to the porch. "Have you lost your goddamn mind?"

I just looked at him.

"Stef, get your ass off this porch and come with us. Nick and I are leaving now, and you know we got an hour drive in front of us back to the B and B. We all need to start gettin' ready."

"The wedding ain't 'til six o'clock at night." Tyler yawned. "What on earth could Charlotte need so long for? I tell you, a nice shot of tequila will calm her down some."

I nodded my agreement.

Ben pointed at me. "You're bein' an ass, and I don't know why, but y'are."

"I just… don't all the girls have to go to the salon and get their hair done and their nails and all that? I mean, why would I need to be involved?"

"I thought you guys enjoyed gettin' groomed."

I didn't even dignify the comment with a response; instead, I just looked back out across the ranch at the sky and the sea of clouds.

"You best get on back up to the house, boys," Tyler grunted. "Leave the men be."

They left without another word as Charlotte's mother took a seat on the other side of me. She passed me a slice of peach cobbler.

When I turned to look at her, she smiled warmly.

"You and Charlotte didn't have any last night, and I think that's because she was busy telling Ben and Rand about what happened those many years ago when she was attacked."

I stopped breathing.

She tipped her head at Tyler. "We both know. I told him after the hospital called me. She was covered under my medical insurance, after all, Stef."

I had never once considered who had paid the medical bills when she was taken to the hospital to be checked out. It had never even crossed my mind. "I'm sorry."

"For what? Are you sorry for saving my baby's life, which is what Rand said you did when I asked him about it this morning? Are you sorry for helping her pay her college tuition? Are you sorry for being there for her when her family couldn't and being the one person I could always depend on to do the right thing by her? Tell me… what precisely are you sorry for?"

I couldn't even speak.

"Perhaps you're sorry to be having peach cobbler with beer? Is that it?"

I smiled at her, even though I could barely see her through the tears filling my eyes. "Yes, ma'am, that's what I'm sorry for."

"That's what I thought," she said, leaning back in the cedar rocking chair.

"If you two are done jawin' over there," Tyler complained, since he was trying to nap, though he wouldn't have admitted it.

We both apologized as I started eating, and May Holloway patted my leg.

AROUND FOUR that afternoon, I made it back to the bed and breakfast, where the wedding party was staying. I got a ride over with Charlotte's mom after looking in on Phil before I left. The calf looked better than I did—he was cleaner, and he smelled nicer. I promised Tyler that we would do tequila shots at the wedding, and he assured me that he would not forget.

In the house, the bridesmaids were all sitting out on the covered veranda that looked over the man-made lake. It was beautiful, and they all looked stunning. I waved in passing but never made it to the stairs.

"Stefan!" Alison snapped at me. "Where have you been? Charlotte is a mess, and her hair's not done, and her makeup is—"

"Then get up there and help her out." I squinted at her. "You guys should—"

"Stef!"

We all looked up, and there, at the top of the stairs, was Charlotte. She looked like hell. Her hair was all piled up on top of her head, she was without a drop of makeup, and her eyes were red and puffy.

"What are you doing?" I asked as I climbed the stairs.

"It's because you think I don't need you," she sniffled. "You get like this. I just never thought for a second that you would think I was like everybody else."

"What're you talking about?" I asked as I stopped a step below her.

She stared down at my face. "In your head, everybody's going to leave you, nobody sticks around, and so the second you think somebody's bored with you or that they don't need you, you do the patented Joss disappearing act and are never seen again. You did it all the time in college. Even now I sometimes get guys that I've met once or twice calling me asking what they did because you don't answer your phone or e-mail them back. You know Cody called me just a week ago asking if you had told me what went wrong because you never actually broke up with him. You just disappeared."

"I did not break up with Cody because I thought he was going to leave me."

"Technically you didn't break up with him at all!"

"What I mean to say is that he wanted more than I was ready to give."

"Fine, whatever, the point is you just disappeared, never to be heard from again."

I scowled at her. "What's your point?"

"The point is that you do not get to treat me like that!" she shrieked.

I stepped up to her, and she grabbed me, clutching tight, the sobbing instantaneous. "Oh, for crissakes, Charlotte," I grumbled, lifting her up, her legs wrapping instantly around my hips as I walked us down the hall.

"You don't have to be my knight in shining armor for me to love you dearly, desperately, and totally. I love you, Stef," she cried into my shoulder, dampening my already disgusting and crusty T-shirt. "And not just because you saved me, not because we shared this secret, but because of all the rest… all our history."

I was smart enough to know I left people before they could leave me. It was bad, but I did it anyway. My mother was the first and last person that ever left me; I was the one who had all the power after that.

"We know so much about each other, we've shared so much… all of that makes us more than just friends, Stef. I know how you need quiet in the morning, and you know how I like my coffee and that I like pickles but not cucumbers. I know how you held me the night I was attacked… after you brought me home to your apartment and made me tea… how you wrapped me in your arms under the covers, and I was so safe…. Oh Stef, do you really think I could ever not need you or not want you or not love you? Is that even fucking possible?"

No. The answer was no. It was not possible. I was permanent. I squeezed her so tight she farted. "Charlotte!"

The crying turned to laughter instantly, and when I put her down, she couldn't even breathe.

"God, you're disgusting."

Her head was back, tears rolling down her cheeks as she laughed and laughed. When I looked over my shoulder, the entire bridal party was there.

"You two are so weird," Ben grumbled.

"Not me." I scowled at him. "Just your girlfriend."

But his look, the softness in his eyes, let me know that when he was looking at us, it was the pair of us together that he just didn't get.

"You two better hurry the hell up," he barked at us. "The party can't start without either one of you."

Since it was true, I grabbed Charlotte's hand and tugged her after me down the hall. The heavy sigh was not to be missed followed a second later by a quick cough.

"What?" I asked her.

"I don't know." She scrunched up her nose at me. "What the hell is all over you?"

"Why?"

"You reek."

"Oh, this morning I helped deliver a calf."

"And you let me touch you? Oh my God, I've gotta shower all over again."

"Sorry. Birth is both a beautiful and horrifying experience all at the same time."

"Yeah, I can see that," she said, picking at something on my T-shirt as we hurried down the hall. "Gross."

As I helped Charlotte into the back of the limousine, a sharp intake of breath made my head snap up. The look on the face of Tina Jacobs gave me pause.

"What?"

"You look… good."

I was confused; Charlotte was the one who would stop traffic. "You mean her."

"What?"

"Char," I reminded her. "She's gorgeous, right?"

"Well, yes, but… Jesus, Stef."

It took me a second, but the way she was looking at me, I understood. I arched one eyebrow for her. "Oh, I'm the pretty one."

Her mouth was open.

"Goddamn, you clean up nice," Kristin assured me. "And that hair of yours is just… something."

"Oh Stef, you're beautiful." Alison breathed out the words.

"And I'm what, chopped liver?"

We all looked at Charlotte.

"Seriously, diva, do you need a minute?" I asked her.

She growled at me, which was funny considering how stunningly elegant she looked.

"Nothing and no one is as beautiful as you are right now. You're glowing."

"Apparently it's reflected glow," she said, gesturing at her bridesmaids, who were all staring wide-eyed at me. "Why couldn't you have just kept the hideous white tux that all the rest of the guys were wearing?"

"You know the answer to that." I waggled my eyebrows for her. "When have I ever been like the rest of the guys?"

She rolled her eyes as her bridesmaids all giggled. Pretty soon after, as I was ready to walk down the aisle before her, she grabbed the back of my tuxedo jacket so I couldn't.

"This is *so* not the time to get cold feet," I warned her as I turned around to face her.

"No, I know it's not—I just wanted to say that you look really nice. I'm sorry I didn't tell you earlier."

I was wearing a tan polished cotton tuxedo with peak lapels, and I knew I looked good in it. I had had my assistant, Christina Wu, go to my apartment and ship it overnight. The fact that Charlotte was taking the moment when I was supposed to be walking down the aisle to give me a compliment was somewhat odd.

"Char, you need to let him go now," Uncle Tyler told her. "We'll meet him down there in front in just a few minutes."

Charlotte had asked her uncle to give her away in her father's stead, and I was sure he had been seeing it as an honor right up until the moment when she lost her mind. The look he was giving me was one of concern.

"Do you feel weird?" she asked me suddenly. "I mean, I never once even considered that this all might make you feel weird."

There is no planning a revelation; they come when they want. I understood at that moment that I could never lose my place in Charlotte's life. She needed me for her sanity. I was her touchstone. Of course there would be pieces I would never know that only husbands and wives shared, but I would still be on board for breakdowns like the one she was currently having.

"Char," I said gently, cupping her face in my hands as I stepped in close to her and looked down into her eyes. "I'm fine. You know me, crowds, whatever—none of this scares me. You're the one who's having a meltdown."

"Maybe"—she started panting—"a little."

"What is it, the walking?" I asked, because I was pretty sure that was it.

"Yeah… I think so… yeah."

I understood. Walking slowly down a long aisle, there was lots of time to screw up, roll your ankle, stumble, and fall. She was not all that coordinated to begin with; she tripped over her own feet all the time. I was forever catching her when we were in college. Standing there with her, staring into her big blue eyes, I thought of a solution.

We ran down the aisle. There was less room for error if you were moving fast. Charlotte wanted either perfection or a total wipeout. She was an all or nothing girl.

No one even had time to stand for the bride before we were there in front of Reverend Ellis. Ben's smile was huge, Nick was shaking his head, and after a moment, when the reverend was still just staring at the bride and groom, speechless and flustered, I got things going by taking a quick step up and giving the man a smack on the shoulder and telling him to go for it. We were all driving the poor man crazy.

"Uh… okay… who gives this woman to be wed?"

"Me and her brother." Charlotte's mother chuckled as she stood up in the front row, "and her uncle, who's still comin' down the aisle."

The reverend looked over at Tyler, who waved from where he was, almost to us.

"Nobody counted one-two-three go," he grumbled. "They just ran."

The hall resounded with laughter, and when I turned to look at Charlotte, I saw her sigh before breaking into the huge smile I knew. She was happy, and that was all that mattered. It was how it was supposed to be.

After the ceremony, pictures had to be taken. Charlotte had not wanted any taken of her and Ben together before the wedding. She was certain it was bad luck. So while the rest of us stood around waiting, they posed for shot after shot.

"Stef."

I was so busy watching the interaction of Ben's family with Charlotte that I hadn't even noticed that Rand was behind me. "Hey." I smiled at him, my eyes flicking to his mother and Uncle Tyler, who had appeared with him. "You guys ready for your turn next?"

Rand reached out to touch the lapel of my jacket. "We were thinkin' you should be in the photos with us."

"Oh no." I shook my head. "I'll be in the pictures with the bridal party. That's enough."

"I was thinking it wasn't," May Holloway told me. "I'd like you with us, Stef."

I looked up at Rand as he stepped in close to me, his hand wrapping loosely around my throat. Where the emotion came from, I wasn't sure, but suddenly I could barely breathe.

"Me too," he said, his voice low and husky. "Come take the picture."

When the photographer called for the bride's family, before a word could be spoken, Charlotte yelled my name.

"You, too, Stef!"

Which basically shut the door on any protest I might have made.

"You look great," I told Rand as I took my place beside him, turning and smiling.

"Do I?"

"Yessir," I assured him, taking the moment when no one was looking to let my fingers touch the end of the bolo tie he was wearing. "And this is a nice touch. Only you could get away with an Armani tuxedo and this instead of a bow tie. It's very you."

He turned to me.

"What?" I chuckled, my voice dropping low. "You know you're the most beautiful thing I've ever seen in my life."

His stunned expression, which I knew I caused, sent fluttering heat all through me.

"Guys," the photographer called out.

I moved fast, closer to the others, leaning in, letting out a breath. "You."

I looked back over at him.

"It's hard to keep my hands… off." The muscles in his jaw clenched. "Can't leave you alone… won't."

My head turned back to the photographer quickly as I heard Rand take a sharp breath. It was satisfying to know that I was the cause of the man's inability to make his lungs work.

"Stefan Joss, you better be smiling," Charlotte warned me from where she was standing in front and to the side of me, unable to see what I was doing, as we were separated by many aunts, uncles, and cousins. "I don't want any of that arty-angsty bullshit."

"I'm smiling," I said as a warm hand slid over my ass. "I swear I am."

Her grunt made everyone laugh.

IT WASN'T a wedding, it was a triathlon. There was bride and groom dancing, and speeches, bride and uncle dancing, groom and mother dancing, and every other special spotlight dance you could think of, then dinner, and then more dancing, cake cutting, cake eating, garter catching, bouquet tossing, and even more dancing. Christ. It was meant to be endured, not enjoyed, as far as I could tell. The slideshow was cute, and all the speeches were good, even mine, but really, after the fifth hour of celebration, I was done. The ceremony had been at six, and it was eleven, and everyone was still partying.

"You havin' a good time, Stef?" Nick asked me as he walked up beside me.

I made a conscious decision to lie. "Yep."

"Goddamn," he breathed out, draining the last drops out of his Heineken bottle. "This has gotta be the best wedding I've ever been to, including my own."

It probably had a lot to do with the open bar, the horde of people still there, and the packed dance floor. I had done hardly any dancing myself, as Charlotte had put me in charge of the photographer, the videographer, and coordinating with the catering staff. As a result, I was busy while everyone else was playing. I consoled myself with the fact that as her faith in me was absolute, she was free to enjoy her special night. Since there was no special dance for best friends, I really wasn't missing anything except for Rand.

I needed to put some mark on the man so that every woman in attendance would know that they had no chance with him. The problem was that after our earlier flirting, the man had not looked for me once. Every time I breezed into the room, he had a different woman hanging all over him. He did a lot of slow dancing, flirting, and even had each and every one of Charlotte's bridesmaids in his lap at one point in the evening. While logically I knew that being jealous was a ridiculous waste of time, I found that the murderous rage that rose up in me didn't respond to reason at all. I was so flustered that I didn't hear Charlotte's mom call my name, making her have to grab hold of me as I tried to streak by her.

"Oh—sorry." I forced a smile, taking a quick breath.

"Honey, since Rand's leaving shortly, do you think that you can give Tyler and me a ride back to the house in Charlotte's car?"

"Rand's leaving?" I was surprised, since I was supposed to be going with him when he left. "When did he—is he gone?"

"No," she said gently, pointing over my shoulder. "Not yet, but he's leaving with Jenny, and I think they're about ready to go."

I turned around, and there was Rand holding hands with a woman I had never met.

"Isn't that his ex-wife?" Ben asked as he walked up beside me, one arm thrown across my shoulders to steady himself.

"Yes, Benjamin, it is." May Holloway chuckled, patting her new son-in-law on the back.

"She wasn't on my half of the guest list," he informed her.

"I asked Charlotte to include her," she explained. "She and Rand parted on good terms, and she was a part of our family, even if it was for a very short time."

"Is she visiting or what?" Ben asked as he turned to her.

"I have no idea." She sighed. "But from the looks of things, I'd say maybe she's going to stay a spell."

"Hey, lady." Ben's smile was out of control as he looked at his wife's mother. "You wanna cut a rug with me?"

She laughed at him. "Absolutely."

I watched Ben crook his arm for his new mother-in-law, and after she took it and he led her away, I was free to look at Rand and his ex-wife.

Jenny Holloway was beautiful, and no one had ever mentioned that fact before. She could have been a model with her height, her long, thick brown hair, and her cornflower blue eyes. Her dimples were deep, her skin creamy and flawless, and her curves were accentuated by the fitted dress she wore. If I had been asked to conjure up the perfect woman for Rand Holloway, she would have been it. When she laughed and wiped some frosting off his upper lip with her fingers, I understood that she would be the one in the man's bed later. It was almost a relief when my phone rang. I answered as I turned away from the dance floor.

"Stefan Joss?"

"Yes?"

"This is Gracie Freeman."

I sighed as I ducked under the tent and started across the grounds. It was cooler away from the crowd of people. "Hey there, Mrs. Freeman." I smiled into my phone. It was nice of her to call and remind me that I had a life beyond ranches and cowboys, a life that I would be returning to in the next forty-eight hours. "How are you, ma'am?"

"I'm sorry to call so late, Stefan, but I had to speak to you."

"No, it's fine," I assured her. "What's on your mind, ma'am?"

She took a breath. "Could you come by and see me first thing tomorrow morning instead of waiting until Monday?"

"Is everything all right?"

"Yes and no... would you come?"

"'Course." I yawned. "Whatever you need."

"Really?"

"Yes, ma'am," I assured her. "What time would you like me?"

"Nine?"

"Absolutely, I'll see you at nine."

"Oh, that's wonderful," she breathed out. "Thank you, Stefan."

"May I ask what you've decided to do?"

"Yes… I'm going to sell you the ranch. I spoke to my neighbors today, and they were all very persuasive."

"Oh, why do I not like the sound of that?"

"No, no." She chuckled. "No one is threatening me—no one would do that."

"Okay."

"You don't sound pleased."

"I'm pleased." I sighed. "I'm just surprised."

"So was I, really."

"Well, I'll see you in the morning, ma'am."

"I'll see you then, Stefan."

After I hung up the phone, I took a deep breath before calling my boss. He didn't pick up, so I left a message and gave him the good news. I called him out on his lie about other people going to see Mrs. Freeman as well.

"You didn't have to make up shit to make me go see the nice lady," I scolded him, laughing at the same time. "You could've just told me the truth—you know I would have done it anyway. I've known you over four years, Knox; I would hope you'd know me better by now."

When I finished, I turned around to look back at the party tent. I was surprised to find Rand standing there, staring at me. He looked good, all rumpled from his evening. His shirtsleeves were unbuttoned, his collar undone, giving a glimpse of the white T-shirt underneath, and the thick, glossy black hair had fallen into his eyes. He looked like he'd been ravished, and that thought made my mouth go dry.

"Was it your idea to drive my mom and uncle home?"

The question, so casually spoken, was illuminating for me because in that moment I understood with absolute clarity what I meant to Rand Holloway.

Instead of just simply going with what he had been told, instead of accepting things at face value, Rand was checking. We had a plan, and as far as he knew, I was changing it because of what his mother had said. I thought he wanted to change it because he had been holding his ex-wife's hand earlier. Both of us were making assumptions. But just before everything blew up, just before we fell back into old habits of thinking that we knew what was going on in the other guy's head, right before everything ended… he was checking.

"No," I called over to him. "It wasn't my idea."

"Okay."

"And Jenny?" I asked.

He cleared his throat. "Jenny came to make sure I was okay... she's gettin' remarried."

Oh. "Your mother thought you guys wanted to be alone... she thought you were leaving early. She asked me to drive her and Tyler back to the house."

He nodded, hands shoved down into the pockets of his tuxedo pants.

"So I guess I'll give your mom Charlotte's keys and you can run me back over there tonight so I can grab my stuff and pick up the rental car."

His gaze on me was unwavering.

"Would that be all right?"

"Yep," he agreed, digging the toe of his boot into the dirt. I had to love a man in a tuxedo and polished cowboy boots. Not many could pull it off. "That sounds about right."

"I'll look for you after Charlotte and Ben leave."

"Good," he said, turning to go.

And just like that, everything was back on course. "Rand."

He looked over his shoulder at me.

"Thanks for making sure what was going on. I wouldn't have."

"I know," he said solemnly, changing his mind about leaving, instead crossing the twenty feet or so of yard separating us.

I waited as he closed in on me, wondering about the scowl on his face. "Why're you mad? I'm not mad, and I'm the one that should be."

He stopped inches from me, so close that I had to take a step back, or would have, if he hadn't grabbed hold of my arm to keep me there.

"Rand?"

"Why should you be mad, and why would you just go ahead and assume the worst of me? I'm the one who should be mad at you for thinking whatcha did."

"Oh?" I snapped back at him, irritated now, rolling my shoulder so he had to let go or hold tighter. "And what exactly did I do?"

His hand tightened as he took another step closer, and I had no recourse but to tip my head back to meet his gaze. The man was big, and it was not the time that I wanted to be reminded.

"You don't just go round thinkin' the worst of people, Stef. That dog don't hunt."

It took me a minute. "What?"

"You know what I mean!" he growled at me, his other hand moving to the back of my head, fisting in my hair. "Don't just think bad shit about me. I ain't a bad man."

Somewhere in the evening between me thinking he wanted out of our previously agreed-on plans and his ex-wife telling him she was getting remarried, Rand had been reminded that he could be an asshole.

"No, you're not a bad man," I said, putting my hands on his hips, sliding them up under his rumpled, untucked tuxedo shirt to the hot skin and rippling muscles underneath. "And I am sorry I didn't come ask you what was going on. I do assume the worst, always have. It's a terrible habit. I'll work on it… forgive me."

I felt the muscles clenching under my wandering hands, heard his breath falter, saw the way he was looking at me, like I was food.

"I thought maybe you wanted Jenny's legs wrapped around you in bed," I murmured, taking a breath before I leaned forward and kissed the pulsing vein on the side of his neck. "But I'm thinkin' now it's me you want under you… am I right? I'm just checking."

He didn't answer. He grabbed me instead, crushing me against him, his face buried in my shoulder, arms like steel wrapping me up. I had my answer.

Long minutes later, he let me go and followed me back into the tent. I didn't worry that anyone would have thought the embrace odd. It was a wedding, after all, which all manner of weirdness could be attributed to. Being overly emotional or drunk covered a multitude of hallucinations. No one would have thought twice about Rand Holloway hugging me in the dark.

Inside, I took Charlotte's keys to Rand's mother and told her that Rand was driving me back to the house to collect my stuff because he was going with me to see a client in the morning. I was surprised when her face lit up and she took hold of my arm.

"Oh thank God," her breath rushed out. "You keep that girl away from him, Stef. I can't stand the doubt and self-loathing she plants in him."

"I thought she was a nice girl," I reminded her of her words earlier in the day. "You said that she was sweet and a homemaker and—"

"I know what I said." She slapped my arm. "But it's crap. She broke the man's spirit with whatever she did or said, and I don't want her back, you hear?"

"Yes, ma'am." I grinned at her. "I'll protect him."

"See that you do."

I hugged her tight, and she gasped at the sudden movement. "She told Rand she's getting remarried. She just wanted to tell him."

"She's full of crap—she came to tell him she's gettin' hitched to see what his reaction would be, and that's all."

I eased her out to arm's length. "You're so distrusting."

Her head snapped up so she could look up into my eyes. "Stef, I know my children well, and if you think I don't know what's good for them and bad for them… you're a fool."

I nodded, my hands dropping away from her.

"When I first met you, I didn't understand about being gay. I was certain that given enough time, Charlotte would wear you down and you two would be married."

I was going to say something, but she lifted her hand to stop me.

"I understand more now. I've gone to meetings and such."

Why? What would prompt her to attend meetings about being gay?

"Don't look at me like that," she warned me. "I need to be… I know what's fixin' to happen, so just don't you be so sassy."

Me? "What'd I—"

"I love you," she said suddenly, hand on my cheek as she stared up at me, daring me to say even a word. "You are a good boy, Stefan, contrary as all get out, but still… very good. Whatever happens, I approve."

Air. I needed air. "You—"

Her hand fell off me, and she turned and walked away without another word. I really was in *The Twilight Zone*, I just knew it. Before I had a chance to recover, Rand walked by, grabbed my bicep, dragged me over to a table, and shoved me down into a chair before taking a seat beside me. Looking around at the group, there was no one I knew except Jenny, and we had never been properly introduced.

"This here is Stefan Joss, Char's best friend," Rand grunted, his thigh plastered against mine under the table. "Stef, this is my ex, Jenny Stover, and her cousin Kim, and my cousin Travis, and his wife Donna."

"Nice to meet you all," I greeted them.

"Your speech was the best one," Kim assured me.

"Thank you." I accepted the compliment because I was hoping it was true.

"And you look amazing," Jenny said, her voice smooth and lovely. "I don't think I've ever seen a tan tuxedo before."

I arched an eyebrow for her. "Gotta be different."

Her smile was warmer than I expected, genuine. "Absolutely." She sighed before turning to Rand, her hands closing on his bicep. "Come dance with me."

He had no choice: she was tugging on his arm, and everyone else at the table was urging them on. As he started standing up, though, the music died, and the DJ apologized before he said that the bride needed her best friend out on the dance floor.

"That would be you," Rand said to me, tipping his head toward the floor.

Standing up, I made my way through the crowd of people to find Charlotte on the dance floor with her hand out to me. I heard the first chords of "Cruisin'" as she grabbed me.

"You're insane," I assured her.

Her arms lifted, locking behind my neck as she stared up into my eyes. "And you will always be my first love."

I took her into my arms as the song began, my eyes locked on hers. It had to be confusing for some people, the way she looked at me, the way I held her, since the love was there, a tangible thing that anyone could plainly see.

When the song ended, I bent and kissed her forehead, and there was cheering.

"One of these days," she said wickedly, "before I die, I will get a real kiss from you, Stefan Joss, and I will know what the big deal is all about."

I smirked, and she giggled before the DJ announced that the car had arrived to take the bride and groom away to their honeymoon. Being ready to call it a night myself, the novelty of her wedding having worn off hours ago, I gave her a tight squeeze before turning her toward Ben as he jogged across the dance floor to us. I was surprised that he had to hug me before he left, and I watched them as the crowd surged around them to see them off.

Outside on the gravel driveway, everyone clustered around as they climbed into the limousine, and Charlotte blew kisses before the door was finally closed and the car rolled away. When I turned to go back inside, I was suddenly face to face with Ben's father.

"She's Charlotte Cantwell now, sir… she's a member of your family."

"Yes, she is, and I'm very proud."

I smiled and went to move by him, but he stopped me with a hand on my arm.

"You let me know if you ever think about leaving that big fancy firm you're with now, Stef. I could use a man who knows people and the value of things."

It was really a very generous offer, as Ben's father owned a very large, very financially sound real estate development company. "Thank you, sir," I said, taking his offered hand.

He tightened his grip when I tried to let go. "What you think you know about me is not the case, Stef. I realize what I said the other day left you thinking a certain way about me, and I am sorry about that. I was upset and spoke out of turn; those were not my true feelings on the Holloways. Furthermore, you being gay does not concern me in the least, and for the record, the insurance at my company covers domestic partners as well as spouses."

I was stunned. I had thought poorly of him after his comment about Charlotte's family, but he loved Charlotte. Clearly he liked her immediate family, as evidenced by his interaction with May and Rand, and apparently he really liked me and didn't care who slept in my bed.

"So you call me if things change with you, Stefan. I would love to talk to you about what you want your future to be."

"Thank you, sir."

"Don't confuse this conversation with me being nice. I am very serious about making money and truly believe you would be an asset."

"Thank you again, sir."

"No, thank you, Stef," he said, patting my arm. "You've been a good friend to Ben, and I value that more than you know."

I was watching him walk away when Rand stepped up beside me.

"What was that about?"

"He just offered me a job." I turned my head to look at him. "Weird, huh?"

The bemused expression on his face made me smile.

"That Mr. Cantwell is a smart man. He sees Char, he sees you.... Very smart man." He exhaled, reaching out to fiddle with my collar.

"So," I teased him, "you ready to go, cowboy?"

"Yessir," he said, nodding, tucking a long piece of hair behind my ear, his fingers sliding down the side of my neck.

We went to say good night to his mother and Uncle Tyler, and they said they would see us for breakfast in the morning. May was going to spend the night at the house where the wedding party had been staying and then drive over to the ranch in the morning. I told her that she should just follow us back and we could get our things and drive over to the ranch together. Tyler thought that sounded logical. The look Rand shot me would have killed me, but I waggled my eyebrows at him, and he couldn't hold the scowl.

On the way out, Jenny and her cousin asked Rand for a ride, but May said that neither of us, neither car, was going back toward Lubbock. We were all headed back out to the ranch.

"And we all know how much you hate the ranch, dear," May said, patting her arm as she walked by.

I looked at Rand as he succumbed to a coughing fit.

"God, your mother just hates me now," Jenny said sadly, looking at both of us.

"Can't rightly blame her," Tyler said as he walked by.

She gasped, and Rand grabbed my arm to yank me after him.

I heard her gasp for the second time and snorted out a laugh. "You're making her think bad things when you manhandle me."

"So what?" He sighed. "She didn't want me. She don't get no say."

As I walked out with him, I wondered about the story of Rand and Jenny and whether I even had the right to ask.

CHAPTER 8

IT WAS late, or early, depending on how you looked at it, but at one in the morning, Rand, his mother, Tyler, and I were all in the kitchen having sandwiches. All of us had showered and changed, and we were all in sweats and T-shirts, even May. I had made her sit while I prepared snacks and served everyone. As I was moving around the table, I told her that she should think about dating, since she was still hot. Tyler choked, and Rand nearly spit out his milk.

"Stefan Joss!" She laughed at me. "My goodness, but you do just speak your mind!"

"What?" I asked as I took a seat beside Rand.

"Are you insane?" Rand was incredulous. "My mother does not date!"

"Why not?"

"Because she's my mother!"

I looked at Tyler, who had made a noise like he was dying.

"What he said."

"That makes no sense," I assured him, my eyes flicking back to May. "You should date."

She took a deep breath. "Actually, I am."

"What?" Rand gasped before he started coughing.

"That's great." I beamed at her. "Tell us all about him."

"You're what?" Rand barely got out, coughing harder.

"I think something went down the wrong hole." May giggled.

Tyler thumped Rand on the back as I laughed at him.

"You're such a prude, man. Your mother's still young, and sex is a very natural part of any relationship that she would be in."

He had to put his head between his knees.

May slapped my leg, trying for all the world to look serious. "You're going to kill him."

I shrugged. "You need to date and have sex and live your life. You just aren't allowed to dress like Ben's mother." I shot her a look.

"Oh heavens, did you see that too?" Her eyes widened as she looked at me. "My goodness sakes, it was horrible! Do you think maybe

Ben's father is tomcattin' around, so she's trying to get his roving eye back on her?"

"Maybe," I agreed. "That would make sense, wouldn't it?"

"Can you two—Christ!" Rand yelled. "What the Cantwells do with—Mother, who the hell are you dating?"

She smiled at him. "Would you like to meet my beau?"

"Well, yeah." He cleared his throat, scowling at me. "If you have a—well, yeah, I need to give my approval."

I scoffed.

"You think I don't?" He glared at me.

"No, I don't." I chuckled.

May pointed at me. "What he said."

"You—"

"But I would love for you to meet him." She grinned. "How about Monday night?" She looked back at me. "Why don't you come too?"

"Oh." I exhaled. "My meeting got moved from Monday to tomorrow, or today, since it's already Sunday, so I'll probably be on a plane home later today instead of Tuesday morning like I originally planned."

"But you could stay until Tuesday," Rand said, bumping my knee under the table. "You could if you wanted."

My gaze hit his.

"Stef... you could."

"I could." I smiled at him.

"Then it's settled." He took a breath. "Stef and me'll meet the beau."

Her smile was luminous as she looked at me. "Thank you, darling."

But I hadn't done anything.

A half hour later, I was doing the dishes, still not tired, just content.

"This is so domestic of you," Rand said as he walked up behind me, his lips finding a sensitive spot behind my ear that seemed to be suddenly and without warning connected to my cock.

"Oh God, what're you doing?"

He moved his mouth to the back of my neck, one arm sliding across my abdomen, his other hand sliding down over my ass.

"Watch yourself," I cautioned him. "They're might see."

His hand slid over my hip on a path toward my groin as he licked a line up the side of my neck.

"Stop." I tried to bump him off me, but he tightened his grip as I felt his teeth on my shoulder.

His deep sigh made me smile. The man liked having me wriggling around in his arms. "You're gonna get us in trouble," I teased him.

"God, you smell good," he said, his face in my hair, inhaling deeply.

"Stop," I said, trying to see from where I was if Rand's mom and uncle could see him groping me. From how the room was laid out and where I was standing next to the sink, I wasn't sure.

"Your skin is so hot," he said absently, cupping me through my jeans.

"Christ." I jerked forward into the cabinet, banging the door.

"Ticklish?"

"Stop."

"Rand," May called over to him.

I felt his warm breath on the back of my neck, knew he had turned to look at his mother.

"Who's Jenny marrying?"

"Some lawyer," he responded, his hands moving on me, sliding up under my T-shirt, over my skin. "Can you hurry up with this?"

I nodded and took a breath, letting my head fall back on his shoulder, closing my eyes to keep my body in check. "Maybe if you left me alone, it would go faster."

He chuckled before burying his face in my shoulder. "I don't think I can... you feel too good," he mumbled, gently biting his way down my shoulder.

My body went up in flames.

"What time we gotta be at your meetin' in the morning?"

"Are you gonna go with me?"

"I plan to spend every second with you from now 'til you gotta go... or don't gotta go."

"What does that mean?"

His arms wrapped me up tightly, crushing me. "You want me to say—I'll say... I want you to stay here with me, Stef. I want you to go home and pack up all your shit and move into my house and live with me. That's what I want."

I couldn't breathe. He stepped back so I could turn around and look at him.

"That's what I want, since you're askin'," he said, his hands on my face, lifting it so that as he stepped back into me, he tilted my chin up. "Stefan Joss, I want you."

Staring up into his gorgeous eyes, I was glad that he had said my name and reminded me what it was. My mind had gone completely blank.

"Speak."

"Rand, honey, I'm goin' on to bed, and Tyler's walkin' back to his place! Night, Stef!"

They were both in the living room, and I hadn't even realized they had left.

"Hey."

The brilliant turquoise of his eyes, the laugh lines at the corners—just looking at the man made me happy, and apparently looking at me did the same for him.

"I will settle, if I have to, for you sayin' that you'll be back in a week after you fly away. I have a ranch to run, or I'd get on a plane and go to you, but I got things I can only do in one place. But it seems to me that you got yourself more options than you figured."

He meant Mr. Cantwell.

"But you think on it," he said, smiling at me. "Right now I need you to wash off your hands, leave them dishes, and go on upstairs and get in my bed."

"But Rand, your mom—"

"Go on."

I studied him.

"What are you tryin' to see?"

"How can you just change your whole life in a couple of days?"

"'Cause I've had a whole lot of time to think on it."

I nodded before turning back to the sink. "I gotta finish cleaning up, and you've got stuff to check on before bed, so I'll meet you upstairs."

After several minutes, I realized he was still standing there.

"What?"

He just shook his head and went out the back door.

It was peaceful being alone in the huge kitchen, wiping down the counters, putting pots and pans from earlier in the day away, and watering the herb garden growing in the windowsill. Everything was in its place, and all the lights except the one over the stove were off when I was finally pleased with how it looked.

Walking out of the kitchen and through the living room to the screen door, I stood silently looking out at the darkness, realizing that the sky was a deep cobalt blue, but with the full moon, I could still see everything, hear the sounds of the cattle, see the lights of the stockyards in the distance, and smell wet earth and wildflowers. It was peaceful, relaxing. There really was something to be said for life on a ranch.

When I heard Rand whistling, I knew he had the dogs with him. Since I'd seen Charlotte do it many times, I went to the chest that doubled as a coffee table in the living room and got out the blankets. In the winter, the dogs slept in front of the fireplace. In the summer, they slept in the same spot, just without the benefit of flickering flames. I heard them whimpering at the screen door, heard Rand telling them to hold on, and walked over and let them in. I was of great interest, and once I had greeted all four of them, patted them, and given them all love, I led them to the blankets. Trained well, they were all down, tails thumping, as Rand came in the house.

"Oh." He was surprised, smiling at me. "You got 'em settled."

"I filled up their water bowls in the kitchen," I told him before heading for the stairs. "I know you still gotta lock the house up, so I'll see you upstairs."

"I'll be right there," he called after me.

"Yes, dear."

"Hey."

I looked over at him before I started up. The smile on his face was surprising. "What?"

"That just sounded real nice, is all. I think a man could get used to having you around to take care of him and his home."

"Me?"

His smile made his eyes sparkle in the low light. "Yes, you."

But I never wanted to take care of anyone. Simple things, small things that other people did, took for granted, I never even thought of. Men I had dated complained because I would make myself something to eat and not even offer. I was cold and uncaring because I didn't run errands or cook or clean. I was the opposite of domestic; I normally ate standing up unless I was out to dinner, and I never lifted a finger in the home of anyone that I dated. Not ever, for any man, but three days of Rand Holloway's attention and I was going soft. Shit.

"Stef."

I looked back over at him.

"Go on up."

In the upstairs bathroom, I washed my face, needing to clear my head, and heard Rand in his bedroom. Moving to the doorway, I looked for him in the darkness. The moonlight streaming in the window made him easy to see. Turned away from me, he was holding his left wrist in his right hand over his head, and without realizing it, he made me catch my breath. The man was a work of art, a study in power and strength. The rippling muscles in his shoulders and back, the smooth skin, the jeans riding low on his narrow hips… I was ready to fall down and worship him if he asked it of me.

"Rand."

He dropped his arms, turning to look at me.

"You're really beautiful, you know."

The deep grunt made me smile. "Ain't but one of us beautiful." He gestured me close. "Now c'mere and lock the door behind you."

When I was almost to the huge king-sized bed, he dived onto it.

"Rand, what're—"

But my voice was cut off as he grabbed my wrist and yanked me down on top of him. I scrambled out of his grip and had him flat on his back a second later. The way he looked up at me, his eyes heavy-lidded, full of need, was very arousing. I leaned over and nibbled up the side of his neck, and the answering groan made it sound like he was going to die. When I moved to his mouth, he let out a deep sigh and wrapped his arms around my neck, holding me close. I kissed him long and languidly, taking my time because he seemed to need the closeness just as much as I did. When I felt his hands finally start to stray, clutching at my back, my ass, urging me to move, I did. I rose up off of him, and he was up instantly, yanking at his jeans, frantic to get everything off as quickly as possible. I had to smile because it was pretty heady stuff to know that I was the reason for his speed. He wanted me that badly. I laughed when he pounced on me, dumping me over onto my back before he stretched for something in the drawer in the nightstand.

"What're you—"

I got a piece of paper from a clinic in Lubbock that said he was free and clear of any sexually transmitted diseases and a brand new bottle of lube.

"Aww." I smiled up at the man who was grinning like an idiot, hovering over me. "Is this for me?"

The answer was a deep animal growl before he dropped down over me, pressing his body all along the length of mine.

"Rand," I breathed into the side of his neck, my arms falling open on the bed.

"Say what you want," he demanded.

"Oh God, Rand, please."

His hands moved quickly over me. The lube was snatched away, and I heard the crinkling of cellophane as the bottle was opened. He lifted my legs roughly over his shoulders and bent me in half.

His breath caught. "Please, what?"

"Please, baby," I almost whined, but I didn't care how I sounded.

"Beg me," he said slowly as one slippery finger slid between my cheeks.

"Please, Rand... I'll do anything."

"Anything," he grunted before he leaned forward to kiss me.

I was surprised that he didn't just impale me as he so obviously wanted to but kissed me first, apparently needing the closeness just as much. I opened my mouth for him, and his tongue drove inside so hard that his teeth bumped my lips painfully. The copper taste of blood had no effect on the bruising, grinding, devouring kiss. He didn't stop until I moaned, like he was waiting for the sound. He was rough with me then, his fingers digging into my skin as he yanked me forward, thrusting to the hilt with one hard stroke. It felt so good, and I clutched at him, wanting him deeper, wanting it harder and faster. He complied with my demands even though I couldn't speak more than the litany of his name.

CHAPTER 9

YOU HAVEN'T lived until you've stood clinging to a fence watching as a cowboy, *your* cowboy, rides by you in a blur of speed. Lasso spinning, mount at full gallop beneath him, the man was breathtaking. Seeing the raw power of the horse, the strength of the man, and knowing that if either of them faltered that they were both dead—it was a rush, and I was absolutely riveted. When he came back by me, leading the horse he had ridden down, he touched the hat pulled low over his eyes as he rode by. It was hot, even more so because the man in question had had me plastered to the wall of his shower just an hour before.

Going back inside, giving up on stalking the man I had barely let get out of bed that morning, I helped May with breakfast before I went down to the barn to check on Phil. He was happy to see me. So was his mother, and it was there, in the stall, that Rand found me.

"What're you doing?"

I was confused. "Brushing the cows."

"Stef, you don't brush cows," he told me. "We're fixin' to eat them, don't forget."

My expression tickled him.

"Oh, for crissakes, c'mon an' eat, we gotta go visit your friend."

"You know," I said, as I hung the brush back up and came out of the stall, "if you're too busy you don't have to go with me."

He stopped me so he could pull pieces of straw out of my hair. "How did you get all this in… Jesus, Stef, you're like a little kid."

The look on his face, like I was just endearing and mesmerizing all at once, it was too much for me to resist. I stepped into him, my hand around the back of his neck as I eased in close and lifted up for the kiss. I took my time and made sure that he felt how much I wanted him. When I pulled back, he swayed just a little before his eyes fluttered open. The look I got was hard to read.

"Did I—"

"Jenny said that sometimes, in bed… I'm no better than an animal."

All at once, I understood what Jenny Stover had done to Rand. She had made him feel like his ravenous sex drive was a bad thing. At that moment, I could have killed her. "Oh yeah?"

"Yeah." He swallowed hard. "I mean, she never said I hurt her or nothin', but after a while I was afraid to, ya know? I quit sleepin' with her."

"Huh."

He reached out and curled a piece of hair around my ear, the backs of his fingers trailing down the side of my neck. "I ain't never hurt you, have I, Stef?"

"No," I promised, reaching for him, sliding my arms up under his, hugging him tightly, pressing into him, showing him that I was telling the truth.

"Stef, I—"

"You have never hurt me," I promised him, "and for the record: you can manhandle me whenever you want."

He made a noise back in his throat.

"And I like it rough, Rand... you can fuck me any way you want."

"Jesus." His breath caught, even though the eyes on mine were suddenly wounded. She had certainly done a number on his psyche.

"You wanna do me here? Now?"

He bent and kissed me hard, his hand wrapped around my throat, holding me but not tightly, with just enough pressure so I couldn't move. The mere hint of restraint was very arousing. My guess was that Jenny Stover liked her men gentle, sweet, and romantic. There was nothing wrong with that, but Rand Holloway was, as a rule, stoic, sarcastic, blunt, and unaware of his own strength.

Leaning back, breaking the kiss, I saw that Rand's eyes had changed from pained to heavy-lidded and filled with heat. The words that tumbled out of him, how his ex-wife had said that she didn't like being attacked and mauled, how she wanted him to make love like he had before they were married... restrained, careful, and fast. The foreplay was fine; the act was not something she enjoyed.

No good could come of bashing Jenny. I asked Rand if he had investigated or just given up.

He squinted down at me. "Pardon?"

"Did you ever think maybe that somebody might've done a number on Jenny to make her like the kissing and fondling part of sex but not the act? Did you even bother checking?"

"No, I... I just left her alone."

I shrugged. "If you care about somebody... you check."

His hand went to my cheek. "I know."

The comment told me the most important thing I needed to know about his relationship with his ex-wife. She was over, and I was the one up to bat. I was good with it. When he yanked me out of the stable with him, I realized that I was not getting screwed in the hay. He reminded me, as we walked together back up to his house, that it was not like it was in the movies. Straw was apparently really itchy.

I kept scooting over to his side of the truck as we drove over to see Mrs. Freeman, and I finally got a very frustrated growl of warning.

"You're gonna be sorry," he growled at me. "I am fixin' to put you over the hood of my truck if you don't quit."

Never in my life had I had a lover like Rand Holloway. The men in my bed had been hot, their perfectly chiseled gym bodies toned and cut and hard, but none of them could compete with the pure masculinity of the cowboy who sat beside me.

Rand's thighs were like granite from riding a horse, his hands callused, and the veins in his arms prominent from working all his life. His father had been a big man, so he was too; he didn't lift weights or swim or do anything but make his living as a cowboy, and that had created a body to die for. Now that I had permission, I could barely keep my hands off the rippling muscles, the long legs, and the dimple in his chin. I was acting like I was in heat, but it didn't seem to be bothering Rand. His deep chuckle made me whimper with fresh need.

"What're you gonna do Tuesday when you gotta fly away from me?" he asked, his arm sliding down my shoulder, tucking me up against his side.

I licked behind his ear, breathing out, making him shiver before kissing a wet trail down the side of his neck. The taste of the man's skin was intoxicating.

"Jesus, Stef," he grumbled, and I felt the truck swerve on the highway. "Are you tryin' to get us both killed?"

"No, just never mind me, watch where you're going."

"It won't matter if somebody saw us." He chuckled. "Gettin' in an accident ain't the only thing that'll get us killed out on this road."

He meant it to be funny, but the thought was a sobering one, and I retreated to my side of the cab. Sitting there with the wind on my face, my brain finally kicked in, and I remembered where I was. This was Texas, and I was in cattle country, and I had actually thought, for a half a second, that living with Rand Holloway on his ranch would be fun and without repercussions. I had forgotten that being gay could get him forced off the road and shot.

"I just didn't wanna wreck," he told me, his voice deep and sultry. "I didn't mean you should take your hands off me. C'mon back."

"I'm an idiot," I said without turning to look at him. "What would your neighbors do if they found out about me?"

"I dunno," he grunted. "I expect some would call me a lot of things behind my back as well as to my face. There might even be a few who come after me or my place or my men."

"Jesus."

"I already had some questions 'bout why you was stayin' with me, and Declan Crawford don't wanna sell me no more feed."

"Holy shit," I breathed out, turning to look at him. "Rand, you—"

He put up his hand. "Here's the thing about all that, Stef: my ranch ain't small. A long time ago, I changed things up so that I don't do all my business in one place. I only buy what I have to for emergencies from anybody in town. Most of what I need gets trucked in from Lubbock."

"What—what're you—"

"Listen here, I have a very lucrative hunting business and got me two guides that take people out. That girl I was talkin' to the other night—the one you was jealous over—"

"I was so not—"

"That girl is gonna start bringin' people out from Dallas to do some huntin' on my land. I already got 'em comin' from Lubbock and Amarillo, and now, with her bringin' folks from Dallas… I might need me another guide."

"Rand, you—"

"You should take a look at the website my publicist came up with."

I squinted at him. "You have a publicist?"

His smile was wicked. "Yessir, Endo Masami, helluva nice guy— works out of Amarillo, but he comes up and sees me once a month or so."

"Rand—"

"You can hunt deer or quail or dove—though I don't really get that, but—"

"Rand—"

"And turkey, of course, and geese, and wild boar, and—"

"Rand, what does this have to do with—"

"Some people bring their own dogs, but they can use mine if they like. I don't let people hunt coyote or bobcat on my land 'cause I figure those critters been hunted enough."

"I don't understand what—"

"I told all the fellas that I was fixin' to ask you to come stay with me, and I told them they was all free to do whatever they felt was right. JC McGraw, he spit in my face and cleared out, but all the others don't mind none, and Chris even said that I didn't seem to be my usual asshole self since you been 'round. I take that as a good sign."

Jesus Christ.

"My ranch is different from a lot of others, Stef. We sell cattle on the Internet, I have the huntin' business like I told you, and I supply a lot of restaurants all over Texas with their beef. You know as well as anybody that after my father died that me and the ranch both went through a rough spell. What I come to when I decided that the ranch was mine to save was that I had to sell the ranch as a brand and make it marketable and known for quality. It's only been ten years, but I got that done."

I knew the ranch was profitable; I just had no idea how profitable. "So you're saying that what the people in town think or don't think... you couldn't give a shit."

"Yessir."

"Because what they do or don't doesn't impact you."

"It don't bother my wallet none, but if they go about spittin' on you like they did Tom Hutchins the other day... I might be a bit chafed."

"Shit, is Tom mad at you?"

"Why would Tom be mad at me?"

"Because of me."

"Tom heard that when you went out to see Mrs. Freeman that you didn't push her to sell, instead you told her that she had to decide what to do, since she knew what was best for the community and not you."

I just stared at him.

He arched an eyebrow for me. "That sounds like a man that wants what's best who ain't concerned about his own wallet."

I had no idea what to say.

"You know Tom Hutchins was born on a ranch in Oklahoma that his father threw him off of when he was eighteen."

"Why?"

"Well, when Tom turned eighteen that was when he married the sweetest little Mexican gal you ever met. She and Tom got three kids, and now he has a house on my land where his boys can grow up. I'm missin' two hands with Pete and JC gone, but Tom's got a brother comin' out in another day to fill one of the spots, and you heard Tyler say that Chase has got a cousin to take the other. Both men, Chase an' Tom, are thankful for my ranch and the job and the roof I put over their heads. When all you know about is bein' a cowboy, you need a ranch to work."

"So Tom and Chase and everyone, they're all happy to be here with you."

"I expect so."

"And they don't care that you're sleeping with me?"

"What I do in my bed ain't their concern, just like what they do in theirs ain't none of mine. We all got us an understanding."

"What about your foreman, Mac?"

"Mac's more worried that you'll be bored out here with nothin' and no one to see. He don't like you 'cause you're from the city, he don't give a damn who fucks you."

"That was lovely."

He shrugged. "Had to be said."

"So when were you going to tell me all this?"

"I just did."

"Rand—"

"This is it, ain't it?" he asked, slowing the truck, taking a turn down the long dirt road that led up to the house. He made a noise like a derisive sort of half grunt, half click in the back of his throat.

"What?"

"Her cows look lean. This here's the growing season from April to October, and my cows are twice as big already as hers."

I had no idea; I just climbed down out of the truck and headed toward the house.

"I'll wait here," he called after me. "I don't wanna make her feel bad since you said she's decided to sell."

The screen door was unlocked, so I went inside. It took me several long minutes to realize what I was looking at. Mrs. Grace Freeman was lying faceup in a puddle of blood. Her sightless eyes were trained on the ceiling, her body frail and broken. In death, she looked small, whereas in life, her vitality had filled the air around her. I could barely breathe, and I had no idea what to do. But I knew who would.

"Rand!" I yelled loudly. "Rand!"

"Stef!" he called back at the same time as the sound of the truck door slamming shut.

It was too much. I bolted for the door, and there was a popping sound behind me and shattering glass. There was a yell as I dove for the screen door. It collapsed under my weight, and I scrambled up, feet sliding around for a few seconds before I regained my balance and shot off the porch.

My heartbeat was like a freight train in my ears, a roar of sound as I ran toward the safety of the pickup truck. Rand was almost to me, running to reach me, but I was terrified that whoever had just shot at me would hit him. I didn't want him to get hurt. He could not get hurt.

I was aware of a motor revving behind me. Rand yelled my name, his hands gesturing me out of the way. I leaped sideways as the car flew by me, fishtailing in the dirt before barreling down the road toward the highway. I saw the cloud of dust as I got to my feet. Rand was there seconds later, grabbing me tight, crushing me to him as I trembled in his embrace. Seconds later, I realized that I was not the only one shaking. Rand was too.

"What the fuck was that?" he yelled, shoving me out to arm's length to look me over. "Jesus Christ, Stef!"

"She's dead," I told him, looking up into his eyes. "Mrs. Freeman's dead."

"And from the looks of things, you were gonna be next."

Someone had just tried to kill me.

"What the hell is going on?"

His guess was as good as mine.

IT WAS the way Rand was touching me. If he could have kept from squeezing the back of my neck, brushing the hair out of my face, or sliding his hand over my thigh, the deputies would not have given me a second look. But the second Rand started showing everyone that I belonged to him, their attitudes changed. There were whispers and snickering, smirking glances, and normally I would not have cared at all, but this was where Rand lived. The deputies, the sheriff, they were responsible for his safety, so I didn't simply tell them all to go to hell.

I had been helpful; I had answered every question I was asked for three solid hours. I explained what I was doing there. I told the sheriff about the deal with Armor South, and it came down to basically two choices. Either Grace Freeman was killed because she was going to sell or because she wasn't. I told Sheriff Colter that she told me she was selling.

"Then I'm confused," he told me. "All her neighbors wanted her to sell. They all wanted the payout from the developer."

"Maybe somebody wanted her to keep the land so they didn't have to sell. Maybe someone got cold feet after but didn't want to be the one spoiling the deal for everyone else."

"That's possible." The sheriff looked at me. "I can't think why someone on the developer's side would want her dead, especially if, like you said, Mr. Joss, you had told 'em that she was going to sell."

"Yeah, that doesn't make any sense."

"So it's gotta be someone here," he said to both Rand and me. "Have you had anybody following you around, Mr. Joss, or threatening you?"

"No."

"Yes," Rand chimed in. "The other day while he was running, someone nearly ran him off the road."

"That was you?" Sheriff Colter pointed at me before turning to look at Rand. "I hauled your stupid-ass cousin in here the other night on a DUI—and by the way, Rand, his license is gone, so if I see him behind the wheel, he's goin' to jail."

"Why're you tellin' me?"

"'Cause you're the head of your annoying family, and I told you months ago to put that boy to work on your ranch."

"He's an idiot."

"Don't I know it!" Sheriff Colter raised his voice, looking back at me. "I threw Bran in a cell to let him sleep off his drunk, and he starts runnin' his mouth about savin' some boy from bein' hit by a truck. He says that if he hadn't'a blown his horn that you would be lyin' dead at the bottom of Hatter's Gulch—is that right, Mr. Joss?"

"He was drunk," I told the older man. "I think he nearly hit me."

"No, sir." The sheriff shook his head. "I don't think so. There was another truck, 'cause I been out there and saw the two different sets of tracks myself. I just didn't know who you were, and Bran couldn't rightly remember."

Rand let out of huff of breath.

"He's your cousin—why wasn't he invited to Char's wedding?"

"Because he tried to cripple the groom," Rand told him. "So what the hell are you gonna do, Ed?"

"I don't think I like your tone, Rand. I—"

"I don't give a good goddamn what you like. I wanna know what the fuck you're gonna do about finding the person who's trying to kill Stef."

"Well, for starters, Mr. Joss," he snarled, turning back to me, "until further notice, you best not go back home to Chicago. We have us an open murder investigation that you are smack-dab in the middle of, and I cannot think of a safer place for you than out there on that ranch with Rand Holloway and the criminals he calls ranch hands."

"What the hell are you talkin' about?" Rand yelled at him.

"What the hell am I talkin' about? You got some of the hardest men I have ever met in my life working with you out on that ranch of yours, Rand Holloway. With it still growin', soon it'll be like you got your own army."

"We're a family."

"JC McGraw told it different in town a few days back."

"JC McGraw is a homophobic piece of shit."

"That's what I heard from Kate Tunston, who I guess is your new feed supplier, seein' as Declan Crawford is refusing to do any more business with you."

"What does that have to do with—"

"Nothin', I just wanted you to know that what you do out on your ranch is your own damn business."

"Well, thank you very much."

"And I know that you can protect Mr. Joss better'n I can."

"I have no doubt."

"With all that said: if he sets foot out of the state, I will throw the both of you in jail for obstruction." He turned to look at me. "Am I makin' myself clear, Mr. Joss?"

"Yessir, Sheriff Colter."

He smiled widely, gesturing at me. "He's a helluva lot more respectful than you, Rand Holloway."

"Give it time." Rand smirked at him. "He'll hate you too."

I sighed deeply. "Sheriff, I have a life to go home to."

"This here is your life now, Mr. Joss."

Rand could not have looked more pleased.

I CALLED Knox on my way back to the ranch. When he didn't pick up, I tried to e-mail him from the computer in Rand's den.

"This is so weird," I told the man hovering over me. "I mean, he's never gone, and he always answers my e-mails right away because he's always online. He can answer from his phone if he wants."

"Which, to me, is givin' up way too much of your time," Rand assured me, flopping down into the leather chair in front of his desk, across from me.

"Crap, I have a shitload of things to do at work."

"Well, I suggest you call someone and get to it."

"What're you talking about?"

"You have your laptop, you can use my fax machine and my Internet, and you can even use my phone if you need to. I don't see what you can't do from right here."

"Rand, I don't actually do my work in a vacuum. I go outside and meet people and look at property and—"

"Not this week, you don't," he said. "Besides, it's Sunday, and we both know"—he stopped talking to yawn—"that you don't normally work on Sunday."

"You work on Sunday."

"Not usually. I had to this morning because of all the wedding crap that ate into my time, but Sunday's my normal sittin' around and do nothin' day."

I squinted at him.

"What?"

"There's no way you ever just do nothing."

"Oh no? You don't believe me?"

"No, I don't believe you."

"Well, how 'bout you fix us somethin' to eat, and I'll run on into town and pick us up some movies, and we'll waste the day."

"You're on. I can't wait to see what kinda movies you pick."

"Well, I like action movies," he said, like that was a surprise. "And you like, what… musicals?"

I flipped him off.

"Chick flicks?"

"I will seriously end you," I said, answering the e-mails that were flooding my inbox.

I thought he had left, but he suddenly ran a hand through my hair. Looking up, I received a kiss on my forehead.

"Stay inside the house, you understand?"

"Yessir." I couldn't control my grin. "Nice that you're worried about me."

"I almost lost you today," he said, his hand stroking my hair. "And any second now, this nice frosty composure you got goin' on is gonna crack wide open and you're gonna be a basket case. Just wait until I get back to freak out so I can hold you, all right?"

The image of Mrs. Freeman lying in her own blood came back to me, but I pushed it aside, thinking of work instead. "I never lose it."

"Okay," he agreed, bending closer to me. "Now gimme a kiss."

I turned and kissed him, and he licked his lips as he straightened up.

"Anybody ever tell you that you taste like peaches?"

"I do not," I grumbled, shoving him away from me.

"Yeah, ya do," he said, the deep voice rumbling in his chest as he crossed the room away from me. "And I love peaches—peaches are my favorite."

"I want ice cream too," I called after him.

"I eat a lot of peaches."

"Give it a rest!"

"Yessir," he yelled back from the stairs.

Peaches. What the hell was that about?

I worked for an hour, e-mailing everyone I knew at the company to try to find someone to tell me where Knox was. It was a really bad time for my boss to be MIA.

When I got bored, I strolled downstairs and out the screen door to the porch. I was surprised to find two men there, one with a shotgun across his lap.

"Hi," I greeted them, trying not to sound as nervous as I felt.

The first man touched the brim of his cowboy hat before returning his gaze to the road leading up to the house. The other man smiled wide and walked over to me, his hand out.

"Hey there." His grin was effortless and infectious, and I found myself having to return it. "I'm Dustin, Dusty, and you must be Stefan Joss."

I took the offered hand. "I am. Who's your friend?"

"That there's Everett."

I nodded. "What is it that you guys are doing here, Dustin?"

"We're just watchin' out for you until the boss gets back."

"I see." I smiled at him. "And if someone you guys didn't know came up the drive, then what would you do?"

"We would see who they were and then—"

"Are you sure?" I asked him.

He let out a quick breath. "I know you think you know all about Texas, Mr. Joss, but we don't really shoot first and ask questions later. We're all God-fearin' men, and we don't just kill people with no cause."

"He doesn't," Everett agreed, looking over his shoulder at me. "I'm a shoot first kinda guy, Mr. Joss. Any car I don't know starts up this drive and they're dead. Those were my boss's words to me, and he is the law on this ranch."

"But you would have to answer to the real law, the law of the state of Texas, if you did something illegal to someone even on this ranch."

"Not likely," he said, returning to his vigil. "It's called trespassin', Mr. Joss."

Which basically contradicted everything that Dustin had said only moments before.

"He's not right in the head," Dustin assured me. "We don't let him talk to people much."

They were both there simply to keep me safe. I was very thankful and told them both so.

"I reckon as long as you keep the boss man lookin' how he's been lookin' these past four days that we got us a fair trade, Mr. Joss."

Everett didn't even turn to look at me when he spoke.

I looked over at Dustin.

"Mr. Holloway is a fair man and a good boss. He pays an honest wage for an honest day's work, but 'til this week, I ain't never seen that man smile or even heard him laugh."

"I kinda like it," Everett spoke up before shifting his feet on the porch rail, trading which ankle was on top. "Normally nothin's right, and these past four days… everything was."

"We all had us a good week, Mr. Joss," Dustin told me, smiling wide, hands shoved down into his pockets. "Why don't you go on back inside, unless you're fixin' to go down to the barn and visit your calf?"

"Maybe later," I said. "Thanks again for being out here."

"It's our pleasure," Everett told me.

I stood there a few more minutes, watching as Dustin took his seat back beside Everett, seeing them take sips of slowly melting glasses of iced tea.

Back inside, I wondered about their attitudes. No matter what they thought of me being gay, they accepted me because of Rand. He was important to them, and so because I seemed good for him, they were fine with me being there. It was a lot to take in.

I realized when I was in the kitchen that I was almost asleep on my feet. The adrenaline rush of running for my life, coupled with how late I had been up the night before, had taken a toll on me. Climbing the stairs to the second floor, I walked into my bedroom, but for whatever reason, I couldn't make myself go in and lie down. I staggered to Rand's room instead and collapsed onto his bed. It smelled like him, and that was comforting as I closed my eyes.

Something smelled amazing, and my stomach growling finally woke me up.

"I went ahead and stopped and got some pulled pork sandwiches for lunch." Rand smiled down at me. "I got coleslaw and potato salad and lots of beer."

I sat up, staring at him. "Why did you stop, I was going to cook?"

"Because I figured you were more tired than you let on," he explained, smiling at me. "And I hoped you'd rest which you did."

It was terribly thoughtful and I was so very touched.

"Everett and Dusty freak you out?"

"No," I yawned. "It was sweet of you. Are they still there?"

"Yep."

"Everett's a little spooky."

"Yep," he agreed.

"Is he the scariest guy on the ranch?"

"No sir, I'm the scariest guy on this ranch."

I chuckled. "I'm sure."

"Then Mac, then Everett."

I nodded as he put the plate that he had been holding back on the nightstand.

"You doubt me?"

I shook my head.

"You do, you think I'm fulla shit."

"No," I teased, moving over to him, shifting so I was straddling his thighs.

He moved one hand to my hip as he reached up and brushed my hair out of my eyes with the other. He looked worried.

"What's wrong?" I asked as I leaned down and kissed him slowly, taking my time, the kiss becoming consuming, devouring. I let the need build in him, in me.

"I almost lost you," he breathed out. "I was really scared."

"But I'm fine."

"You were just lucky."

"I've always been lucky."

"Promise me you'll be careful from now on."

"I promise."

He took a shaky breath. "You hate bein' stuck out here."

"No," I said truthfully. "It's actually kinda nice."

"You're lyin'."

"I am not," I growled at him. "If I hated it, you would so know."

"Oh yeah?"

"Yes, Rand, I promise you. I show my feelings to you. I don't hide shit from you."

"Show me," he ordered as he pushed up into me. "Show me you love it here."

I leaned over to the nightstand, and he shivered when he heard me fumbling in the drawer, knowing what I had retrieved.

"What's with you?" I husked, bending over him.

"I want you."

"You got me," I said, my voice husky and deep beside his ear.

His groan was primal and desperate as I kissed down the side of his neck. When he moved under me, lifting up to dump me down onto the bed, I smiled up at him. Looming over me, pushing his groin against my crease, his eyes narrowing in half, the man was the sexiest thing I had ever seen in my life.

"Rand."

"Could we just… can I just be inside you? I really need to be in that tight ass of yours. I need to be in you so I can feel your heart."

I started stripping under him.

"I can't… wait," he growled, yanking my jeans to my knees before flipping me over on my stomach. I came up on my hands and knees in the middle of the bed, and he snatched the lube from where I had dropped it. There was a quick creak of the lid before a finger slid down between my cheeks. "Is it okay?"

I gave him quick permission, begging him to forgo the usual readying, the foreplay unwanted, unneeded, as my only desire was to have him inside me.

"Rand, I need you too," I demanded, letting my head fall down between my arms. "Fuck me, please, I—"

He silenced me by driving inside, pushing into me, a guttural cry torn from his chest. "Christ, Stef, you feel so good," he groaned, stroking out, then in, pounding into my hole, making me yell his name. "You're so tight and hot…. I just wanna be right here like this…. I never wanna be anywhere else."

"Rand," I whimpered, writhing under him, urging him on, faster, deeper, and harder. "Rand… please—please."

But after the initial rush, he slowed, tender with me because even though I thought I wanted it rough and hard and fast, I didn't. I wanted, like he did, to reconnect, and his closeness would reassure me, not being pounded down into the bed. And when I finally broke down, he pulled me into his arms and held me tight. Later, when we were tangled together so tight that it was hard to tell where I began and he ended, I fell asleep in his arms.

THE FOOD was good, the man's skin next to mine even better. I could not for the life of me stay awake after being made love to and eating. Even with the faraway sound of other voices, I still couldn't lift my head off his chest.

I woke up later alone, but I still was not able to open my eyes. When the door opened, I thought it was Rand until I felt the soft hand on my bare back.

"Poor thing," May Holloway said softly.

My eyes drifted open, and I turned my head without lifting it off the pillow. "You're not mad?"

"About what?"

"Me… being here… in your son's bed."

"No, darling, how could I be mad? You make Rand so happy, and I don't have to guess what kind of man you are, because I know already. You've been in my life for over ten years, showing me your heart and how wonderful it is."

"I love you," I said, sitting up fast, turning to grab her, squeeze her tight.

She giggled. "Oh sweetie, me too."

"You're not worried about Rand getting hurt?"

"Hurt by you?"

"No, by homophobic assholes who—"

She snorted out a laugh. "If you get a bazooka, you can hurt Rand. Barring that, I'm not concerned. I'm actually more worried about Tate."

I leaned back. "I'm sorry, who?"

"Tate Langley, my beau… he's downstairs."

"Wait, I thought we were meeting him on Monday night?"

"I know, but he got a wild hair up his butt and decided that today was the day, since it's the six-month anniversary of our first date."

I smiled wide. "Aww."

Her answering noise of disgust made me smile.

"He loves you."

"It would seem so, yes," she said irritably.

"But we're not happy about this why?"

Her hands were suddenly on my face. "I'm so sorry about Grace Freeman, and I'm terrified for you. My God, what would we do without you?"

"No, no, no." I brushed her hands off me. "Why aren't we happy?"

"Well," she cringed, "what if he decides he wants to marry me?"

"That'd be good, wouldn't it?"

"But then I wouldn't be Mrs. James Holloway anymore."

I let out a deep sigh. "It doesn't mean that at all. You'll always be the wife of the father of your children, but he's gone, and do you really think that he would want you to be alone when you have so much more love to give?"

Her bottom lip quivered. "I loved Rand and Charlotte's father with all my heart. I wanted to go into the ground with him when he passed."

"I know you did. I remember."

She put her hand on my cheek. "You see, this is what I mean. We have history already, you and me. You being with Rand—how could you think I would object?"

I sighed. "I wonder what Charlotte will think?"

"I think Charlotte will either be over the moon or devastated."

"What makes you say that?"

"Because her brother will know something about her best friend that she never will," she said. "Charlotte is never going to be in bed with you, Stef, and knowing that Rand is… as ridiculous as it sounds, as unreasonable… she'll be crazy jealous."

"God, she will." I looked at May. "You know your daughter well."

"I should hope so."

I tipped my head toward the door. "So you're comfortable leaving your new man downstairs with your son?"

She jerked like she'd been struck with lightning. "Oh my lord, what was I thinkin'?"

I chuckled, watching her rush from the room.

After a quick shower, I changed into a pair of khakis and a baby blue short-sleeved collared shirt. I wanted to be presentable to meet May's gentleman caller. I didn't mess with my hair as much as normal, figuring that it was more important to hurry up and get downstairs. Since I couldn't find any clean socks, I went barefoot. When I walked into the living room, Rand and Tate were playing with the Wii. They stopped the game immediately.

"Sorry," I said, walking over next to Rand. "I didn't mean to interrupt."

"You're… not," he said quickly, swallowing hard, licking his lips. "You sure you should be up, Stef? You had quite a—"

"I'm fine," I said. "Can I play the winner?"

He nodded, looking me up and down, and I stared at him until he looked away.

"Okay, so lemme introduce you to Tate Langley."

Mr. Langley was fifty-eight to May's sixty and had three daughters and a son of his own. He was just thrilled to meet me, and his warm handshake let me know that the feeling was genuine. He was a handsome man, shorter than both Rand and me, with pale blue eyes and silver hair. He told me that he had an insurance business in Lubbock and a car dealership in Amarillo. I told him that it must be nice to sell the car and then insure it. I liked the wink I got in return.

Dogs barked, and the screen door opened as another cowboy walked into the living room. The man was lean and lanky, handsome in a classic way, with deep-set eyes and chiseled features.

"Chris," Rand said.

"It looks like Mr. Langley's family has arrived."

He nodded quickly. "Show them in."

Chris looked over at me, touched the brim of his hat, and turned back for the door.

"I didn't know he could talk," May said as the screen door banged shut. "And he actually acknowledged you, Stef—alert the media."

I was going to say something, but May suddenly gasped.

"What?"

She ignored me, turning instead to Tate. "Did he just say that your family was here?"

"Yes." He smiled wide. "I was telling Rand that I would love him to meet my family soon, and he said that there was no time like the present, so I got on the phone and invited them on out here. Isn't it wonderful?"

She looked like she was going to pass out.

I cleared my throat. "Have you even met his family yet?" I asked May.

"No," she barely got out, quickly turning a very sickly shade of gray.

I tried not to smile as I led her over to the bookcase. "Quick, shallow breaths," I advised her, showing her, modeling it so she'd know what to do. "Funny, I figured at sixty this kinda shit wouldn't happen anymore."

She swatted me hard.

I laughed at her, and she did it again.

Tate Langley's family was just as attractive as he was. His daughter Sophie was stunning, her husband Eli charming, his daughter Amanda was crisp and flawless, his son Tristan looked like he should have modeled suits in a magazine, and his daughter Candace, the beauty of the whole bunch, took one look at Rand Holloway and decided what she wanted for Christmas.

Her lovely copper-colored eyes slid over Rand from head to toe, and she started gushing about the ranch.

I arched an eyebrow for May. "She likey."

"Stop."

"What?"

"Oh good heavens." She sighed, walking to Tate's side when he called for her, still doing the semi-Lamaze breathing that I was making her do.

"Who knew that was gonna come in handy again, huh?"

"You're an evil thing, Stefan Joss."

This was not news.

I darted into the kitchen to pull out some of the leftovers from Charlotte's rehearsal dinner. There were still platters of barbecued beef and pork left over, and I went to work preparing a salad. The baked beans just needed to be warmed up, and the potato salad and coleslaw that Rand had bought for lunch were added to my menu.

When the door swung open, I was surprised to find Tristan there.

"Hi," I said.

"Hello." His smile was huge as he crossed the kitchen to me. "I'm Tristan."

I shook the hand he extended for me. "I heard your dad introduce you."

"And you are?"

"Oh, Stefan, sorry."

"Stefan," he repeated, covering my hand with his. "It's a real pleasure."

I nodded as he released my hand.

"You need some help?"

"That'd be great."

He was articulate and funny, and as he was a marketing manager for a PR firm, we had a lot to talk about. When his sister Amanda poked her head in and asked if she could lend a hand, he told her no before I could say yes. She gave me a perfunctory smile and left the room.

"I hope she didn't feel shafted," I told him.

"Amanda's just being Amanda. She wants to see if I'm making any progress in here."

"I'm sorry?"

He looked at me oddly. "Stefan, you must know, I didn't just come in here by accident. I followed you in here."

"Well, that's very flattering."

He slid closer to me. "You are without a doubt the most beautiful man I have seen in a very long time, and I would be remiss to let an opportunity like this slip by."

"An opportunity like what?"

"To ask you out."

I smiled slowly. "Oh, okay, well that's a very nice offer, and normally I would take—"

"Don't say no," he said. "You have to eat. Let me take you out—I know some great places in Lubbock that—"

"I'm sure," I told him, "but I'm seeing someone right now."

He leaned close and grabbed a handful of my ass. "You are going to look so great in my bed.... I can't wait to see your skin next to my sheets."

It was not the cheesiest line I had ever heard, but it was right up there. Someone somewhere had done the man a grave injustice at one point and told him he was smooth. It was like the people who auditioned on *American Idol* because their "friends" said they could sing. You're sitting at home wondering, *Why?* I try never to humiliate anyone because it's bad karma just waiting to happen, but this was a day on which I had almost been killed. I was not in possession of my usual emotional stamina. Between Rand's upheaval of my life and nearly being gunned down, I was slightly unhinged. All I could do was put my head back and laugh. I should have thanked him for the release, because laughing was certainly better than the alternative.

"What the hell is so—"

"What's goin' on in here?" Rand asked as he strode into the room, Candace close behind him. "What're you doin'?"

"I'm cooking," I gasped, wiping at my eyes with the back of my hand, the tears from laughing blurring my vision. "And Tristan here is entertaining me. He's funny as shit."

"Is he?" Rand scowled, walking up beside me, his hand on the back of my neck, massaging. "Well, that's right neighborly of him... to entertain the help."

I smiled up at him as he tangled his hand in my hair. "The help?"

"Yep." He chuckled before giving my ass a hard slap and strolling out of the room. I was left with Candace staring at me with huge eyes and a dumbfounded Tristan beside her.

"Sorry, he's kind of a jerk."

Candace pointed after him. "Rand's gay?"

Technically, Rand was bi, but I didn't have time to answer her before the door swung open again and the man in question returned. I was grabbed hard from behind, arms wrapping around my waist tightly. I smiled crazily as he pressed against my back before rubbing his chin on my shoulder.

"You smell so good," he said gruffly, his face pressed against the side of my neck, nuzzling, his hands slipping under my shirt, clutching at my bare skin.

It was hard to concentrate with him so close to me. I got that almost queasy feeling in my stomach.

"Rand?" Candace said.

My head rolled back on my shoulders as my jeans tightened uncomfortably. His effect on me was instant. He burned me up.

"Hi," Rand said cheerfully as he pressed a hand against my stomach. "He's mine, did he tell you?"

I recovered enough to look up, tried to smile even as Rand pressed his groin into my ass. The movement sent an electric shock through my entire body. I realized then that we should have just stayed in bed all day. This thing, whatever it was between us, was still too new for us to be capable of socializing. We needed to be alone because I was on sensory overload.

"You're his boyfriend?" Tristan asked, giving me a look.

"Yeah." I smiled lazily, loving the feel of his hands on me. "It's new."

"I had no idea that... does Dad know?"

"Sure," I said cheerfully.

"Yeah, he knows." Rand laughed, kissing my ear before letting me go. "Everyone knows this man belongs to me," he finished before walking back out of the kitchen.

"Oh my God," Candace breathed out. "I feel so stupid."

"Don't," I told her. "He's hot as hell—if I were you, I'd want a little of that myself."

Her smile was huge as she grabbed my hand. "You're very charming, and now that I know I have no possible chance with your boyfriend—can I help you?"

"That'd be great." I grinned at her.

We both looked over at Tristan. He said nothing before he left the room.

"So," I teased her, "tell me all about yourself."

I had more fun talking to Candace than I had her brother. When we called everyone in to dinner, having set up the food like a buffet, they were all appreciative. I took plates out to Chris and Paul, who had relieved Everett and Dustin, and told them to call over to the bunkhouse to see if anyone else wanted to eat. When I was back in the kitchen, Rand appeared at my side. Turning to look at him, I realized for the hundredth time how beautiful his eyes were.

"What?" he asked me after a minute of silence.

"Nothing," I said, smiling at him. "I think I need to go back to bed."

"Okay." He grinned at me even as his eyes clouded.

"What's wrong?"

He looked suddenly like he wanted to be anywhere but with me.

"Rand?"

Deep sigh from him. "This ain't gonna work."

"What won't?"

"This. I can't play at this because I want it so bad."

Without warning, my choice was upon me.

He took a breath and dived in. "You can't make it so being here without you will be bad for me. I can't take that; I can't feel like that in my own home. Jenny wasn't able to do that, to make me hate the ranch, because I never felt like she fit here. Every day after we were married, she was miserable standing in this kitchen, talking to the men, even riding beside me… she wanted to run away, and instead she ended up marrying her jailer."

He had actually done the digging I had thought he'd missed.

"Jenny hated how we were together because she didn't want anything to do with me. She needed everything to be bad so she would have a reason to go. She didn't want to enjoy being in bed with me because she never wanted to stay. She hated ranch life, but her family an' friends all thought it was in her blood. I saw that after we were married, knew she wanted to be gone, so I made it easy for her and let her blame it on me."

No doubt about it, Rand Holloway was a very good man.

"But now I see how it was supposed to be."

I swallowed down the emotions welling up inside me, realizing that suddenly, without warning, I was in the middle of a life-making or life-breaking decision.

"You, Stef... you make me love my home more," he whispered, his voice going out on him, "because whether you know it or not... you love it here."

I could only stare at him.

"You're so beautiful, Stef... and cold and hard and fiercely independent... it's scary how careful you are not to need anybody."

He was right, I was very careful with my heart.

"But this mornin' when you first opened your eyes and looked at me, just for a second before you remembered that you're supposed to be on your guard with me... the trust that was there... Jesus, Stef. Your eyes were so soft and the way you look at me, the way you always do, like I'm a gift... how could I not be in? How could I not want you right here with me?"

He was going to kill me.

"I love you Stef," he exhaled, "and it's killin' me."

I had no idea what to do.

"After just one day of your smell on my sheets, of your hair in my face, of you biting my bottom lip when you don't want the kiss to end... I don't want to live without it."

"Rand—"

"Just.... I love touching your skin. I love how rough I can be with you in bed and how gentle you are with me, and I love how you feel inside when we—"

"Okay," I cut him off, having trouble breathing.

"What? You know that you were made for me."

He was right: together, in bed, we were amazing.

"So I need you to stay. Will you stay?"

This thing with us was a minute old, and I had no idea if it was real or just a lifetime of crazy, mixed-up desire.

"I know I said I would settle for you comin' back after a week, but I don't think I can." His voice cracked, deserted him.

I turned to face him, and he put his hands on my shoulders.

"Think hard now," he said before he bent and kissed my forehead.

Seconds later, I watched him walk out the door.

IF I thought about Rand, I would lose my mind, so I went upstairs to check my e-mail and see if I had a response from anyone about Knox. There was nothing. When my phone rang, I answered it without looking.

"Stef."

"Holy shit," I breathed out. It was unbelievable that my boss was just somehow on the phone. "Where the hell are you?"

"I need to see you—talk to you. I'm in trouble."

"In trouble for what?"

"I'd rather not say on the phone."

"I'm sorry, is this a party line? Are you worried about your phone being tapped or—"

"No, I just—"

"Just fire me already, because this is bullshit. Donna said she hasn't heard from you in a week."

"You talked to Donna?"

"Well, yeah. I mean, if I can't get ahold of my boss, then I need to call my boss's boss to try an' get some goddamn answers! What the fuck is going on?"

He didn't answer for so long I was tempted to check and see if he was still there.

"I'm in trouble."

"Yeah, I figured, because in four years of working for you, this is the first time I ever couldn't get ahold of you."

"Shit."

I changed tactics. "Please tell me what's going on."

He cleared his throat. "Just come see me."

"Fine. Where are you?"

He explained about the motel where he was and how he needed to talk to me and that if he didn't, he was sure he was going to completely lose it. The strained, broken sound of the man's voice, normally so filled with absolute confidence and conviction, scared me to death.

"It's okay," I soothed him, grabbing a hoodie, pulling it on, and zipping it up. Everything seemed to be taking forever. I felt like I was moving underwater. "It'll be all right. Whatever's wrong, we'll figure it out, okay?"

He sucked in a breath. "Okay."

"I'll be right there."

I knew Rand would never understand me going to see my boss alone, so I left him a quick note and went out the back door, around the side of the house. Because everyone was eating and talking, there was no one on the porch. I got to my rental car, put the car in neutral, and rolled it a quarter of the way down the long drive. When I was sure I was far enough away from the house that I couldn't be followed, I started the engine but left the lights off. I navigated by the moon to the highway, and almost the second I turned off of Rand's property, my phone rang.

"Why can't I hear your phone ring from somewhere in my house?" Rand asked me, his voice cold and hard.

"My boss called, and he needs to see me."

"Fine, come back and get me."

"That's not a good idea."

"I think it is."

"I need to see him alone, Rand."

"I can't believe you'd sneak off the ranch, and even worse—"

"I can't believe I did either," I said, the weight of what I'd done suddenly hitting me. "Holy shit, since when and in what realm of the imagination am I scared of you?"

"Stef—"

"Fuck me." I caught my breath. "I honestly care about what you think of me…. I didn't want you to be mad."

"Stef—"

"Shit… I think I love you."

The coughing was instant and loud. "You what?"

"You heard me. Goddammit, when did that happen?"

He was still coughing, sounding more and more like he was choking. "Stef… tell me."

"This is bullshit, I refuse to do this over the phone—it's a cop-out because it's easier, since I don't have to look at you. I wanna tell you to your face."

"Tell me what?"

"That I love you, asshole, have you not been listening?"

The laughter was warm and made it hard for me to breathe. "Jesus, Stef, don't sound happy about it or nothin'."

Just saying the words out loud settled things for me. It was like I had blurted out the vault of my heart. "I don't wanna give up my life, Rand, I still wanna be me."

"No one says you gotta give up any part of bein' you. Why would I want that?"

"I won't work on that ranch."

"All right."

"I'm serious."

"Okay."

"Okay."

"Okay then, tell me where you're meetin' your boss," he demanded. So I did.

THE MOTEL was small with rooms to rent by the hour, and that was strange for me, as my boss always did five stars or nothing. What in the world was going on? The man who answered the door when I knocked looked nothing like the man I knew. It was like he was in disguise, covered in stubble and wearing jeans and flannel. I was absolutely floored.

"What the hell?" I asked him as he yanked me into the room, roughly shoving me sideways so he could lock the door. As I turned to face him, it was only then I saw the gun. "Seriously, Knox, what the fuck?"

His smile was fast and finally reminded me of whom I was looking at. "Remember how I always tell you that you're so loyal that you would take a bullet for me?"

I was suddenly freezing.

"Well, today we both get to test my theory," he said, looking past me at the same time I heard someone behind me. Then there was only black.

CHAPTER 10

I HATE the smell of gasoline. Some people like it; I've never been a fan. When I tried to lift my hand to cover my nose, I found that I couldn't move at all. Opening my eyes, I realized that I was pinned to the floor by a man twice my size. The wide-open sightless eyes made me cry out, and, shoving out from under him, I scrambled back against the wall.

"Scared?"

Looking up, I saw my boss with an empty gas can in one hand and the same gun he had earlier in the other.

"That's Cole Gypsum, if you care. He was my partner in this little adventure. I would have blamed it all on him without you, but I realized that it would have made no sense to people and so they would have searched for the logic. Looking for a connection would have led to me. But with you here, the connection's made, so... no need to do any digging."

His pupils were huge, dilated—he didn't look well. It was like the man I knew was gone, having left a walking, talking shell in his place.

"What did you do?"

"I needed the money."

"What money?"

"Were you always this stupid? I never thought of you as stupid."

I clicked through what I knew before I looked around and saw where I was: in Mrs. Freeman's living room. "Oh shit, Knox."

"It made so much sense. I mean, these people are the salt of the earth, right? Every cowboy movie I ever saw... you never sell the ranch to city slickers. We're the bad guys, they're the good guys, so no way they sell."

"But they did—at least some of them did."

"Yes." He let out a deep breath. "They all decided to sell."

"Except Mrs. Freeman."

He smiled at me. "She was the last holdout. She was my angel... as long as she didn't sell, no one would need the money, and if no one needed it—"

"Then no one would realize that it was gone."

"Precisely."

It was quite a revelation. The money to pay the people who had decided to sell their ranches had been stolen by my boss. Knox Bishop had embezzled over five million dollars from his company, my company, and no one had any clue.

"How did you do it?"

"It's just a question of moving funds around until people lose track."

"They will find it, Knox."

"No one's looking for it, Stef. There's no reason to. No one is selling their ranches."

"But when they find out that Mrs. Freeman died, they're going to want the money back."

"Yes. And this is where you and my dead partner come in."

Shit. "When did you take it?"

"I took it a year ago, when we started this venture. The money was there, this surplus given to us by Armor South, and no one was watching it."

"Someone was."

"Yeah, me," he said cheerfully. "It was my project; I was supposed to get the buyers to sell and pay them out so Armor South could build their Green Light megastore."

"What did you do with all that money?"

He was pacing now. "I have debts and expenses and a life that you have no idea about, Stef. You just… you have no idea." There was a wistful quality in his voice.

"Why kill Mrs. Freeman?"

"I had to," he admitted. "You told me yourself on the phone last night—or the night before, I don't remember—but you said that she was going to sell. It's actually the reason I sent you. I knew if she would sell to anyone it would be you. I tested her, and I was right. Everyone loves you, Stef, I knew she wouldn't be able to resist you."

"But—"

"Or maybe she could." He smirked. "That was the point, right? She would either hold out and I'd be safe, or she'd cave and I'd come out here and kill you both and make it look like you embezzled the money and killed poor old Mrs. Freeman to save your own ass."

It was terrifying, the power of money. I had known Knox Bishop for four years, since I had started at Chaney Putnam, and I had never even seen a glimmer of the evil that lurked just below the surface. The man had been a friend to me; we had pulled countless all-nighters brainstorming together, and when he was in a skiing accident, I had visited practically every day. We had so many memories between us, sometimes just a shared look could bring on raucous laughter. I would miss him.

"Stef?"

I tipped my head at the gun in his hand. "So you're just gonna shoot me?"

"Yes," he said at the same time I saw the butane lighter. "And then I'm going to set fire to this house with you and Cole in it."

I shivered hard.

"For the record, Stef, I never wanted to hurt you. I prayed that Mrs. Freeman wouldn't sell, and so you know… Cole killed Mrs. Freeman, not me."

What was I supposed to say?

"He's also the one who tried to run you off the road."

"Why kill Cole?" I stalled him, watching him play with the lighter, flip it open and closed over and over.

"Cole wanted more than we said at first." He sighed heavily. "He gambled a lot."

I looked up at the man hovering close to me. "Why can't you just run away and disappear, Knox? I mean, all the money that you took… you've gotta be able to live off of that for the rest of your life, right?"

"I told you already," he said sadly. "It's all gone."

"It can't all be gone."

"Enough of it is. I need my job, and with you gone, I can start over, make a clean start like none of this ever happened."

I got slowly, carefully, to my feet. "I don't think you really want to hurt me."

"No, I don't," he said flatly, leveling the gun at me. "But I have no one else. Cole's dead, and it has to be you two in it together."

I felt like I was underwater as he flipped the lighter on and casually tossed it into the corner. In an instant, one side of the living room went up in flames. The fire spread to the curtains, the bookcases, and the beautiful antique rocking chair. It made me sad to think of Mrs. Freeman's home burning to the ground, her whole life, her photographs, her children's baby books, recipes, handwritten notes…. It was all going to be ashes, and her children would have nothing but their memories.

"Don't worry," he said as he advanced on me. "I'm not going to make it your fault. Cole's going to be the one who pressured you. I have a great story about how you guys were in love, but he actually used you, and then you ended up killing him and then killing yourself. I even wrote a note."

"Nobody who knows me at all is gonna believe you." I was many things, but tragic was not one of them.

"It's romantic, in a sick, twisted sort of way." He shrugged. "They'll believe it."

I didn't think, I just bolted for the archway. I wasn't going to stand there and get shot. How sane was that? I ran into the kitchen, came careening around the corner, and grabbed onto the doorframe so I wouldn't fall. When I turned, I was faced with two doors. The first one was locked, so I tried the second one. It led up to the second floor.

"Stef!"

There was a pop, and a chunk of the door was gone. In my body, the hole would have been bigger. I charged up the stairs and he screamed behind me.

"I don't want to hurt you!"

No, he just wanted to kill me. Obviously as the psychosis had set in, the man's logic had flown right out the window.

I ran down the hall on the second floor, hearing pops behind me, and dived inside of the first room. There was nothing to grab and hit him with. It looked like a spare bedroom, all done in rosebuds. It was so surreal to be running for my life and to find myself standing in a room that looked like it belonged to a nine-year-old girl.

"Stefan!"

I ran to the window and looked out to see how far down the fall would be if I threw myself out, and the blue lights flashed on my face. My head snapped up, and I saw the four sheriff cars and Rand's big, scary pickup. Two men were holding onto him, keeping him from running into the house. I banged on the glass, and his face lifted as he yelled. I couldn't hear it, but I saw all the rage and force, even from a distance.

"Stef!"

The drop from the second floor was straight down. If it didn't kill me, it would hurt me really badly. I darted from the room. There was a "pop," and my shoulder felt like it was on fire along with the house. I ran, even as the throb made it feel like my arm had fallen off, and leaped sideways into another room. That one had another door, and when I went through that, I discovered that the bedrooms were connected like a dorm room. When I peeked out into the hall from the second bedroom, I saw Knox go into the first. Neither one of us knew the house at all, which was working to my benefit. I took the stairs back down to the first floor, hearing him running around above me, roaring my name.

It was like walking into a sauna. Smoke was everywhere, and I wished that Mrs. Freeman's house was laid out like Rand's. I would never again take for granted the back door that led outside from his kitchen to the enclosed porch. But there had to be a second way out, I just had to find it. The front door, engulfed in huge flames, was not an option.

"Stef!" he screamed, and then I heard his footsteps on the stairs.

There was no way out. Everything was too heavy for me to pick up and launch at the only remaining possibility, the enormous bay window.

"Stef!"

I turned, clutching at my shoulder, the blood oozing between my fingers. "You can't get out either, Knox."

"I will, Stef! Watch me!" he shrieked at me, lifting the gun.

I braced for the impact; any way I dove, he had me.

He screamed as blood exploded from his shoulder, arm, and collarbone. I turned to the window in time to see Sheriff Colter wave me out of the way. The chairs Mrs. Freeman and I had sat in just days ago flew through the window, shattering the glass in a downpour of shards.

The third deputy grabbed me through the gaping hole where the window had once been. He dragged me outside as the others went in after Knox. I was spun around and shoved hard only to find myself crushed against a wall of solid muscle. Looking up, I saw that the usually bright blue eyes were almost black.

"I just wanted to save him, Rand."

He nodded and tucked me against his side before bending fast and sliding an arm under my knees, scooping me up. He walked me away from the house toward his truck.

"He shot me."

"I know. I heard it."

"Why're you mad?" I asked, reaching up, touching the clenched jaw.

"Oh, I dunno, the man I love finally tells me he loves me and then goes on and gets himself shot."

He was adorable.

"What should I say?"

"What should you say? You're askin' me what you should fuckin' say?"

It had actually been somewhat rhetorical.

"Goddammit, Stefan!" he roared, squeezing me so tight I made a very unmanly squeak. "How 'bout 'I'm sorry as shit, Rand, for taking ten goddamn years off your life'?"

I lifted my head and kissed under his jaw.

"All that bullshit about not workin' on the ranch, you know that's off the table now, don't you?" he muttered angrily. "You'll be lucky if you get to leave the ranch to do your goddamn Christmas shopping!"

The bluster was kind of cute, because it was obvious he had been worried, scared to death, and it was there in his voice, in the way he was clutching me, and in the chin rubbing against my hair. I wanted to hear him rant and rave at me, but suddenly I was more tired than I had ever been in my life. I could not keep my eyes open, even when Rand threatened me.

CHAPTER 11

IT WAS different from how I thought it would be. The fallout from Knox's crime tore Chaney Putnam apart. Apparently there was more scandal than I knew about, and the FBI came and took people and files away. As soon as I was cleared to travel, I had to return to Chicago to help put things in order so that the office could be closed. There was no time to return to the ranch and spend time with Rand. I simply had to go from being in a hospital for two days to the airport. I could have refused to go, but the company had been good to me, and I felt that I needed to do as much as I could. Rand did not understand.

"You need to stay," he said on my last night in the hospital.

"I need to go help, Rand," I said, still coughing from smoke inhalation. My lungs were recovering, but it was slow progress.

"You need to stay here with me."

It was a good fight, but in the end, it was one he lost. He was more upset than I felt he should have been.

"I'm coming back. I told you I was. What more do you want?"

"I want you now."

"You got me."

"You're going away."

"For two weeks, tops."

"I don't believe you," he said flat out. "You'll get back there, there'll be exciting job offers, and you won't come back. You're easily taken in by smoke an' mirrors."

"Well, it's nice to hear you think so highly of me."

His hands went to my face. "There's no one I think more of. Just stay here."

"I told you I love you, and since I've only ever said it to my own mother, Charlotte, and your mother, never to a man, you need to accept it as the gift it is."

"Stef—"

"I will come back because you're going to be my home."

"Stef—"

"Do you wanna be my home?"

"It's all I want."

"Well, then, I don't see the problem."

Rand's mother and Uncle Tyler came to visit me at that moment and interrupted him. They were both very concerned, even as I made them swear not to call Charlotte on her honeymoon and tell her. It took some convincing—they were afraid of what she'd do to them when she found out the truth—but in the end, my charm prevailed.

Saying good-bye to Rand at the airport was harder than I thought it was going to be. Funny, but now that I knew whom I wanted to spend the rest of my life with, I was ready for my life to start. Back in Chicago, back at work, I would have flashes of Rand. I would think of him standing in the breeze, hair tousled by the wind, or looking down at me with his molten eyes, or feel again his hands on my skin. I wondered how he could ever think that I would not go home.

"Stef?"

Looking up, I saw my assistant, Christina Wu, standing in the doorway, looking at me oddly.

"Yeah?"

"Are you all right? You look weird."

What could I tell her? That I missed my boyfriend? "I always look weird."

She gave me a smug smile. "It's true, and it's nice that you're admitting it. That's the first step to getting help."

"You're hysterical."

"I'm aware."

I crossed the room to her, grabbing her hard, hugging her tight. "What are you going to do now? Where are you going to go?"

Her brows furrowed. "Stef, you're the one that got me a job working for your friend Dave Barron. I start next Monday."

David Barron had been more than a friend. I had slept with him and only him for six months before he decided he wanted to keep me and I disappeared. I had felt weird calling, even more so when he had so obviously thought that the reason for the contact was romantic and not the business that it was. It had been nice that he wanted my assistant, needing a good one. I had given him a great one.

"Sorry," I said, letting her go. "And sorry about that…. I know you don't like to be touched a whole lot."

"Make me sound like a basket case, why don't you. I simply don't like to be touched by people who aren't family or friends. I don't discourage all human contact."

"Sorry."

"And besides," she said, surprising me by wrapping her arms around me, "you're the exception to the rule, Joss. I'm crazy about you—everyone is."

"Knox used to say that."

She nodded. "Well, Knox will have a lot of time to think about it while he's serving time for his double-homicide and fraud. Or is it theft? What is it?"

"I have no idea." I sighed. "I wonder how long he'll be in for?"

"My guess is a very long time," she said. "But don't worry about that. He's gone, he can't hurt you, and everyone knows what he tried to do to you. If we actually had a company anymore, you could write your own ticket."

"Weird that we're closing."

"I'm just glad that I work for you, one of the good guys, and not one of the bad ones. Some of the other assistants have to testify against their bosses and go through and give dates and times of meetings and all kinds of stuff."

"Lucky for you I am one of the good guys," I teased her. "'Cause trying to remember what I'm doing on a day-to-day basis would be a pain in the ass."

"Yes, Mr. Scattered, it would be."

It was nice that some of the things in my life didn't change.

I WAS into my third week in Chicago before I realized that time had gotten away from me. Rand had been right, the job offers came flooding in, but as I felt disjointed and not myself, it was hard even to call people back and politely decline. I sent e-mails instead.

My conversations with Rand were short and sometimes terse. He had moved quickly from understanding to sullen to silent. When he stopped answering his phone, I checked in with May. She informed me that he had taken a trip to hire the men for winter grazing and was not expected back for at least a couple of weeks. Before I could get off the phone, she wanted to know why I myself was not returning Charlotte's calls.

"I'm just not ready to rehash everything and explain about Rand."

"Well, you best get ready before you have a very hurt and angry girl on your hands."

"Yes, ma'am," I said solemnly, hanging up minutes later after telling her I loved her too.

How was I going to explain being madly in love with her brother to Charlotte? She had missed the beginning, and now I was supposed to catch her up? It was daunting just thinking about. She would be pissed that I had hidden things from her even in the midst of all the wedding craziness. Walking home from work that night, I realized that for the first time in ages I did not have my best friend to reach out to. Normally Charlotte was my touchstone, but as it was, I didn't have her to turn to. When my phone rang, I didn't even check the caller ID, I just answered.

"Are you out of your mind not answering my phone calls?" she yelled at me.

"Sorry."

She growled.

"I am."

"Oooh, I should beat you!"

"Come see me and you can."

"Okay—poof, here I am!"

Looking up the street to my brownstone, I saw her waving from the steps. I flew down the sidewalk and up the stoop into her waiting arms. I hugged the life out of her, and she giggled.

"If Mohammad won't drink from the stream—wait—" She stopped herself. "That's not right—how does that go again?"

I just laughed into her shoulder as she clung to me. When she finally stepped back, her face lifted to mine, I watched her eyebrow slowly arch.

"Crap."

She grunted.

"I had no idea, Char," I told her. "I mean one minute I think he hates me only to find out that he never did? It's still surreal, you know?"

"Yeah, that's great, but first I wanna hear about your boss."

"You do?"

"Well yeah," she said, like it was understood. "I heard there was shooting."

"You're like a rubbernecker on the road."

"Yeah, and?"

I made a noise in the back of my throat, but the pouty lip made me spill. Who could resist the boo-boo face and the Bambi eyes?

"And then what?" She pressed me for more details, still riveted an hour later as I recounted my experience with Knox Bishop and the fire.

We talked and ate, talked and had dessert, talked and went out for second dessert, and the whole time, she was careful to tiptoe around all reference to her brother. She told me all about her honeymoon and how she had locked herself in the hotel bathroom for three hours when the doorknob fell off. She cackled evilly as she recounted how Ben had managed to get stung by three jellyfish in one day and how sick she was of having sex. She just wanted to play video games instead.

Finally, at two in the morning as we walked back to my apartment, when I could not trade snappy banter with her a second longer, I grabbed her and looked into her face.

"God, what?" She laughed at me.

"Jesus, Char, don't you want to know all about Rand?"

"Aww, honey, I already know all about Rand."

"You do?"

"Of course I do."

"But how? Have you talked to him?"

"I don't need to talk to him to know what's going on." She smiled widely.

"You don't?"

"No, honey, I don't. I knew it was going to happen sooner or later. It's just timing." She sighed deeply, her hands on my face. "I knew someday Rand was going to grow a pair and tell you how he felt. I just always hoped you guys would both be in the same place at the same time."

I was absolutely stunned.

"Close your mouth, Stefan. You look like a fish."

I snapped it shut.

"Please, I never saw so much sexual tension between two people in my life. You could cut it with a knife," she assured me. "I mean the way Rand always looked at you like he wanted to eat you and kill you at the same time, and the way you always had to find an excuse to pick a fight with him? C'mon, what am I, stupid?"

"I... I thought he hated me."

She cackled evilly. "Oh, my poor, dumb baby, were you dropped on your head when you were little?"

"Charlotte!"

She dissolved into laughter.

"Char!"

"Stefan Joss, my brother is crazy, head-over-heels in love with you! He has been since he was twenty-one and he walked into that room and saw the most beautiful eighteen-year-old boy that he'd ever seen in his life."

"I—"

"He's thirty-one now, and you're still the most beautiful thing he's ever seen. But it's lucky for you, huh?"

"What is?"

"It's lucky that you're pretty, 'cause wow—really not bright."

"Char!"

She cackled again.

"You better fly home to your husband; he's probably pissed at me for taking you away from him already."

"Are you kidding? That was the longest goddamn honeymoon in recorded history. He's so glad I came to see you he can barely stand it. I said, 'I'm gonna go see Stef,' and he said, 'Yeah, go visit your boyfriend'."

"You guys are like an old married couple already."

"Yeah, super."

I put my arm around her shoulders as we closed in on my apartment. "Hey, did you meet your mom's lover?"

"Eww, you just said 'lover' to gross me out. That's mean."

My turn to cackle. "His son Tristan hit on me."

"Did Rand hurt him?"

"No, Rand doesn't know."

"Oooh good, lemme tell him. I like to see that vein pop out in his neck."

"God, you're horrible."

"And you're actually okay." She sighed. "And I'm so glad. I was so worried. I thought maybe this thing with Knox had made you nuts or something."

"No."

"Well, it makes sense. I mean, hello—were you answering my calls?"

"No, I wasn't."

"You see, do those sound like the actions of a sane person to you?"

I squeezed her tight. "No, they don't."

"I rest my case."

"I will always pick up the phone from now on."

"See that you do."

She was very bossy, and I loved her like mad.

"So when are you leaving?"

Her head turned, and her gaze captured mine. "The better question is when are you leaving?"

It really was the better question.

"What are you still doing here, Stef?"

I stopped walking and froze where I was, looking at her like I was seeing her for the first time. "Shit, what am I doing here?"

"Stalling."

"Why?"

"Because you're scared," she said. "It's okay to be scared, but you gotta dive into the deep end sometime and trust that you're not gonna drown."

"I love him."

"I know." She nodded. "He's the only one you've ever cared enough about to fight with. That's how I knew, that's how I always knew."

"Why didn't you tell me?"

She scoffed. "Men don't listen to women, straight, bi, or gay, not at all."

And she was right, at least in my case. I would have never believed that Rand Holloway wanted me for anything at all.

"So?" She prodded me, the warm smile on her face that I adored.

"So I think you should stay here and help me pack."

"I think that's a phenomenal idea."

CHAPTER 12

DRIVING A truck with a trailer is harder than it looks. The whole adventure becomes particularly dicey when turning. I had cut the angle too closely, and now I had to back out to try another shot at it. I was outside looking at both the trailer and the signpost for the ranch, so entrenched with how to make the turn that I didn't hear the truck stop behind me.

"What the hell are you doing?" someone yelled.

I turned around, and you could have knocked me over with a feather. "Rand."

He closed his truck door as he got out and walked around the front to the gravel. I moved forward, but I wasn't quite sure how I was doing it. I stopped a few feet away and stared at him. He had never looked so good.

"I repeat," he snapped at me, "what the hell are you doing?"

"Well, I just got back from dropping Phil at the Winston Petting Zoo, and out was fine 'cause it was a straight shot, but in...." I winced, turning back to look at the trailer. "I mean, I can't back up and go straight because there's that dip on the other side of the road, and if I cut it too sharp, then—"

"I meant what are you doing here?"

"I just got back from dropping off the cow." I scowled at him. "Were you not listening?"

"What cow?"

"My cow."

"You don't have a cow," Rand assured me.

"Not anymore, no," I agreed.

"Wait. When did you have a cow?"

"I had Phil."

"I'm sorry, what?"

"Phil," I reminded him. "Phil was my cow and he went to a petting zoo today."

"What?"

"Why are you having trouble grasping this?"

"Are you—Jesus, Stef, that was not your cow to—"

"Tyler said since you let me name him, he was mine, and Chris and Everett agreed."

"Did they?"

"Yessir," I said, breathing in his manly scent, taking a step closer to him. "How did the hiring go? Did you let someone else talk to the guys, too, since you know you suck at it?"

"I suck at—"

"Tyler said you suck at hiring, remember? And you have to admit, Pete was a really bad choice."

"You never even met—"

"You know, I think I got this," I said, turning to walk back to the cab of the truck.

I was grabbed hard and spun around to face the man.

"What are you doing here, Stef?"

I squinted at him. "I live here."

His eyes widened. "You what?"

"Isn't that what you said you wanted? I could've sworn that's what you—"

"I thought you weren't coming."

"When did I say that?"

His breath came out in a rush of air. "I thought I...." A hand came to my face, and he brushed a strand of hair back out of my eyes. "I was sure I missed my shot."

I stopped breathing, and my throat went completely dry. "Why?" I croaked out.

"'Cause you were gone for so long I... and then I was cold to you, and I didn't wanna be, but I couldn't... help it."

"You missed me," I got out, even as my heart started pounding like a drum.

"I missed my chance ten years ago," he said slowly, his voice husky as he cupped my face in his hands. "I will not let that happen again."

"You were young, Rand." I smiled through tears I didn't realize had filled my eyes. "Give yourself a break. We both needed time to grow up."

"I can't lose my love twice," he whispered to me, his jaw clenching as he spoke, the muscles flexing. "That's just stupid."

His love. I just stared at him. It was all I could do. His love.

"Say something."

I reached up and wrapped my arms around his neck and drew him down to me. I felt like I was freezing; my teeth were chattering, and I was trembling, terrified the moment would pass, unbearably happy that I was there with him.

It was not a smooth Hollywood embrace. I clutched at him, keeping him close, my hands in his hair, on his back, making sure he couldn't get free. When I kissed him, I felt the sigh of pleasure just come up out of me. I had been holding on for so long, holding it together and being strong. I didn't want anyone to feel sorry for me; I let no one see a trace of uncertainty or fear. There was only my iron will and my strength, my drive, my purpose.

"I was mad at you for so long," he said into my hair, holding me close, pressing me tight against him. "And with wanting you at the same time... damn."

"You should have told me," I heard myself say, breathing him in, kissing his throat as he spoke.

He moved me suddenly out to arm's length, and I smiled in spite of myself. He was treating me like I belonged to him, and I thought my heart was going to explode from my chest.

"So where is all your stuff?" he asked me.

"In the house."

"And where do you work?"

"In Lubbock, with Ben's dad."

"Really."

"Yes, really, I have an office and everything. It's working out great."

He grunted. "That's quite the drive you have every day, Mr. Joss."

"I know." I smiled big at him, absolutely adoring him. "And your truck gets shitty gas mileage."

"Best we get you somethin' else to drive."

"That'd be good."

He was thinking about a lot of things. I could tell as all the emotions blew across his face. "So." He cleared his throat, pulling me close again. "This is where you're gonna be?"

"Yessir." I sighed, my cheek against his chest. "If you still want me."

He didn't say a word for several minutes, so even though I was terrified at what I would see, I stepped out of the embrace and looked up at his face. His eyes were so dark, and he was just staring down at me.

"So do you... want me?"

"Do I want you?"

I waited breathlessly.

There was the heat of his breath on my face before he grabbed me and kissed me like he was a drowning man and I was the air he needed to breathe. One hand was in my hair, tangled deep as he tugged it gently back, his other sliding over my ass as he deepened the kiss, his mouth slanting over mine. It was ravenous, and as he pressed me tightly to his chest, I felt the shudder that tore through him.

"Please," I begged him, tearing free, needing it to be clear between us, "can I stay?'

He lifted his face to the wind, and the breeze blew his hair back from his face. I watched him take a deep breath, and then he looked down at me hard. I lost myself in his eyes and heard the prayer in my head. *Please give me this man. He should be mine. I don't deserve him, it's true; I've messed up a million times, and I've broken my share of hearts. But I know the real thing when I see it, and this is it. Give me the real one. Give me the man I'm going to keep forever.*

And then suddenly he smiled, and it was a good one. It lit his eyes and took my breath away. "Oh, you're staying." He beamed down at me. "You think I'm lettin' you off this ranch a second time? You're mine, you belong to me, and that's how it's gonna be, 'cause I ain't fixin' to worry about this no more. We're done with you bein' anywhere but right there with me."

I watched the relief as it washed over his face, saw it lower his shoulders, smooth out his entire stance. He looked, finally, relaxed, at ease for the first time in all the years I had known him.

"Go get in my truck, and I'll drive this one in."

I bolted for the other truck only to be grabbed and yanked back into the man's arms. "What?"

He just waited.

And it came to me, what he needed. "I love you, Rand."

"I love you, Stef."

I arched an eyebrow for him, and he rolled his eyes before he shoved me away. I laughed all the way over to the truck.

He made driving the truck and trailer look really easy. I was scowling when he made it back up to the house from where he had parked it. His knowing smile was not to be missed.

"You'll practice," he said as he came up the steps.

"Like it's a skill I need to have on my resume," I said irritably, walking into the house, letting the screen door bang shut behind me.

The squeak came a second time, and he was suddenly all over me, grabbing me tight, lifting me to press against his chest. I wrapped him up in my arms and legs, taking the black cowboy hat off and putting it on my head as he carried me up the stairs, his hands cupping my ass.

"I'll get you a hat," he said. "It looks good on you with all that pretty blond hair you got."

"You just like it because it's your hat on my head, Holloway. It's that simple."

He growled, leaning in, bumping my chin with his nose so I had to let my head fall back to give him access to my throat.

I smiled as he licked and bit down my neck, loving how possessive he was, how he needed to mark me. I kissed his eyes, his face, his temple, his chin, his throat, and finally his mouth. His smile fired his eyes, and I did not miss the fact that he couldn't seem to stop.

When I squirmed free, I backed him up against the wall and made quick work of his belt buckle, snap, and zipper. The cock I released was hard, already leaking, and a beautiful sight to behold. I traced the vein on the side with my tongue, licking, kissing, and breathing in the scent that was Rand's alone, spicy, like smoke and rain mixed together.

"God, Stef, don't... tease, just... oh."

For the teasing comment, I swallowed him down my throat. He moaned hoarsely as he bucked into my mouth. Pulling back, I laved the length of him, making him slick with saliva before sucking faster and harder, missing no part of him.

"Stef... I can't... stand," he barely got out. "I'm gonna come if you don't stop."

I wrapped my slick hand around his penis and jerked him off while my mouth did wicked things to the flared, throbbing head.

"Fuck," he roared, grabbing me, lifting me up in one fluid movement and hurling me down onto the bed.

I watched the quick striptease, unable to tear my eyes away from each glimpse of golden skin and rippling muscles that he uncovered. Every inch of the man was gorgeous, and now he belonged only to me.

With a growl, he came down on top of me, and I was very pleased to have caused such a violent, visceral reaction. I made him crazy, and that was very good.

"Get your clothes off and wrap your legs around me."

I made quick work of my jeans and T-shirt, and in seconds I was naked under the man of my dreams. I watched him squeeze lube into his palm, and seconds later, a finger slid between my asscheeks. Instantly, I pressed back, wanting more.

"Don't do that," he cautioned me, "unless you want another."

"Please."

He caught his breath as he added two more fingers to my quivering, needy hole, and groaned as I pleasured myself on them.

"Jesus, Stef," he groaned. "You're so beautiful."

"Show me."

"Shit… it ain't gonna be… it can't be—"

"Slow?" I asked him, smiling playfully.

"Yeah, I can't—I missed you, and—"

"I got it, cowboy," I told him, my eyes narrowed in half. "Fuck me through the mattress."

He let out a low, primal groan before he withdrew his fingers and gripped my thighs as he parted them, lifting my knees up over his arms, angling me against him.

I felt the head of his shaft against my passage for a second before he buried himself inside me deep and hard. Arching up off the bed at the same time he pounded down into me, I had him farther inside than ever before.

"Fuck, Stef!"

I clutched at him with arms and legs as he plunged in and out of my body, bent over me, one hand fisted on my cock. He supported all his weight on his other as he thrust into me, shifting his angle so he slid over my prostate with each new lunge.

There was no other way for me to show him how I felt about him, how much I craved him, how I needed him, how much I loved him and wanted to be with him always. Words were meaningless in the face of passion.

"Christ, Stef, you feel so good."

He was filling me, stretching me as most other men could not, his thick shaft causing my muscles to grip him tightly. The hammering thrusts built heat inside me, sizzling up my spine until I was ready to explode.

"Come for me, Stef," he whispered into my ear, his breath wet and hot.

I yelled myself hoarse when my back bowed, and just for a second, I thought I'd died before euphoria infused every cell of my body. My shuddering orgasm, my muscles bearing down on him, clenching tightly, proved more than he could take. He thrust to the hilt one final time, and I felt liquid heat fill me, overflow me, and run down the crease of my ass. He collapsed on top of me, pressing me down into the bed.

"Kiss me."

The demand made, I lifted my head for his blistering kiss. He bit and sucked and devoured my mouth, his tongue tangling with mine as I returned all the heat I was given. In me, he did not have a passive partner, and I could tell he loved it.

"You were made just for me," he said, leaning back and panting, staring down into my face. "Only for me… this is gonna be a forever thing, Stef, me and you."

"Me and you," I agreed, offering up my heart to him. "I'm not gonna run away. I don't want to. I'll stay as long as you want me."

"Then you're done, 'cause like I said—I want the forever."

"I'll try not to make you crazy."

"Don't do that," he said, rolling off of me, pulling me sideways into his arms. "I don't want you to change. I like you just how you are."

"I love the ranch, Rand," I said, coiling around him.

"I know you do," he said, holding me tight, close to his heart. "It's one of the many reasons I can't live without you."

His words, his actions, filled me with peace. It was so good to be home.

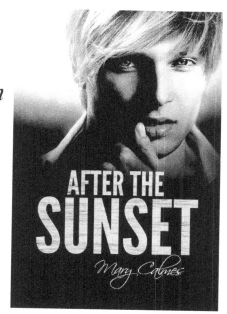

CHAPTER 1

EVEN THOUGH it was late for it, just after seven, I had stopped at the local market to pick up groceries on the way back to the ranch. I wanted to surprise Rand when he got home, with me being there and with dinner. Originally I had told him that I would have to stay late for a department meeting, but it had been cancelled, and instead of going for drinks with the others, I bailed. Even after two years, I still got excited at the thought of going home and being there when the man I loved walked through the door at the end of the day.

So since I had decided to cook, I had to stop and pick up supplies, and I was standing in the checkout line when Mrs. Rawley, who owned the store, came out of the back to see me. It was nice of her to make the effort.

In the small community of Winston, where her store was, the people were divided between those who didn't give a damn that I was gay and lived with my boyfriend, rancher Rand Holloway, owner of the Red Diamond, and those who were vocally and adamantly opposed to the idea. And while those who whispered when I walked by, muttered under their breath, or tossed off slurs when my back was turned were in the minority, there were still enough sprinkled around town to make me conscious of where I chose to conduct my business and spend my money.

After so long, I knew where I would and would not be accepted, but now and then, people still surprised me. What was nice was that more often than not, someone who I thought was just waiting to do or say something hateful or snarky was actually just looking for the opportunity to offer a warm handshake or a smile.

"Can I have Parker carry that out to the car for you, Stef?" Mrs. Rawley offered.

"I was gonna ask," Donna said, clearly exasperated. "For crap's sake, Mama, I wasn't raised in a barn."

I enjoyed the mother-daughter interaction, which was mostly exasperated and sarcastic. "I'm good," I told Mrs. Rawley. "Be nice to your kid."

"Thank you," Donna snapped.

"Respect your mother," I said, grabbing my bags.

"What he said," she shot back at her eighteen-year-old as I left with the jingle of bells at the front door.

As I started toward my car, my snazzy red-and-black MINI Cooper, I saw the police cruiser parked beside me and the SUV that had me blocked in.

"Really," I called over to the two deputies in the car. They could not miss the irritation in my tone.

Both men got out, both smiling at me, and I noticed that one of the deputies, Owen Walker, had a cup in his hand. He moved fast around the front of the cruiser, and as I reached him, I could smell the chai as he offered it to me.

"C'mon, Stef, you know this ain't our call."

I took the warm cup, and he took the bag of groceries and looked inside.

"What're you makin'?" he asked me.

"Just some breaded pork chops and a salad, Deputy."

He looked up at me. "That sounds good, and it's just Owen, all right?"

"Sure." I nodded, smiling at him.

"There's wine in here too."

"And wine," I quipped with a chuckle. "Can't have good food without wine."

"I guess."

I smiled at him. "If it wasn't so late, I'd invite you and your family over."

"Maybe you'd like to have us another time," he said, his eyes suddenly on mine.

I wasn't sure if he was serious. He looked it, but I decided to test. "Maybe one Saturday we could barbecue if you want. The kids could see the horses."

"They would certainly love that, and my wife is dying to see how the house runs with the wind turbine system and the solar panels you all put in. She wants us to go green as well."

"Okay, then, I'll give you a call."

"You do that." He nodded as he lifted his hand, motioning with his fingers.

"What?"

"Gimme the damn keys so I can put this in the trunk for you."

"I can put my own—"

"Just give 'em to me," he growled, grabbing them from my hand.

"This is harassment," I told him.

He flipped me off.

"Stop yelling at him," the second deputy, James, *call me Jimmy*, McKenna ordered me.

I turned to look at him, and he pushed his hat back on his head. "Is it true?"

"Is what true?" I yawned, so glad it was Friday, so ready to just sit and veg and do nothing for my long three-day October weekend. Monday was Columbus Day, so I had it off. Not that my cowboy would be observing a federal holiday, but at least he would probably take off early to spend the evening with me.

"Is Rand really going to build a school in Hillman?"

My eyes watered as I rubbed them a minute before I turned and focused on Deputy McKenna. "Who told you that?"

"All your hands know, Stef, and most of 'em got wives and kids. How long did you think it would be 'til the whole town knew?"

I exhaled before I took a sip of the chai latte.

"Why does that smell weird?" Deputy Walker suddenly asked me, turning my attention back to him as he passed me my keys.

"It's chai," I told him. "You ordered it. How could you order it if you didn't know what it was?"

"I didn't order it. I went in and said gimme what Stefan drinks, and the girl, whatshername with the messy hair—"

"They're dreadlocks, Deputy."

"Owen."

"They're dreadlocks, Owen."

"Whatever. She gives me this smile like I made her day and gets to work, and five dollars and twenty cents later, I'm carrying around something that smells like cinnamon and cloves and somethin' else."

"How did you guys know I was stopping in town instead of going right home?"

"Lyle's out on the highway, camped behind the 'Welcome to Winston' sign, and he saw you drive on by and make the turn toward town."

I nodded. "How is Lyle?"

"He's good. He and Cindy are expecting again."

My eyebrows rose. "Really?"

He grunted. "Don't I know it? That's number five he and my kid sister are havin'. I told him they should take up bowlin' to give them somethin' else to do together."

I couldn't stifle the snickering.

"I thought my mama was gonna explode."

"I bet."

"I think the sheriff was hopin' to have a word with you," Jimmy chimed in. "It's why we're here interceptin' you."

"That's right," Owen agreed. "And back to the coffee," he began, and Jimmy rolled his eyes. "I really don't get why everyone loves that new place so much. My wife wants to live there, and my daughter stops in every afternoon now after school, and there's gettin' to be a line."

The new coffee/bakery/sandwich shop that had gone up four months ago between the bed and breakfast and the senior center had been, for me, a blessing. I made sure to stop in every morning on my way out of town to grab my chai latte and a homemade blueberry scone. They saw me coming and made my drink, the four people who worked there all knowing my face and name on sight. It was nice.

"They knew what you wanted when I said your name," Owen told me.

"Not a lot of chai drinkers in this town," I assured him.

"I expect not."

I tipped my head at the SUV blocking me in. "Where is the big man?"

"The sheriff is picking up his campaign posters from Sue Lynn's."

"Why?" I asked them. "No one is running against him. Why does he need campaign posters?"

"I suspect he likes to see his face really big," he said, gesturing, showing me how mammoth the sheriff's head would be on the banners. "I mean, shit, that's your tax dollars at work there, Stef."

I laughed and saw how at ease both of them were in my presence. "Listen, Deputy McKenna—"

"Jimmy," he corrected me like he always did.

"Jimmy," I sighed. "Why do you guys care if Rand is building a school? How does that affect you in any way?"

"I just think it's funny that he's building in Hillman instead of in his own town, is all."

I leveled my gaze on him. "He was kicked off every committee in this town as well as having his property lines rezoned so that the Red Diamond is no longer even in Winston but in Hillman instead."

"Yeah, I—"

"So your question makes no sense, as Rand is actually building in the town that the Red Diamond resides in."

His eyes narrowed. "Rand's been making a lot of donations and changes to Hillman lately. Do you know anything about that?"

"You know I do," I said, taking another sip of my latte.

He cleared his throat. "I heard the new school was gonna be a charter, but I ain't sure what that is."

"It means that they can pick and choose the curriculum and—"

"The what?"

"Curriculum is what you get taught, idiot," Owen snapped at him. "Go on, Stef."

I couldn't control my smile. "Rand wants things that the elementary school in Winston doesn't offer. He wants them to learn agriculture, which makes sense, and he feels that Spanish should be taught to the English-speaking kids and English taught to the Spanish-speaking kids. He wants them all to be bilingual."

"What for?" Jimmy asked.

"Because it will help them culturally and economically, and learning a second language improves your mind."

"Does it?"

"Yes," I assured him. "And little kids soak up language. It's easier to teach a little kid a new language than it is an adult."

"And so Rand's gonna build a school in Hillman just for that?"

"Right now all the kids on the ranch go to Winston Elementary, but there's no bus that comes all the way out to the Red Diamond, so they're all carpooling. But if Rand builds the school at the south end of Hillman and buys a couple of buses, then all the kids on the ranch as well as the ones who live on the north side of Winston can all go to school in Hillman. The bus can pick them all up every morning."

"When he builds the school, I want my kids to go there," Owen told us.

"You do?" Jimmy asked him, clearly surprised.

"Sure." He shrugged. "I think learning a second language is a great idea."

"There you go," I said, turning back to Jimmy. "It just makes sense."

"Rand sure has made a lot of changes since you got here, Stef," he told me.

"I think the sheriff wants to talk to Rand about that and about maybe taking his seat back on the community board of directors," Owen said softly.

But Rand had been voted off. When he had outed himself by moving me onto the ranch with him two years ago, the Winston community leaders had booted him from the seat that his father had held before him. They didn't even take the time to make it look good; instead they let it be known that the reason for revoking his seat was because of me, because Rand lived with me. The Red Diamond Ranch was the largest in Winston as well as in the outlying areas of Croton and Payson, as well as many others, but that had not stopped the mayor and the rest of the city fathers from finding a loophole to get rid of my then boyfriend and now partner. They were homophobic assholes, every last one of them, and when they had rezoned the county three months later, officially relocating the Red Diamond to Hillman, that had been the last straw. I had been surprised that Rand didn't fight it, but when he explained, I understood.

The day the rezoning had gone into effect, the mayor of Hillman, Marley Davis, along with her entire staff, had made a special trip out to the ranch to welcome Rand and the Red Diamond to her county. She had been the one to give her permission to have the county lines redrawn; she was thrilled to have Rand join her community and just knew he would be thrilled about it too. She was hoping that Rand would come to the next city council meeting, as they would be interested in hearing any thoughts he might have. He was also more than welcome to bring me.

I was stunned, and Rand's smile had been huge as he recounted the events that Friday when I got home.

"Everything happens for a reason, Stef," he told me, drawing me into his arms. "I never thought too much of Hillman before, but suddenly I can't think of them enough. I feel like we got us a home all of a sudden, and I think I wanna help those folks out. I got some money that I think will do us all some good if you help me. I mean, you got the background in acquisitions and finance and all. Will you take a look at some things and see what you can do?"

Of course I could, and would, and did.

And while it had been hard for Rand, severing all ties with the town he had grown up in, his warm welcome in Hillman twenty miles to the east had been overwhelming. Hillman had not been able to boast of having a large, thriving, three-hundred-thousand-acre ranch in their county, but since the home of the ranch was wherever the main house sat, now they could. I had thought at first that it was the money he represented that they were responding to, but it was also the man himself.

Hillman had become Rand's new hometown and, as a result, was reaping the benefit of both his philanthropy and his loyalty. He made a generous donation to the senior center, built a huge gas station/mini-mart with his friend AJ Myers that had already increased traffic in town, and donated five tricked-out computers complete with scanners and printers to the county library. He built a feed store, and put a new roof on the gymnasium of the high school when he found out it leaked during the last thunderstorm. In the next year, there were more city improvements in the works, and the proposed elementary school was at the top of the list. When Rand had been invited to attend school board meetings, he had been very touched. He was an important citizen in Hillman, his voice appreciated, his opinion courted, and his patronage eagerly anticipated.

"Stefan!"

Wrenched from my thoughts, I found myself standing in front of Sheriff Glenn Colter. "Oh, Sheriff, what can I do for you?"

"You bought the Silver Spring from Adam Weber last week."

I had to catch up with the conversation that we were apparently having.

"Didn't you?"

"I didn't," I told him, taking another sip of my latte. "Rand did."

"Adam said that you negotiated the deal."

"That's what I used to do, Sheriff," I said, watching the lines in his face tighten. "And even though I teach school now, at Westland Community College, apparently it's a skill I still possess. The whole background in acquisitions thing doesn't just go away."

"Well, Adam said that you were real fair with him so that's why he sold, but that he didn't mean to include the parcel of land down by the Dalton place."

"That's not what he told me."

"Well, he wants it back."

"Really?" I asked drolly. "You talked to him in Vegas, did you?"

"What I mean is," he said, then cleared his throat, "that's what he was fixin' to tell you before he left."

"Uh-huh."

"Stefan."

"You're talking about the parcel that butts up against the Coleman piece, right?"

He grunted loudly. "We both know that those folks from Trinity want that piece, because the way it's zoned now, if Rand sells them the Silver Spring and clear down to the highway, then they can make their own drive and not run through Winston at all."

"Yes, I know," I told him. "And with the gas station in Hillman and a resort between the Red Diamond and Hillman... why would anyone even go through Winston?"

"Rand bought up the land, and now he's fixin' to turn us into a ghost town."

I shook my head. "The people from Trinity—"

"That son of a bitch, Mitch Powell, wants to build a resort and a golf course and God knows what else out here, but only if he gets the land to the east where—"

"Rand sold it to him," I said, because it was no longer a secret and would actually create a whole slew of jobs for all the neighboring towns. Mitchell Powell, golf pro turned entrepreneur turned multimillionaire, was going to build *the* resort in the area. He was about to put Hillman on the map, thanks to Rand, who had basically collected a monopoly that no one had wanted or given a damn about, and sold it for buckets of money that he was poised to do great things with.

The Silver Spring, Twin Forks, and Bowman ranches, none of which had been working ranches in years, would all be converted into a huge, sprawling, 250-acre monolith of wealth and prosperity. It would be a very posh, very exclusive, very expensive resort, catering to the rich and famous, that would be far enough from the ranch as to not adversely affect it or change the lives of the people who lived there. The Red Diamond would remain the same, and the land that Rand had bought would finally be put to good use. And even though the town of Winston itself would not see the boon directly, as there were no civic projects planned, the people who lived there would benefit directly from the hundreds of new jobs about to be created.

If you didn't work on a ranch, there was nothing to do in Winston. You had to drive to Lubbock, just like I had to, to work. But now, thanks to Rand Holloway buying and selling and Mitchell Powell building, there was about to be a great influx of employment.

"Rand sold all three ranches to Powell?"

"Yessir, he did," I said, walking around him to the driver's side door. "Now move the cruiser. I wanna go home."

The muscles in his jaw tightened as he followed me. "How could he do that to the town he grew up in?"

"He just created thousands of jobs for the people of the town he grew up in," I told him. "Buildings will go up, and when that's done, there will be jobs at the resort to fill. This community just got saved."

"But where the resort would be.... Hillman will be the town the resort is located in, not Winston."

"Why does that matter? The people you serve will be better off for the influx of jobs."

"And Hillman becomes the point of interest between Midland and Lubbock while Winston is left as it is."

"What would you have Rand do about that, Sheriff?"

"You're a smart boy. You understand what I'm saying to you."

I squinted at him. "Papers have been signed, Sheriff. Mitchell Powell has come and gone with deeds and rights and more lawyers than Rand said he ever saw in his life. The people who sold their property to Rand did so under no duress. We both know that the Silver Spring and the Twin Forks have been dead for years, and the Bowman place... well, all Carrie wanted to do was sell and move to Oregon to be close to her son. Running a successful ranch in this day and age is hard work, and for some it's easier to simply get paid and get out. Rand found use for land that was going to waste, and because of that, his own ranch can be that much bigger and that much more lucrative and even more capable of supporting the men and their families, who live and work on it. Now I understand that you're concerned about Winston, but Rand had to do what was best for the Red Diamond, and in the process, he ended up doing right by the town."

"The mayor doesn't see it that way."

"I suspect Rand won't give a damn."

He scowled at me. "I suspect you'd be right."

I smiled back.

He visibly deflated.

"It's not your fault, you know. I know that you weren't one of those who wanted Rand off the board."

His eyes searched mine.

"I know your only reservations with Rand stem from the fact that sometimes he can be kind of an ass."

"Sometimes?"

I chuckled, smiling bigger, unable to stop myself. "It's late, Sheriff. Are you not eating at home tonight?"

"No. Mrs. Colter is visiting her sister in Abilene."

"Well, would you like to come by the house and have some dinner? I have more than enough for three."

"No thank you, Stefan, but I do appreciate the invite. I've got to go over to the Drake place and talk to them about Jeff."

It took me a minute because nothing at all ever happened in Winston. It was why Rand and I had been such big news. "Oh, the drag racing," I said snidely, baiting him.

"It ain't funny. They could get themselves killed doin' that."

"On the tractors," I said, trying really hard not to sound patronizing. "Yes, I'm sure they could."

He thrust his hand at me to shake. "Call me when you're makin' the lasagna again."

"Yessir, Sheriff, I sure will," I promised, taking the offered hand in mine.

He gave me a smile before I turned to get in my car.

"Stef."

I looked back at him over my shoulder, opening the door.

"Call me if you're makin' the pot roast too."

"Oh, okay," I teased him. "I didn't realize you had favorites."

"Damn right," he told me before he suddenly froze. "You ain't makin' any of those tonight, are ya?"

"No, sir, I'm not."

He grunted before he got in the mammoth car.

It was actually really nice that the man had favorites. Before I began my life with Rand, my culinary skills were basic at best. But the restaurants in Winston were both barbeque places, and while they were good, sometimes variety was nice, so one of us had to learn to cook, and of the two of us, I had more time. He really enjoyed it when I slaved away in the kitchen for him; why, I had no idea, but the look on his face when he came in the house and found me in the kitchen was enough to melt me through the floor. He really enjoyed the hell out of me being domestic.

I watched as the sheriff moved his SUV, honking as he drove away. The deputies both followed suit, and when I was headed for home, I had time to think about the transformation my life had gone through in just a short amount of time.

MARY CALMES lives in Lexington, Kentucky, with her husband and two children and loves all the seasons except summer. She graduated from the University of the Pacific in Stockton, California, with a bachelor's degree in English literature. Due to the fact that it is English lit and not English grammar, do not ask her to point out a clause for you, as it will so not happen. She loves writing, becoming immersed in the process, and believes without question in happily-ever-afters, and writes those for each and every one of her characters.

ALL KINDS OF TIED DOWN

Mary Calmes

Marshals: Book One

Deputy US Marshal Miro Jones has a reputation for being calm and collected under fire. These traits serve him well with his hotshot partner, Ian Doyle, the kind of guy who can start a fight in an empty room. In the past three years of their life-and-death job, they've gone from strangers to professional coworkers to devoted teammates and best friends. Miro's cultivated blind faith in the man who has his back… faith and something more.

As a marshal and a soldier, Ian's expected to lead. But the power and control that brings Ian success and fulfillment in the field isn't working anywhere else. Ian's always resisted all kinds of tied down, but having no home—and no one to come home to—is slowly eating him up inside. Over time, Ian has grudgingly accepted that going anywhere without his partner simply doesn't work. Now Miro just has to convince him that getting tangled up in heartstrings isn't being tied down at all.

www.dreamspinnerpress.com

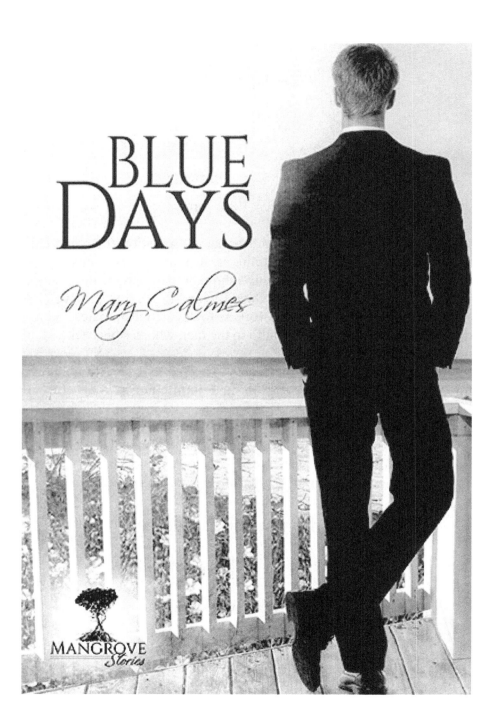

BLUE
DAYS

Mary Calmes

MANGROVE
Stories

Mangrove Stories

Falling for a coworker is rarely a good idea, especially for a man getting a last chance at salvaging his career. But from the moment Dwyer Knolls sees the beautiful but socially awkward Takeo Hiroyuki, he seems destined to make bad decisions.

Takeo's life is a string of failed attempts to please his traditional Japanese father. Unfortunately, succeeding in business turns out to be just as difficult for Takeo as changing from gay to straight. In fact, the only thing Takeo seems to truly excel at is taking notice of Dwyer Knolls.

When Dwyer and Takeo head to Mangrove, Florida on a real estate buying trip, their tentative friendship combusts and becomes much more. Is their sudden connection real enough to bank their futures on, or should they chalk the whole thing up to the daze inspired by the blue ocean breeze?

www.dreamspinnerpress.com

LAY IT DOWN

Mary Calmes

Paradise can be hell.

Most people would say being stranded in the villa of Spanish shipping magnate Miguel García Arquero on the beautiful isle of Ibiza wasn't such a bad deal. But Hudson Barber isn't one of them. To him, being stuck without a passport in a foreign country far from home is a nightmare, made worse by the fact that the person who did the stranding was his flighty twin brother.

Unwilling to turn Dalvon in for identity theft, Hudson is forced to wait, but meanwhile he discovers the chance to rehabilitate Miguel's failing local businesses—enterprises left to Dalvon's inexperienced care. The flagging ventures are a badly wrapped gift from heaven, and if Hudson can turn them around, he might be able to leverage the experience to finish his MBA.

Then Miguel returns to Ibiza, and instead of finding a boy toy, he discovers Hudson has turned his cold villa into a warm, welcoming home. Miguel's path is clear: convince Hudson to lay down his defenses and let love in.

www.dreamspinnerpress.com

ROMANUS
Mary Calmes

Stopping to offer help one sultry summer night, Mason James is unprepared for the change that this simple act of kindness will bring. After giving an old man a ride home, Mason discovers a new, magical, and even dangerous world he cannot hope to understand. But he also finds Luc Toussaint and is intoxicated at first sight... and even the secret Luc protects won't be enough to keep Mason away from the truth of his heritage and their love.

www.dreamspinnerpress.com

Made in the USA
Monee, IL
10 March 2021

62375864R00115